Christine

Enslaved

Magik

Enjoy!
with love
Carys

Carys Bateman X

NOVEL
EXPERIENTIA

First published in Great Britain
by Novel Experientia Ltd.

www.novelexperientia.com

. . .

. . .

ISBN: 978-1-9196145-0-2

Acknowledgements

To my first reader, Ian.
Told you it had changed a bit.

To the members of DAC (Disability Arts Cymru)
Writers Group who first heard of
this book a long time ago.

Especially to Alan, Denni, Wendy and Mari.

To Ali and Gill, who read later versions and gave me
the boost to continue when I had almost given up.

To Dafydd who told me about Novel Experientia.

To Novel Experientia and all who sail in her,
especially my editor Andrew, who really got this
story, and Amin who works so hard trying to sell it.

To you folks for buying this
and taking a chance on me.

Thank you!

For

My Nain and Taid for love.

The Boy Wonder for belief

And

My Littlest and Best for love and everything else.

Look what I made!

Chapter One

Pok, pok, pok.

The sound echoed out into the night and Weasel pulled himself deeper into the shadows as he waited for the figure to come closer and pass before he crept silently across the narrow roadway behind her. He grinned to himself knowing that this woman was also breaking curfew and, as such, would not be able to complain about anything done to her this night. The rain began falling more strongly and the mist came in heavily, making his grin even wider. The Night Watch would stay warm and snug inside their tower in this weather, allowing Weasel and other lawbreakers to do whatever they wanted.

Squinting, he moved quietly down the roadway, keeping deep within the pools of darkness and watching for anything that might trip him as he moved up behind her. He made sure to step in a wide circle around the floating black columns that hung in the air. This was Mýste, one of the most dangerous manifestations of magik.

He had seen more than one curious fool step in too close, mesmerised by the faint sounds coming from within the swirling pillar; delicate, sweet noises like the murmur of voices singing a hymn just too quiet for the ears to recognise. Without realising it, the poor sap would edge closer and closer, none the wiser to the slim tentacles of wispy black smoke touching a bare ankle or wrapping itself around a wrist. Even, as Weasel had heard once, sliding into a partially opened mouth.

Where the Mýste touched didn't matter, the results were always the same: the victim would be paralysed, only the eyes showing the horror and full knowledge of their predicament. Fear and panic soon changed to overwhelming pain as the tentacles began silently draining their victim: blood, tissue, muscles and internal organs all drawn up through the whisps of dark magik. Those watching would see the victim becoming thinner, drying and shrinking down, skin becoming withered and mummified, hair falling out, clothes sliding down as their body shrank even smaller. Eventually, after just a few short moments, or a lifetime, depending upon your perspective, the tentacle would release the desiccated husk and slide back into the dense pillar once again. All that was left was an empty shell to show where a human being had stood not so long before.

In the early days, before people learned caution, some idiots would race forward to pull the victims free. Instead, the hopeful saviour would become caught within the same spell and sucked just as dry. Once or twice the Mýste connection had been broken but the victim died anyway, either because too much of their insides had been sucked out or the shock and horror was just so unbearable that they were unable to cope. No matter what the reason was, no-one survived the Mýste so now even the foolhardiest scavenger avoided the black stuff.

The Mages, the only magik users allowed in the Coalition States, were supposed to keep the Mýste at bay according to some. According to others, Mages were the ones causing the Mýste in the first place. Weasel didn't know which version was true and cared even less, he just knew to be wary and avoid the floating death.

The young woman he was carefully pursuing continued walking in the same steady manner, not bothering to keep watch around her. The small man had seen that she held a parcel close to her chest as she walked along, adding inducement to his interest in her.

'Hello darlin', what you doin' out on a nasty night like this, then? It ain't right you being out in the dark. Don't you know there is stuff around 'ere that could kill you without even blinkin'? And yeah, I do mean the Watch.' He chuckled lightly, trying to sound both harmless and humorous. 'How come you is out without an escort? No matter, I can do that for you, darlin', I will get you safe back to where you need to be. For a price, a'corse.' He raked his lascivious gaze up and down her body as he spoke.

There was no acknowledgement from the woman as she continued walking at exactly the same pace as before and Weasel frowned as he skipped to keep up, irritated at the lack of response.

'I'm speakin' to you, you dumb bint!' His voice no longer carried any of the false obsequiousness it held before as his quick temper began to rise. 'Is you deaf? Or is you something much more tasty? Let's have a proper look at you.'

Grabbing hold of the girl's arm, he dragged her to the next lighted street lamp. Within the feeble glow of burning oil, he pulled the damp shawl away from her head and body and dropped it onto the dirty ground. The girl stumbled a little at his rough handling but held tightly to the parcel in her hands.

'Well, well, well, Weasel, me old mate, haven't we got us a lovely prize 'ere then!' He swept his gaze up and down the girl standing in front of him while her own eyes stayed blank and unfocused. It was a gaunt face, without animation, her hair hidden beneath a brown bonnet tied loosely under the chin. Uncaring about her painfully thin body or the scars marking her, he saw enough of a shape under her dress to make his mouth water. Now the shawl had been pulled away, Weasel could also see her slave collar, a wide and delicately wrought gold filigree choker adorned with fine gems sparkling in the dim light. His muddy eyes lit up in salacious pleasure as he murmured to himself.

'A slavey! Well, bless me, you must have someone rich prepared to ransom you, wearing that particular bit of fancy. Let's have a closer look; gold linked chain, pretty and worth its weight but not any good to me' As he mumbled to himself his dirty, cracked, fingers slid with surprising delicacy along the girl's neck. Now he had stopped pulling at her, she stood as still as a statue. He looked more closely, noting the selection of jewels: black, blue, green, amber and…yes! Just what he wanted to see!

'A fireheart! A blimmin' luvverly fireheart! This means you are mine, you little beauty…a slavey, trained for pleasure and out after curfew without a Keeper! What could be more perfect?' Eagerly he pushed her against the wall, clawing at her clothes and pulling her already low neckline down even further to bare her breasts to the night.

'Oh, they is sweet,' he mumbled, continuing to wrench at her clothing and tugging at his own, scrabbling urgently with his buttons, already hard and wanting to be inside her. Sex with a woman would make a change to having to use his own fist and he was almost dizzy with eagerness and expectation.

'I am going to show you how a real bloke does it.' he said, giving up on trying to pull her dress down and instead lifting her long skirts up, showing off thin legs, encased in thick woollen stockings and ending in the battered boots whose sound had first caught his attention. Lifting the material higher, and trying to free himself from his britches, proved to be a problem for the small crook, who began cursing under his breath.

'Bloody hell, you stupid bint, hold up them blimmin' skirts so I can see what I'm aiming for.' Desperately, he finally managed to free himself and pinched at her thighs, trying to separate her legs. Leaning back slightly, he studied her face for a reaction but could read nothing, her eyes still focused on something far away. Well, he would make her scream by the time he had finished with her. A bit of how's your father followed by a good bloody beating might even get rid of some of the burning anger he carried within himself. How dare she sit in the lap of

4

luxury and want for nothing while him and his mates scrabbled for basic crusts and died by the hundreds? Weasel felt his anger growing and so began grabbing and squeezing the slave's breasts viciously. Still she did not respond in any way.

'We die like animals in these streets, you listening? We *die*. Some of us starve to death, some of us are killed for the little bit of crap we carry. My mate Trotter, he was the best mate a man could have; he got knifed for crap that I would have thrown away before the plague. Yet you stand there, wearing your posh clothes, your comfy boots and that collar that'd feed a family for months and you don't even care, do you? You *tart*, you bleedin' *slavey*!' His voice had become louder as he vocalised his litany of pain; conveniently forgetting that it was he himself who had pushed the knife in between Trotter's ribs and had stripped the man he called a friend naked, before selling off the booty for a few brass coins to buy grog. Breathing heavily, Weasel realised that he had begun to lose readiness in his temper. He took the slave's free hand while her other still held fast to her parcel.

'Rub it, you cow, rub it 'til I am big and hard. Think about how it's going to feel when I shoves inside you.' His breath became unsteady as the slave's hand wrapped around his penis and began to move back and forth. His hips began to move with her rhythm and his breathing became heavier as he began pulling at her skirts, eager to start causing the bitch real pain.

Suddenly, he found himself propelled backwards as a heavy weight was placed on his shoulder. The would-be rapist gave a howl of agony as the slave girl continued gripping hold of his manhood until it was ripped away from her tight grasp. Weasel curled up whimpering in pain, cupping his groin, his deep fear of what he would, or wouldn't, find turned to sheer relief as his hands found that he was limp, sore but intact. He gave a strangled gasp of sheer terror as he recognised the big man looming over him.

'Well, well, well, if it ain't my old mate Weasel. Just what is it you are doin' here?' The voice was deep and not as rough as the smaller man's. It came from a barrel chest, belonging to the biggest man Weasel knew.

'*Void it*' he swore, knowing he was in trouble now.

'Bloody hell, you sick bastard, you was going to tup a slavey? You dirty animal' Full of disgust, the huge man swung a hammer-like fist catching the smaller man in the stomach just as he managed to get to his feet. Weasel lost his breath, followed by his small dinner and all that he had drunk that day, as he collapsed and vomited. Another brick-like fist hit the side of his head and he fell flat and lost consciousness for a brief second or two. As he recovered he saw the man he had been avoiding for days, making sure the slavey was covered up and decent, Mr Poole.

'This is your last warning, Weasel. Get yourself to somewhere else, out of Harmony or off Bisra completely, because if I see you again, I am going to hurt you. If you want sex, the bloody Leadership provides us with Bawdy Houses on almost every street corner. You can get what you want there for just a few pennies. You don't have to rape, especially those who can't fight back. Now go on, get lost, you disgusting little scav.'

'She's a slavey! How the hell can I rape a slavey? She has to do what I tells her so I can do whatever I bloody well want, so how can that be rape? It ain't rape if they let you!' The whine in Weasel's voice emphasised his genuine puzzlement.

'Shut up, scum. I warned you days ago to use the Bawdy Houses and nothing else. No woman deserves to have your tiny, diseased, pecker anywhere near her.' At Weasel's scowl, Mr Poole bared his teeth, taking a deep, calming breath before continuing. 'Now here is something you will understand so you better be listenin' with both ears. You have crossed me for the last time, so I am going to put a real effort in finding you come sun up. If I catch you, I am going to do worse to you than kill you.'

'Oh yeah?' Weasels voice was fainter but full of bravado, grabbing at his chance to back away. 'What could be worse than you killing me, *Mister* blimmin' Poole? I have seen your work, remember? And my life ain't so full of sunshine that your beatings are going be a problem.'

'Well now," the burly tough smiled grimly 'I can think of something that should be a worry to you, Weasel. The Ringmaster is looking for a new spectacular at The Best Show. His old one just killed himself. Would you like that, rat-boy? Being stripped naked, gagged and tied to that bench, your virgin arse bare and open for any bloke who wants a taste? Being swived again and again, so much and so hard you begin to shit blood? I have seen some real tough men break down and beg after just three days of that. I will start laying bets on you if you reckon you can last longer.'

'If you are in the city after first light then me and the boys will be able to find you and…' Mr Poole's voice trailed away as Weasel fled into the night, throwing loud curses back over his shoulder. The noise of his rapid footsteps fading away, moving faster than any who knew him would previously have believed possible.

The big man turned around and looked sadly at the young woman who was standing frozen in place, one hand still outstretched. He studied her and noted that she was older than he had originally thought. The light from the overhead lamp, although dim and flickering madly in the damp air, was enough to show her features. He saw eyes so dark they looked black. There was scarring to her left cheek and eye and he wondered if the girl had had been marked before being bought at the Auction House or after. If before, he would bet a month's pay that the scav that bought her had demanded a discount.

Mr Poole checked her from head to toe, pulling up the neckline of her dress again to make sure that her breasts were covered properly. Her full skirts, draping her body to mid-calf, showed just a little of her legs and her ankles. He looked at the slave collar and its obscene beauty and sighed loudly.

'Oh, sweet lass, what a bloody world we live in. Right, we best get moving before I get sent to the Punishment Square for stealing you. Here, wrap this shawl around you. It is wet and a bit muddy but will help keep some of the wind off you. Thank the Gods that the rain is letting up again. Now, my name is Mr Poole. If you ever need any help of any kind, you get word to me. Tell any cabbie, inn keeper or newsboy and the message will get to me and I will do what I can for you. Remember: Mr Poole.' The big man grimaced and shook his head before he continued softly to himself. 'What am I saying? She can't ask me for a bloody thing, not with the drug they feed her.' He sighed again, even more deeply than before.

'Alright, you ready to go now? Let's get you back home. You lead the way, poppet. Are you allowed to tell me where you need to go? What family you belong to?'

The girl looked at him blankly, but then a tiny spark seemed to light up her dark eyes. Hesitating, she looked at him then swallowed.

'I need to go to Tranquillity Road in High Town. I have a parcel for Lady Willoughby.' Her voice had no life or inflection although there was the faintest trace of an accent underneath the rustiness of lack of use.

Mr Poole thought deeply, trying to remember the layout of the city centre. He knew his way around his own tangled alleyways but he rarely ventured into the richer part of town.

'Alright, I think I know where you need to go. You sound a bit like you were from Cryllek, gel, probably caught out on the wrong side of the border sea when all the shouting started. No, you walk near the wall, my lovely, not near the roadway. We don't want that black Mýste stuff getting friendly with us, trying to make our hair curl,' he grinned at her, his shaven skull gleaming under the occasional light as they walked. 'That Mýste will suck you down to the Void quicker than that bastard who is using you can.'

As they walked down the street Mr Poole tried to think of any way he could help this blank-eyed woman. Eventually he shook his head, knowing full well that, when he had taken slaves away from their "masters" in the past, the poor buggers had died in great pain from the drug withdrawal. Some had even literally lost their heads, as had the locksmiths who tried to remove the damned collar. There was nothing he could do unless she wished for death and she was too damn drugged to even make that choice now.

'If you ever start coming to your senses, lass, you get in touch with me and I will do what I can to help, even if it is only giving you a quiet and painless death.' Mr Poole spoke on impulse, not understanding why he needed to repeat information that the slave would never retain but he felt a little better for it.

The sound of marching feet pounded loudly in the night and so he swiftly caught the slave's hand and tugged her down into an alleyway.

'You stay quiet, lass, just until these gits get past,' he whispered as a group of ten men marched past the alley entrance. 'Huh, glad they stayed indoors for a bit; if they'd have caught you with bloody Weasel, they would have used you cruelly.'

Mr Poole took a broken piece of mirror out of his waistcoat jacket and held it out cautiously, using it to see the back of the marching men as they moved away. Seeing them go around a corner he tugged on the girl's hand and walked her carefully but, swiftly, towards her destination. Broken stones and hard packed mud slowly gave way to better repaired streets. Buildings changed from one room hovels made from anything that could be scavenged, leaning together for strength, to neat one and two storey cottages with gardens and on to higher three level buildings with plentiful grounds. The instability of the earth ensured nothing was built above three storeys.

As they walked through the dark, wet, night Mr Poole found himself musing on how some people thought that it was alright to take children from the local orphanages and drug them until any will had gone. That in itself was bad enough, the Gods knew, but using mage-made collars that could give either a quick snick of pain, or a continuous stabbing massage of agony that lasted as long as the button on the control box was pressed was inhuman to his way of thinking. There was also that one setting, the one that sent magik slicing straight into the carotid artery so that the victim bled to death within minutes, the magik sucking out all blood within the body until not one drop was left.

There was also the final indignity of putting a pinch of explosive powders into the catch of the neck ornament. If anyone tried to remove it without the proper skills, it would end up killing the slave as well as crippling or killing the would-be rescuer.

Unhappy with where his thoughts were going, Mr Poole began telling stories; fables he had told his own little girl before his world had imploded. He kept his voice low and his ears pricked for anyone else out in the night. He was in the mood to use his blackjack on someone if they tried it on with him. After two hours of walking, the rain tailed off completely just as they reached the imposing front of the house where the slave resided.

Mr Poole stopped just outside the light of the many shining street lamps that lit up the Square and watched as the slim figure moved towards a stately house, ready to go down the alley to the rear of the building. Still clutching her parcel tightly, the girl moved quickly but, just before she was out of sight, he saw her stop. He watched as she turned slightly, his amazement drowning out the frustration from seconds before. In the stillness of the night, her words floated to him on the breeze.

'Mr Poole. I will remember your name.' and she disappeared from view.

Chapter Two

On Bisra, and the other Coalition States, the rich provided support for the worship and priesthood of Kintrelle, The Shining One. The Mages belonged to the Church and, in theory, used their magik to make the world better for all. In practice, it was only the priesthood itself and the richest in Bisra that actually felt any benefit. Anyone else caught using magik, apart from the Mages would be sent to the Punishment Square for public torture and, probably, death as an Abomination.

The world was still recovering from the upheaval that had caused huge land masses to break into smaller islands. There were places from the Before Times, over one hundred years before, that had completely disappeared, whereas others changed shape or size. Natural disasters such as hurricanes, tsunamis, earthquakes and fires had all contrived to kill many and to reshape the world. As things began to settle down and the survivors came out of their hidey holes, there was a death of technology as magik rose. Creatures previously only known in story books stepped up out of the rubble of broken lands and damaged lives, taking their own place in the new world. Beings that were once dismissed as fantasy now had to be acknowledged as real.

Then, only a few years ago, there was the Plague outbreak. Still watching the now empty alley way that the slavey had gone down, Mr Poole's mind went back to his beloved Lottie, the woman he had loved from childhood, and the way she had died.

He remembered holding her in his arms, careful not to tear the paper-thin skin and add to the lesions that covered her body. Bending close, he used to listen as she tried to tell him of her love for him and their daughter as tears rolled down his cheeks but her own eyes were dry.

She had spoken so quietly, struggling to draw breath as the virus tore through her. He did his best to never show her the pain he had felt as she faded. Where once she had been a plump, bustling, cheerful busybody, she had become a skeletal stranger.

When the headaches had first appeared, she had known what would happen, even as he would not, *could* not accept it. His anger with her had been explosive when he arrived home one day to find that she had sent their young daughter away to relatives.

As the end came nearer, and she breathed her thoughts into his ear, he tried to give his Lottie the reassurance of his love for her. He struggled with his tears as she admitted that she had begun to crave for the sweet taste of human flesh. That, even as he held her, she wanted to sink her teeth into his neck and tear away the meat of him. Her eyes were clouded with the thick growths that hindered her sight and she had no tear ducts left to allow her own pain to flow but he felt her sorrow and knew it was time to let her go.

There was no cure for the Plague, apart from death, and he wouldn't allow any other to do what she begged for. He had promised her that she would not progress to the last stage of the Plague, the mindless hunger. Horror stories abounded of the sudden change from victim to Necrotic, monsters that had lost all humanity and saw humankind as the only food source to curb their insatiable hunger. He had leaned down and kissed his Lottie gently, ignoring the rotten stench from her cracked lips and body that no amount of bathing could disguise. He could never decide if she had truly whispered her thank you or if it had been his imagination but he allowed himself the cold comfort of the words.

An hour after her death, he had walked away from the loving home he had known with his wife and child. As the flames crackled loudly behind him, Elias the cooper of Frank's Pool had become Mr Poole, the future leader of a pack of Low Town cut-throats.

He quickly shook himself free of the sad memories. If ever he slipped up and said that he missed his wife and child out loud, he could be flogged or worse. He had to be particularly careful of his habit of mentioning the old Gods as he had noticed himself doing a lot lately. Since the Eternal Faith of the Shining One had taken over as the only religion allowed on Bisra, no-one could mention missing the dead, or speak of other gods, unless they wanted punishing. According to the Servers and the Speakers of the Church there was only Kintrelle, the Shining One, and it was the people's job to live knowing that when death arrived it would bring with it oblivion and complete rest only for those who had made true and proper penance when living. The rest of humanity would go to the Void as slaves to the Shining One's minions, forced to work in the netherworld or to be reborn again and again until enough punishment was given. If anyone questioned the beliefs of the Servers, Searchers, Speakers, Mages or the Preceptor himself, or acted as if they doubted this view, they were punished severely with beatings, torture, slavery or death.

As Mr Poole turned away, he found himself praying for the slavey and wondering about his own girl-child, what would she look like if she had survived? Did she live? He had found out, before Lottie's death, that his daughter had never arrived at her uncle's. Since that day, despite constant searching, no one had heard of her and even Mr Poole's now immense resources couldn't find her.

'Hey, Boss!' The quiet whisper made him turn and see one of his informers from the Watch standing in the shadows.

'Hello, Wates,' Mr Poole's voice was just as low. 'What's up?'

'The world is going out that the Speakers are going to be preaching against Abominations tomorrow.'

'So? They have been preaching against magik and anyone and anything like it ever since the beginning, son, what difference will tomorrow bring?'

The Watchman gulped. 'They are doing more than just saying that Abominations are unnatural, they are now saying that we gotta be careful not to get too close or we might catch whatever turned 'em. According to what I've heard, that means we got permission to kill any on sight and, if we are wrong, then so what?'

Mr Poole remembered the last big change to happen. All the magikal beings had been banned from Bisra and other Enlightened countries, having been accused of bringing the Plague into "civilised" places. Anyone who was not able to prove antecedents for at least three generations had been enslaved to prevent contamination.

Poole felt his teeth grinding in anger. Just when you thought things were bad, it all got a bit worse. 'What will you do?' He asked Wates.

'Not much I can do, can I? I know we might kill some innocents but rather a few of them then letting a whole bunch of Abominations free.'

This angered Mr Poole. He knew that no magik user or shifter, no bloodling or elf, tricksy, gnome or fae that had risen up out of the dust and debris of the broken world had caused the Plague. He knew that the supernatural beings had even tried to help with healing; medicines and poultices given to ease both fever and cough. However, any person who was found to have lived because of using help from the "Abominations" was tortured and put to death so as not to "spread" the Plague further. He decided that Wates had said enough.

The Willoughby slave wasn't taken out as a sweetmeat for others to taste either, much to the surprise of some. The Keeper thought he knew why. Lord Willoughby may not have had as much money as some of his peers so the slavey could have given his income a definite boost, it is true, but Lord Willoughby had no intention of sharing the slave girl with anyone, apart from his son. She was his property and no-one was allowed to touch anything he owned. He never even punished her by using the lovely jewelled collar that every slavey wore.

Now though Samuel patted down her body, hating having to slide his hands inside her gown to make sure no weapon was cupped between her breasts. Then he dropped to his knees and slid his hands up and around her thighs, trying to ignore the flesh and just do his job. A slavey did not wear under-clothing unless it was demanded in the bedroom, so the search was much more intimate than he was comfortable with, even after all these years. Rising to his feet, he leaned down and apologised in a whisper as he usually did.

'I am sorry, girl, I really hate doing that to you,' he said unhappily. 'Her ladyship is in a right blimmin' temper, miss, so I hope you did what you needed to. Right…you ready? Of course you are.'

With a stifled curse, the Keeper tapped on the drawing room door, opened it and spoke without stepping into the room. 'The slavey has returned, your Ladyship,' he announced. 'Should I send her in?'

An impatient voice answered. 'Of course send her in, you idiot.'

The slave stepped through the doorway and heard the door click shut behind her. The room was large, overheated and cluttered. Seating of all kinds fought for space, almost completely covering an ancient threadbare carpet. Small tables stood in various spaces between the bigger furniture. Ancient broken porcelains and shimmering glass of various shapes as well as precious plastics that had faded to a uniform dull grey decorated the tops. In the grate a fire burned sluggishly, adding its choking murk to the musty room. The walls had originally been papered with expensive patterned silk but were now covered in so many pictures and the smoke of a thousand fires, the original delicate rose pink colouring was completely lost. Heavy curtaining covered the tall windows, shutting out the street lighting and hiding the protective metal bars, blessed by the Mages. Three small oil lamps burned dully, vainly trying to bring some brightness into the whole area.

The Mistress of the house, Lady Constance Willoughby, stood in front of the fire. She was clothed in an expensive mushroom coloured satin that flowed down from her hips in delicately embroidered panels. The bodice of the dress was heavily beaded and embroidered, darkening the look of the material which suited her better as it rested against her white skin. Her pale hair was plaited and pinned in a coronet around her head and studded with jewels. Turning, she beckoned imperiously to the girl to come closer. Carefully the slavey walked between the obstacle course of furniture and she reached Lady Constance without having knocked over anything, not something that she always managed. As she stopped in front of her Mistress, the slave's head suddenly whipped violently to the side and a loud *CRACK!* echoed out, heard by the Keeper outside the room who winced in sympathy.

'You are late, you slut! You're lucky that I am so damn forgiving or I would have pressed the button to that collar of yours. Did you think of that while you were dilly-dallying, hmmm? Of course you didn't, you stupid little swiver. You should remember your place, slave, remember that I could make your life much more difficult if I chose.' The strident voice became shriller and louder as she spoke finishing at almost screaming pitch, slapping the girl again and again. Not a sound passed the girl's lips. Each time her head stopped swinging, she faced forward, staring straight through her Mistress.

Lady Constance stopped her harangue abruptly, glaring at the girl in front of her. Seeing a thin trickle of blood from the corner of the slave's mouth caused a frisson of fear even as her chest heaved with the effort of holding back. Hatred flowed through her veins. This bitch had allowed herself to be touched by Lord Willoughby. Now Markus, her son, was doing the same, touching and doing unspeakable things with her. The rage was so strong that, if it were possible, Lady Constance would have torn at the slave's face with her nails, hit her again and again until the vacant face had been obliterated. She calmed down slowly and finally admitted to herself that the damned slave had much less choice in the matter than she did. She was not so much angry with the helpless, unknowing girl standing in front of her but with Willoughby for forcing the situation and with herself for accepting it.

Lady Willoughby turned away from the blank gaze and glared down into the fire. Her thoughts began to calm slowly although the anger still seethed. Glancing over, she spotted the parcel still clutched in the slave's hands and snatching it, she stalked to the sideboard to the left of the room, making tables tilt dangerously with her full, heavy skirts. On the surface of the sideboard was a jug of now lukewarm milk as well as honey, cocoa, an empty cup and spoon. After putting on a mask to cover her mouth and nose, Lady Constance poured the milk into the cup, added cocoa and then honey. After stirring the mixture, she opened the parcel the slave had fetched and removed the carved wooden box from within the wrappings. She was careful not to breathe too deeply as she unlocked the lid, revealing a fine greyish powder within. From the chatelaine hanging from the belt around her waist, she lifted a tiny metal spoon and added two scoops of Numb into the cooling cocoa mixture. A brisk stir and Lady Constance picked up the cup and thrust it at the mute girl who stood quietly waiting.

'Drink this,' she demanded, her tone hoarse from shouting. The slave took the cup and tipped the contents into her mouth without fuss or bother.

As soon as she had emptied the cup, her mistress snapped out her evening orders. 'Go to your room. Wash with the scented soap. Your Master and the young master will be visiting later. Be here at your usual time tomorrow morning. I have no wish to see your face until then. Nine o'clock and no earlier. Go!'

The slave turned on her heel, winding her slow and careful way out of the dim, hot room into the chilly corridor. Shutting the door quietly behind her she turned and headed up to her own quarters without a backward glance. The Keeper felt his anger burn as he saw her reddened cheeks and swollen mouth but he didn't speak as he followed the slavey down the passage way and up narrow stairs to her room. There wasn't anything Samuel could do for her: if he helped her escape, the withdrawal from the drug would kill her with tremendous pain and besides, where could she go? There was nowhere to hide on Bisra for an escaped slave, the reward for their capture too much for many to resist, and the seas were not safe unless one was on an ocean vessel which would cost more gold than Samuel had. *If* he could have found any captain who would take her and if he could have got to a port. No, the poor lassie was trapped with no way out and he couldn't do a bloody thing about it except make her end as quick and as painless as possible when the time came.

The Keeper didn't bother speaking to his charge as he knew that, moments after the drug was ingested, she was a complete automaton again. Not until just before her next dose would her senses begin returning but before true understanding arrived, she would be given more of the stuff.

The two of them walked up the narrow staircase that led to her room. Breaking with protocol, Samuel walked past her and went inside instead of stopping at the door. It wasn't a big room but it was richly furnished. A large bed was made up with red satin sheets and covers. Paintings were on all the walls, heavy red curtains were drawn, hiding the fact that there were no windows. A gilt and white dressing table neatly covered in face paints and perfumes stood along one wall, while a tall cupboard held her clothing. A thick, warm carpet sprawled underfoot from wall to wall. For all its rich furnishings it still felt cold and sterile. She had no personal belongings and there was no way to relax. Not that she *could* relax, the Keeper reminded himself. He went to light a fire, knowing the slave couldn't unless ordered to. At least the poor girl would have some true warmth in her usually freezing chamber for once. The slave stood at the side of the large bed, not moving, seeming to watch him from the corner of her eye. Which was impossible. Even knowing that she was mindless, Samuel chatted to her as he usually did in private.

'There you go, lass,' he said. 'You best go do as the Mistress ordered now and don't forget to put a cold cloth on your face, to help take some of the swelling down and get rid of the blood. I will see you tomorrow, so until then you stay safe.' With that, he patted her cheek gently and froze with his hand still touching her face as he watched a tiny trickle of cocoa slide down from her lips to her chin. His eyes met hers and he saw shock and fear in them, emotions she should not, *could not* have. He felt his own lips stretch wide into a grin. Eyes shining he managed to speak calmly.

'Go and spit that out, drink water then make yourself sick. Do it as many times as you can and get rid of that poison. You know what will happen soon if you follow through with this, don't you?' At her nod Samuel turned her and pushed her gently to the bathroom door. If the slave managed to stop taking the Numb, in three months or so she would be dead. The fact she seemed to

23

know that eased the Keeper's conscience but he would find a way to make sure. Then he would help her as much as he could.

Samuel left the room, struggling to keep the emotions from showing on his face. Standing at his post at the top of the stairs, he waited for the men of the house to make their nightly visit. He wouldn't give her away to the Master, not if he could help it.

As the door shut behind her Keeper, the slave girl almost ran into her bathing room with its integrated water closet. She spat the mouthful of Numb down the toilet and drank a large glass of water before making herself vomit. She started the water running in her bath and drank another glass of water and vomited again. She added some lovely scented salts to her bath before drinking more water before vomiting that up too. The bath filled slowly as she forced herself to eject more of her stomach contents before she finally stopped. Her throat was sore and her body felt bruised and battered. Using the old toilet mechanism, she flushed the disgusting mess away. She rinsed her mouth out and brushed her teeth vigorously before undressing and sliding into the bath and allowing the jasmine scented water to dispel the sour smell of milk, cocoa and vomit that lingered in the room after clearing the latrine. She washed her hair with soap scented the same jasmine as the bath salts before pulling out the stopper and wrapping herself in a towelling robe.

She walked back into the main room and, although still groggy, she found that she was able to comprehend more of what was going on. She was also beginning to get flashes of her past. Drying herself off, and before she could do anything else, there was a faint tap on the door and Samuel opened it without looking in.

'There is a little soup here for you, girly, with a bit of bread. The Master will be coming to see you in an hour, he says, so you'd best be ready.'

She went to the door and pulled it open and looked directly into Samuel's face. She saw his handsome features clearly for the first time as she saw his eyes widen slightly in response to her stare. 'Careful, lass,' he said in an urgent whisper. 'What if Patcher had been here?'

All he got in answer was a slow blink as she deliberately dulled her expression and slowed her movements again, taking the tray from him to place on her dressing table top. Then she turned and looked at him enquiringly.

'What?' Samuel felt confused, unable to keep up with this version of the woman he had spent the last eighteen years with.

'Clothes?' was all she said, her voice raw and husky from the vomiting.

'Oh, right…no, nothing was said about clothes. Just that he will be here in an hour and I have to make sure you are ready.'

She gave a slight nod and then began eating quickly and neatly, the soup and bread disappearing rapidly. Then, as soon as the last mouthful had gone, she began painting her face before taking the towelling robe from her body and hanging it behind her chair.

'Blimmin' Void, lass!' was all Samuel could splutter, looking away from her nakedness.

'I have to be ready and he did not mention clothes.' The girl looked at him with confusion.

'Yeah, well,' He rubbed his hands briskly over his face. 'I need to get hold of myself or I will get us both killed.' He took a deep, steadying breath before continuing. 'Alright, lass…good luck.'

With that, Samuel took the empty food tray and left the room closing the door softly behind him. The slave girl finished her make-up before going to stand at the bottom of the bed, shivering slightly with the chill that still permeated the room, despite the fire burning merrily in the grate. A quick glance around helped to settle her nerves, as she saw that everything was in its proper place. Another look at the door and she took a chance, moving with lightning speed to add two more logs to the fire before returning to the foot of the bed again.

The girl stood and allowed the dullness to flood her mind. Whatever happened, she could not show that she was coming out of her drugged state. It would be a death sentence if the men realised that she had any spark of intelligence flickering inside her. Samuel would also be in danger. Standing motionless, she found herself remembering the last few hours and how, and why, her mind had begun to clear.

'Did he tup you?' was all Markus seemed to want to know. He sighed with relief as she shook her head, still staring off into the distance.

Lord Willoughby then barked out a question about the damage to the slave's face and the girl spoke about the Mistress's anger when she had arrived home with the fresh Numb.

A few minutes went by as Lord Willoughby forced himself to calm down. He knew many subtle ways to show his wife his displeasure and by the Shining One, she *would* feel his wrath. Markus continued to lean against his father's back, barely breathing until he felt the older man begin to relax. Giving a sudden grunt, the old man grabbed the girl by the hair and forced to her hands and knees, her rear facing them. Markus watched eagerly as his father pleasured himself within her body, touching and squeezing her buttocks as he thrust into her, quickly and roughly before grunting out his release. With one last groan of effort, he emptied himself completely before pulling out and lying down at her side, wheezing heavily. She stayed on her hands and knees until Markus moved her around so that he could take his own pleasure in a different way. A few minutes later, he too gave a gasp of pleasure as he emptied himself into her.

'Get us cleaned up.' Lord Willoughby snapped and the slave crawled off the bed. She walked into the small wash room, getting a cloth wet with warm, scented, water and rinsing her mouth out quickly. The two men lay side by side as the girl wiped away the bodily fluids on them. She went back into the bathroom and began washing herself, letting the sound of running water hide the small sounds of distress and retching that escaped her.

'I think there might be a problem for me and the Messenger girl, Papa,' Markus began, speaking of his worries. A habit both men had got into since they had begun sharing a slave together.

'Hmmm? A problem? Why is that, my boy?' The response from Lord Willoughby was drowsy. 'I thought that the Makepeace gal was suitable for you. She isn't beautiful, that is obvious, but that makes her more eager, m'boy. Her figure is good and I must say, the thought of you rumping with her is delicious. So, what is wrong?'

'Her name is Messenger, father. And you won't be there with me!'

'What?' The elder man sat up before leaning over his son in the rumpled bed. 'My sweet, dear boy if that is what is worrying you, don't fret. There are ways to make things happen, if it is truly wanted. Now explain in full and I will find a way to make it all better.' The small man smiled.

'You have almost always been here when I, well, you know. I don't worry about not being able to tup her. I want to enjoy myself but I never really do when I'm with anyone without your encouragement. Your words inspire me and I find that my pleasure is so much more. Unlike with our slavey, I cannot have you doing what I need in the bedroom of my wife.'

'That, my darling boy, is where you are wrong.' He looked up as the girl moved silently back into the room, before ordering her to get the Keeper to bring them fresh coffee and pastries to keep up his strength.

'Papa?' The younger man looked at his father, confusion on his face.

'I had the same worries when I married your mother.' Lord Willoughby began explaining. 'My problems were more severe than yours are now. The Searchers came looking in my school for one who was blessed by our most Holy Kintrelle. I was chosen and taken to the Academy when I was seven and stayed until your uncle Jerlane was stupid enough to get the Plague. Upon his death, I was your Grandfather's only heir which meant that I

32

had to leave the Academy. I was both heart-broken and angry. I loved my time at the Academy but at least your grandfather was able to teach me the manners of society.'

'So I will do for you what my father did for me, son. In the same way I showed you how to tup that,' a gesture over his shoulder pointed into the slave girl's general direction, 'he taught me how to act in the marriage bed. On my wedding night, a little dose of Bliss was added to your mother's wine. In such an amount it has a strong effect upon one, especially if they have never used it before. It is done for the woman's protection of course. No proper lady is happy with coupling and those who say they are cannot, by definition, be true ladies.' Both men laughed at this, knowing how many of society's ladies acted one way in the marriage bed and another in a lover's.

'After going into the bedroom,' Lord Willoughby continued, 'your mother undressed and put on her nightgown. By the time she had finished her preparations, she was, shall we say, in a very malleable and excited state. I told her that it was considered normal to tie a strip of fabric around her eyes. I waited a few minutes longer until she had begun to get more than a little flushed, with the Bliss sending erotic pleasure along her nerve endings. My father was already in the room and I watched as he removed your mother's gown. That was the first time I saw her naked. She didn't have a bad figure although she was a little skinny and her paps were too small for my taste. Your grandfather told me later that he had thought the same.'

Markus was sitting up in the bed, concentrating on every word, unable to hide his growing physical response. 'Well? What happened next?'

'What do you think happened, m'boy? Your grandfather had a touch and a stroke, your mother began squirming and panting and then he tupped her, making her squeal as he broke her in. The traditional listeners at the door laughed, went away, and your grandpapa took his time showing me how to act with a society lady. When he had finished, he stood at my side as I had my way with her. You were born nine months later. Your grandpapa enjoyed your mother very much and continued to join us in the marriage bed for the next year or two whenever he came to visit. So you see, you and the whatever-her-name-is girl would have been fine.'

Markus laughed with delight and gave his father a hug.

'Does Mamma know about this?'

'Good grief, no! She hated your grandfather, I never did know why. She seemed to think she was a cut above him yet it was our side of the family that had the title and the breeding. Your mother only brought the money. Thankfully, as well as making one ready for tupping, Bliss removes any true memory of it happening when it is mixed with alcohol.'

'Well,' Markus lay back on the pillows, casually stroking himself as he grinned at his father. 'I am looking forward to my wedding night, after all. I just need to get you to remember the girl's name.'

His father looked at his son gravely before placing his own hand over the younger man's. 'There may be a bigger problem than that, my boy,' he said.

Chapter Five

Before Willoughby could say anything else, there was a light tap on the door as the Keeper returned with the coffee and the pastries. The two men on the bed watched the slave leave her wash room, still naked, to take the tray at the door before carrying it to the little dressing table. Putting a selection of cakes onto a plate, she prepared two cups of coffee which she set ready at the side of the bed ready for the men to help themselves. Nothing was said for a few moments as both men enjoyed their refreshments and the slave returned to her position at the side of the bed.

'Papa, please explain.' Markus finished his meal and listened intently as his father answered.

'There is a terrible shortage of slaves, m'boy, which means those that don't have any are beginning to be in the majority. Lots of whispering is going on, with many people insisting that being a slave owner is degrading. I have been warned by my friends that there is a bill being talked about in the Leadership Conclave which could stop slavery altogether.'

Markus gave a gasp of horror. 'Can they do that? Don't they realise that the slaves don't live for long? What are they…?' His voice trailed off as his father held up his hand for silence.

'When slavery first began, it was a way to ensure the purity of human bloodlines. Many slaves were like her over there; from the foundling hospital, orphanages or from poor families. Nowadays the surgeons take away any chance of these inferior beings having young but there were plenty of brats to continue the slave lines before this. Once we began using Numb slaves began to die much more swiftly. Their deaths aren't the problem. The problem is that we haven't got enough new bodies to take their place. This one here is the exception to the rule; you know she should have died years ago yet she has held on and on. It is one of the reasons that your mother hates her. Your Mamma feels that you have an unnatural attachment to the slave which is why you aren't married yet.'

'Papa, I haven't yet married because there hasn't been a woman who will satisfy Mamma! Anyone I show any interest in, she finds fault with.' With that statement, Markus threw himself backwards on the pillows, sulking and glaring up at the decorated ceiling.

Lord Willoughby gave a slight smile at his son's antics. Now was the perfect opportunity to begin teaching the younger man about their own fortune and what devious dealings it took to make it. Curving his lips into a wider smile, Lord Willoughby shook his head at his son's pouting.

'I know, son,' he said. 'You have to understand, though, that most mothers act in this way when they have sons. She wants you to have an advantageous marriage but, in truth, she cannot bear to let you go so she finds fault. Your grandmother was just the same when it came to me. Although she has now proved to have had a point.'

'What do you mean?'

'Your grandmother said that your mother would never be a true member of society. She would only do all she had to for the sake of duty, and not one thing more. Is that not exactly what has happened? Once Lady Constance had you, she swore she would not have any other children and barred me from the marriage bed. It was only when your grandfather pointed out that I should have another child, just in case of accidents or childhood illness, that she even considered allowing me in her chambers again. Even so, I spoke to her and she refused me three times before I resorted to the Bliss again.'

'Did grandfather…?'

'Of course he did. We tupped the frigid woman for six months before she became pregnant with your sister and, once she knew for certain that she was carrying a child, her chambers again became locked against me. Your grandfather attempted to speak of her duty once again but, when he heard her response, he advised me to get a slave instead. Damn good advice too. A Bawdy House is a great experience but not one I wish to partake in too regularly. Even the higher class establishments run the danger of giving one the pox. And when one goes to the rougher dives, where the Housekeepers are not so particular in taking care of their brood, one runs an even higher risk.' As he spoke, Lord Willoughby rearranged his pillows to sit upright in bed rather than lounging. He glared down at his son and was pleased to see a look of apprehension cross Markus' face.

'Do you think me a fool, boy?' Lord Willoughby's voice was no longer reminiscent or playful but hard and sharp in its intonation. 'You think you can play me, laugh at me, take in the information I give because you think me stupid, before spilling it all to your mewling Mamma? I may look like a doddering fool but, believe me, I am nothing of the sort! I am a mummer, acting one way to get secrets out of others they think I am too unobservant to understand. You would do well to learn the same. Your own features are much too open, and easily readable by anyone.'

Markus gaped in shock. Far from being a figure of fun, he saw the strength in his father that was kept hidden from almost everyone else. Lord Willoughby examined his son's face, reading all the emotions flashing over the younger man's visage and nodded in satisfaction. It had been mainly guesswork, but he had been correct in his summation. Markus was a weak fool and could not be depended upon fully but such weakness meant that he could be manipulated in any way necessary. Lord Willoughby continued in a sharp tone, completely unlike his usual way of speaking.

'Now, listen to me, boy, and do as I say. You won't marry the Merryweather or Messenger chit or whoever the Void she is. In a few weeks time, we as a family will be sailing for Mertam. Once there, you will begin to look for a wife in earnest. I do not care who she is, aside from the fact that she will have to be of our station in life, malleable and with a large enough dowry. You will marry her and breed with her, though I will be there to tup her if you truly wish. Whatever works to get her with child. But know this; if you hope to get anything from me, in any way, you must learn caution. I told you when you came of age at fourteen that I would be a traditional father and I would teach you every pleasure known to man. Although no longer a Mage, I still intend to have everything I want. I will show you how to do the same but you have much to learn if you want to survive.' He paused as he thought about what he would say next.

'There is another reason we must leave.' He continued. 'We have to go partly because of the unsettled times, yes, but also partly because the blond waiter from Bridlington's has been captured and taken to the Watch Tower. He will be naming names within a few days.'

'But, Father! I have never before…I haven't…I didn't…' Markus was incoherent with panic. He truly did not recognise this cold man before him. The weak, pathetic old fool he thought he knew had transformed into a stranger, one with muscles of steel under a soft coating, with an energy that heated his flesh and sent a thrill through him.

'I swear, Papa, no man has ever touched me.' Markus was shocked; he hadn't realised that his father had recognised the attraction that he, Markus, had for males as well as females.

Lord Willoughby glared into his son's eyes and saw the truth. His son did not have the courage to work upon his own desires and would never be strong enough to fight for a prime position within the household. That wasn't necessarily a bad thing. Willoughby would teach the boy all that he could, but now that there was no chance of internal struggles within the household things would flow more readily. Far from being manipulated by the boy and his mother, he – Lord Jervis Ecort Temint Willoughby – was now in full control of his own destiny as well as his son's. Leaning down, he hugged his son before he rolled off the bed. Turning he caught the stunned look on Markus' face as the younger man began absorbing all the information offloaded upon him. Willoughby smiled his shark's grin, knowing he was way ahead of his wife's poorly played game of control.

'Well, Markus. From the look on your face, I could get you to tell me anything I want to know.' Leaning over, he patted his son's cheek. 'Go to your club tonight, it won't be raided for at least a week. Find someone who takes your fancy and spend time with him. Take a packet of Bliss with you. It will keep your cock erect if you take a pinch with water. No alcohol for you, remember! It will overcome any scruples in a reluctant partner if you put a little in their drink. The only thing I expect from you is to be back here by breakfast to help me sort through what papers we need to take with us and those we need to burn. You will learn much about our business in this way. We will leave this house by the middle of next month. Your mother and sister must think that we are off for a short holiday. You can get a small taste of what deviancy is about over the next few nights. If you want more then, when we reach our destination, I will help you to find a lover who is safe for you to have.' Pulling at his lower lip, Lord Willoughby continued. 'Never go for a servant. Yes, I have noticed how you look at the Keeper. We will find you either slave or a man of our own station. The first cannot say no, the second has as much to lose as you do. Another thing you would do well to remember: you are mine. Your first loyalty must be to me at all times. I am a very generous man when things go my way but I promise you, you will not enjoy my punishments if you betray me.'

While he had been speaking, Lord Willoughby had the slave girl wash him and help him dress in his exquisite clothing, transforming him from a man of power back to the silly, ineffectual idiot he preferred the world to see. Once dressed, he walked over to the big bed, where Markus still sprawled on the red satin sheets, marvelling about the man he had never truly known.

With a chuckle, Lord Willoughby moved towards the doorway, needing to begin putting his own plans into operation before the morrow.

'I have many things that need to be sorted out. I have no time for further explanations or even relaxation with you. So, get dressed and get off to your club now, you must take whatever opportunities come your way.'

With that, he walked briskly out of the room, closing the door firmly behind him. Markus lay there, stunned at the changes that had been wrought in his life in such a short time. He paused for a brief moment then began to laugh with delight. For years, he and his father had shared the bed with the slavey, Markus always trying to find out information to pass along to his mother in the eternal game that his parents played. Now though, his father had showed that he was a much more powerful man than Markus could have ever thought.

The young man jumped up and snatched the damp cloth still held by the silent slave and roughly freshened himself before dressing as quickly as he could, fumbling a little over his elaborate cravat. Rushing from the room, he slammed the door loudly behind him and moved past Samuel almost at a run, not even stopping give his usual offensive ogle at the handsome Keeper.

Inside the room, the slave girl began to sink down upon the bed when the door to her room was flung open again. Quickly she straightened up, hoping that Markus was too caught up in his own excitement to notice the change in her posture.

'Get the room cleaned up, change the sheets and give the old ones to your Keeper. When you wake up tomorrow, dress in your uniform and proceed with your usual work. Get the Keeper to build your fire up.' Duty done, the young man again left the room in a rush, wanting to get to his night of pleasure as quickly as possible. He stopped only to put on his heavy overcoat and accept the small parcel held out to him by the butler.

'Your father left this for you, sir. He said you would need it for this evening's entertainment.' The butler, Patcher, stood almost at attention. His naturally servile tone usually annoyed the younger Willoughby, but this time Markus just laughed as he took the parcel of drugs and ran out of the house into the street, calling for one of the cabbies who patrolled about, waiting to pick up a fare.

Inside the house, there was a feeling of confusion and disarray. Lady Constance frowned at the fact her son hadn't even bothered to come in and share his father's information with her, as he had previously. Lady Sophia was surprised at the flurry of her brother rushing past her on the stairs then curious at the way her father disappeared into his study without comment, locking the door behind him.

Up in the attics, the Keeper stood guard outside the slave's room, the door slightly ajar, allowing him to hear her cleaning up. He wanted to go to her but kept to his place in case of any lurking spies, knowing Patcher's habit of turning up unexpectedly. He waited for the used sheets to be put outside the door as usual.

Inside the room the slave's mind still wasn't completely clear but she knew she had discovered some valuable information tonight.

She had discovered that the family would be beginning the journey to foreign shores in just a few weeks. If she tried to escape the household before leaving this land she would still face major hurdles, whereas if she waited until they had crossed the sea, she might have more chance of getting the important three miles away, beyond the collar's punishment range.

She would also be closer to the FreeLands. If she could bypass the magik, find the border, slip past patrols or find a portal, she knew she would at least be able to die free. Stopping the Numb meant certain death within three months anyway but that still left her plenty of time to breathe free air. If she didn't get away, if they shocked her to death, at least she would have died trying.

All of this went through her mind slowly even as her body worked automatically to do what she had been ordered. She slipped on her wrapper and then placed the dirty linen outside the door and looked into Samuel's eyes. With a slight tilt of her head, she mentioned Markus's last orders. The Keeper gave an expressionless nod and walked into the room, making sure that the door was firmly closed after him so that no sound would be heard from outside. Placing his hands on her shoulders, he studied her for any physical hurts as she quickly spoke of all that had happened to her, from the moment Lady Sophia had ruined the Numb earlier in the day right up to Markus's orders as he left. Samuel gave little reaction but his mind flew from one thing to another, planning and preparing.

'You will need help when you run,' he murmured and then grinned at her start of surprise. 'Come on, poppet, do you really think I would expect you to keep being what they want? I will do all I can to help you. Rather die free than die a slave, right?'

She nodded solemnly, her eyes filling with tears. 'I can keep going, keep pretending for now but not forever. I feel sick at the thought of taking that stuff again, even though I know there will be times I have to. If you know I have had it, make me vomit, promise?'

'I give you my word. I promise I will do everything I can to help in any way possible to keep you with us. Now, this bloke who helped you. You said he called himself Mr Poole?' At the girl's nod, Samuel grinned. 'Well, I know a lot about him, alright. Don't know if he can help us or not, but I will find a way to talk to him, ok? You may find yourself free from sex for the next few days as the Master will be too busy trying to plot the journey and Markus will be too busy having his cock serviced by anyone he can drug, so there is that, anyway.'

Looking at him, the girl frowned slightly and said abruptly. 'You like men, don't you, Samuel?'

The Keeper froze. Here was his secret, why he had become a Keeper. The one thing that could get him sent to the Punishment Square as an invert if he admitted it aloud. He stared into the young woman's deep grey eyes and she looked steadily back. After what seemed hours but was actually only a few seconds, he decided that the slave deserved to know his truth.

'I don't know for sure but I think so. I have never touched another man but I haven't touched a woman either. Being a Keeper means I don't have to spread my seed like everyone is supposed to do. I find that the only ones to catch my eye are male so I assume that I am a deviant. I have never tried to find out for a fact. I cannot trust anyone to know me that closely. I trained to become a Keeper so I wouldn't be forced to touch a woman or to breed. You probably don't remember but I came here when you first arrived and expected to watch over you for a few years before giving you an easy death and then going on my way with enough gold to travel into the country to hide from the city officials and their hypocritical rules. Eventually I expected that I would grow old and die as virginal as I had come into the world. You have changed things though, my girl.'

The smile on his face reassured the slave. 'They might allow deviancy in the FreeLands. Samuel, you must come with me and we will both be free. You will have to anyway, to make sure that my body is allowed to fade away as it is supposed to. No crypts and no communal pits please; just lay me under a tree and let my physical self nourish the earth.'

Samuel felt his heart crack at the thought of this woman dying but he knew there was no point in pretending it wouldn't happen and sooner rather than later. He just hoped that this extraordinary person survived a little more than the usual three months so that she could have a true taste of freedom.

'I promise you that I will stand as your family and I will look after you, in life or in death. Understand?' His voice was husky with emotion that surprised him as did the slave girl reaching out and hugging him close, her head buried in his shoulder. A few minutes later, they moved apart, both calmer and more connected than before. Samuel winked at her and kissed her bruised cheek before going and putting more fuel on the fire. After leaving her room, he collected his sleeping pallet and placed it across the entrance to her room.

Undressing quickly in his own rooms that were situated next to hers, he ignored the jug of spirits that the butler had sent up and went and laid down upon his thin mattress, pretending to sleep. A few minutes later he heard soft footsteps and he lifted his head only to hear a quiet curse and then rapidly fading steps retreating quickly. Samuel grinned in the darkness before he allowed himself to fall into a light doze.

Inside the room, the girl put on a wisp of a nightgown that would give her a little protection from the damp air before she climbed into the freshly made bed, thankful that she couldn't smell the two men on the sheets. Trying to sleep, she found another problem with not taking the drug. Her thoughts twisted and turned in her head, her mind raced with ideas, fear and deliberations. Eventually, she sat up and clasped her knees as she began to formalise plans for her short future.

She didn't hear the footsteps of the butler, not having yet remembered that he would sneak in and use her body most nights after the Master had left. She didn't hear the settling of the house and she never noticed herself slowly slip into a heavy slumber. She also didn't notice that for the first time since the collar had been placed around her neck, her cheeks stayed dry and clear of the tears she had previously shed in her sleep as her subconscious dealt with the pain of her life.

Chapter Six

By the time the sun rose the following morning, the slave girl had cleared all the grates in the house laying, and lighting, the new fires before taking the ash outside for the garden. Having emptied the chamber pots from the rooms of the servants she dealt with the bathrooms, scrubbing and cleaning each one until it sparkled. Then it was time for her worst job. She went down to the cellars and changed into the evil smelling rags kept there. Going through a heavy door she stood in a large room that held one huge container, paired with two much smaller ones, connected to the house by a complicated series of pipes. The biggest needed to be filled with fresh water from the well and the other two had to be emptied of the used water and bodily fluids that had been flushed away from the working baths and toilets the day before.

This was the hardest and dirtiest physical work the slave had to do. Topping up the clean water was heavy and monotonous involving filling the bucket at the pump, staggering back indoors to climb the steps to tip the water into the container made her legs and arms ache. What came next was even worse. Unhooking the pipes on the container of body waste, the slave pulled the wheeled container down the gravelled pathway right to the bottom of the garden, leaving it near the back gate for the tanners to collect later in the day. Each step made the viscous liquid slosh and hit the sides of the container, sending up a nauseating stench. As she walked, she made sure to keep her back to the house as she was unable to prevent herself gagging regularly at the stench. This, she decided, was another downside of no longer being numbed. This smell would not have even registered on her senses while on the drug, whereas now she had to fight hard not to vomit again and again.

At the gate there was a replacement container, scrubbed clean and much easier to wheel back and connect to the pipes. The second container was taken out and placed near the compost heap. There she added the bath and washing water to a water butt, so that this waste water could be used on the garden.

Before going back inside the house, the slave gulped in fresh air, trying to lessen the nausea she felt at the stench that seemed to have burnt into her nostrils. Going inside, she changed into her house-work clothes before going back to her room and washing herself thoroughly with a disinfectant soap to cut through worst of the smell before dressing again and continuing with her work.

She brushed all the carpeted stairs, polishing the banisters as she went. This was followed by sweeping the polished wooden floors, knowing that the rugs and carpets wouldn't need the heavy beating to clean them until two days hence. Finally she went back to her room, where she washed up again before sitting and eating her breakfast, feeling almost physically sick with hunger. Samuel had brought her food into the room just a few moments earlier. Without comment, he placed the tray on the dressing table and looked at the dress that covered her completely. With a mute apology the Keeper loosened the ties at her neck, pulling the fabric lower to show more of her creamy skin. With a small smile, and a nod of her head, she accepted the changes to her costume and then sat on the small stool to begin eating.

Oh, the delight of tasting food brought a moan to her lips. Samuel glanced quickly at the door, shut it, and then leaned back against it as he enjoyed the spectacle of the slave eating this basic meal. She obviously enjoyed the tea, sipping the hot beverage and rolling it around in her mouth before swallowing, her eyes closed in ecstasy. The porridge was eaten with a screwed up nose until Samuel stepped forward and added a little honey. This made it a little more palatable but she still ate the cold, heavy gloop without pleasure. Seeing the thick stuff sticking to the spoon Samuel admitted to himself that he would struggle to enjoy that mixture, being so different from the tasty hot bowlful he had eaten an hour before. The cold eggs were also eaten quickly, without much enjoyment, but the thick slabs of bread he toasted for her over her fire before he smothered them in butter and honey were eaten with murmurs of appreciation.

Once the girl had indicated that she was full there were still some bread slices left, so without a word, the Keeper hid them in a drawer, wrapped in a clean kerchief along with the dish of butter. Then he poured out the last of the tea and shared it with her.

'Is that what I usually eat?' She asked the question so quietly that it took a moment for Samuel to recognise it as such. He shook his head and smiled at her.

'What you eat depends on what the servants have left. I didn't bring everything that was on the platters because, once you are told to eat, you keep on doing so until you vomit. I am trying to make sure you have enough to keep you going until your next meal this evening, without over-doing it. I left behind some kidneys and some kedgeree, thinking that now you are awake you only need a little at a time. If you get hungry during the day, I can sneak here and get you some of the bread. It will be a little stale by then, but...'

His voice trailed away as the slave girl held up her hand, her head cocked to one side. Samuel stood quickly and began speaking in the slow loud voice he had been told to use when training her.

'...so make sure this,' he opened the door swiftly, keeping his back to the entrance, 'handle on both sides is polished properly as the Master wishes, do you understand?'

Inside the room, the slave stood facing her Keeper without any expression. Giving a short slow nod, she gazed emptily over

Samuel's shoulder. The butler, Patcher, was standing there and he looked at her up and down. He *knew* there was something different about the slave, but it just wouldn't come to him what it was. While the girl and Samuel were both acting brilliantly and giving their best performances, the slave was unable to hide all of the life beginning to show in her features, no matter how empty and numb she acted.

'What is it, Patcher?' Samuel grunted out the question impatiently.

'The Master wants to see the girl before she has her dose this morning, Keeper. She needs to go to the breakfast room now.'

Samuel raised an eyebrow in interrogation but the older man turned away and began walking to the stairs.

Watching him until he was close to the stairwell, Samuel then called out quietly, 'Mister Patcher? I had a strange dream last night. I didn't drink your gift of brandy for once, sir, as I was just too tired to remember it. I fell asleep soon enough but just as I began to travel to the deeper realms I thought I heard footsteps here. Would *you* know about that, Mister Patcher? If you know of any servant who is trying – or has *succeeded* – in touching the slavey, *you* would tell me, wouldn't you? Unless you haven't noticed, the Master does not like to share.'

The butler did not miss the faint emphasis that Samuel had given to certain parts of the comment and quivered with rage but he understood that he was being given fair warning, something that, by Bisra Law, Samuel did not have to do. As Keeper, Samuel was expected to protect his charge from anything or anyone acting without the Master's permission. The Keeper could simply draw his dagger and kill the butler where he stood. With a nod, the older man acknowledged the warning.

'Don't worry, youngster, the slave won't be bothered again. The Master has big changes planned. Speaking of which, you'd best get a move on before he gets annoyed.' With that, he shuffled down the steps, not once having looked at Samuel or the slave since giving his message. The Keeper exchanged a quick glance with the girl then stepped back to allow her passage. Her face was completely blank and Samuel felt a shiver of fear, wondering if she was getting lost again in the haze of her own mind. His fears evaporated when he heard her whisper something to him as she walked past. He had to call upon all of his training to stop the shout of elation leaving his lips.

She had remembered her name.

Walking into the breakfast room a moment later, Samuel gave a nod to his Master followed by a short bow to his Mistress. The slave girl stood a few steps behind him, her hands clasped together in front of her.

'Mr Patcher said you needed to see the slave, sir?' he enquired.

'Ah, yes, Keeper. There are going to be certain changes happening in the near future and I wanted to see that she was well enough to travel, especially after her ordeal last night.' Lord Willoughby dabbed his mouth with a linen napkin, eyeing the silent girl up and down. 'Is she badly marked this morning?'

Samuel gave a silent thank you to the guardians of life, grateful that he had thought to ask the girl earlier about her injuries. When she had been a walking but empty shell, he had done his job without thinking, it never crossing his mind that what he did had any effect upon her in her Numb trance. Now he knew that she was becoming more and more aware of her surroundings and what was going on, he just could not bring himself to do any of the intrusive checks any more. This morning she had been able to use the lavatory and have a wash without Samuel being in the same room, watching her every move.

'The bruises upon her breasts are small but there is strong discolouration and some swelling. As you can see yourself, sir, the slavey's face has also bruised and will take some time to heal. I applied the Heal-All paste earlier, so that should help.' Samuel kept his voice low and even, not allowing any emotion to show in his words.

His Master sat expressionless as he perused the girl. Both cheeks had turned a delicate purple and there was more bruising along her jaw. Her lips were also slightly swollen and he spotted the small cut to the side of her mouth that he had not noticed properly in the dim light of the previous evening. With great energy he slammed his fist onto the breakfast table, breaking his plate and scattering silverware and foodstuffs. His wife and daughter jumped in their seats and Lady Sophia gave a low cry of fear. Unnoticed by anyone but Samuel and the girl, Lord Markus stepped into the room behind them, waiting just inside the doorway to see what was happening.

When Lord Willoughby spoke, his voice trembled with barely suppressed anger. 'If the girl had been damaged permanently you would be made to pay the price, *my dear*.' The scorn in his voice when he said the last two words was thick and heavy as he sneered at his wife. '*If* she had been permanently disfigured by your actions, I would have had the right to send you away...and *believe* me, madam, I would have done so. You have played your petty power games these last few years, trying to undermine me in my own house-hold. No, you will *not* leave the room; you will stay and listen to me. You have finally reached my limits and now I say enough! This slavey is more important to this household than you are, madam. You have constantly refused me my rights and this slave has ensured that I have taken no mistress to usurp your position. Endanger her in any way again, and I will go to the Conclave and speak to the Preceptor of the Church to deny you as my wife. Don't forget, I have proof of your lack of affection, my dear, which means I would get to keep your fortune and will be allowed to take another and where would you be then? Homeless, penniless and, madam, completely childless!'

Lady Constance had been giving tiny squeaks of astonishment and anger all the way through this speech but when he finished, she gave a great cry of shock.

'No, my Lord, you cannot...you would not be so cruel...' her voice cracked on her words as she felt her world crumble slowly around her.

Her husband sat and looked at her in silence before turning to his daughter and speaking in a much gentler tone. 'Sophia, my darling, do stop looking so frightened and dry your tears for your father's sake, there's a good girl.' His eyes flickered to Markus, raising an interrogative eyebrow, allowing a small smile to appear at his son's answering smirk and satisfied nod. He turned back to his daughter. 'I must accept much of the blame for what has been happening in this household but you all need to understand that, as from today, things are to be very different. To begin with, Constance, you will apologise to the slave girl.' As his wife just continued to stare at him, open-mouthed, he glared hard at her and rapped out; '*Now*, Constance!'

Her Ladyship hadn't moved, stunned at his change in attitude. She struggled to understand what was happening, taking a few seconds for his demand to sink in. Her eyes bulged in horror at what he was asking her to do. He stared coolly back at her, only raising an eyebrow and tilting his head when she didn't do his immediate bidding. Her mouth dry and tasting bitterly of ashes, Lady Constance managed to mumble something out that could have been taken as an apology. Her colour was high with the rage coursing through her and she knew she would never forgive her husband for this humiliation.

'Hmmm, that will do, I suppose,' was all Lord Willoughby said in response to her glare once she had finally finished. 'Now I will explain to our daughter just why this slavey is so important to us. You will stay and listen and be reminded of your place and your responsibilities. I hope I will never have to repeat it again.' Turning again to his daughter, Lord Willoughby's attitude gentled.

'There are many reasons that we have a slavey, my dear. For one thing, she does lots of the nasty work that no servant wishes to do. She doesn't need a wage and will keep going until she drops from exhaustion. My original investment in this one has repaid itself many times over.

The girl herself wasn't very expensive as she wasn't a beauty and had that scar on her face, along with a few others on her body, which gave me a decent discount. The collar cost a significant amount originally and every time a new jewel is added, it costs a little more. Each gem represents a skill the girl has learned, so our slavey has many skills, including those no one else wants to do. The more gems she wears, the more valuable she is to us, and others but the most important jewel in her collar is the fireheart. This jewel means she has been taught how to pleasure her bed partner.'

He glared again at his wife before he carried on. 'The reason this is so important to me is that your mother has refused to allow me into her bed ever since we realised that she was ripe with you. One thing she has never understood is that men have needs. If these needs are not met, aggression and anger can explode from them, causing trouble, pain and even death. Now, as my wife, it is her job to keep me contented and this she has not done. So I turned to a slavey, thereby not causing gossip or shame to her, yet she still acts in a destructive manner towards our property.'

'Markus,' here he nodded to the doorway, including his son into the conversation. 'Markus has been prevented from getting betrothed on at least three occasions because of spurious, petty concerns put forward by your mother. But this has not taken his bodily needs into account. He is, thankfully, a real man who has strong natural urges. Instead of running around in Bawdy Houses and catching terrible diseases, or ending up being forced into marriage by a cheap tart pretending a pregnancy is his, he has the use of the house slave. Because I am there when he releases himself, I can assure everyone that there is no emotional connection between either of them. It is not as if the girl is a real person. She is like this cup, or a spoon, or any other useful household object that has no feelings, no emotions. So the next time you hear your mother making any comments about the slave, I want you to remember that it is my foresight that has kept us at our elevated position in Society. No scandal has ever been connected to us and that is because I am a cautious man.' Lord Willoughby blew out a breath and took a sip of his cooling tea before explain the rest to both his wife and daughter.

'We are going to be going on a holiday across the sea. I am not sure how long we will be gone but I want you to go and begin choosing what you need to take with you. Include your embroidery and a few books, my dears, as there will be times when you will have to amuse yourself on board the ship. Once we arrive at our destination, I will provide money to clothe you in the local fashions so you need not worry about too many dresses. Consider travel costumes, and perhaps two ball gowns and your jewellery in case of invitations. Start making your decisions now as we will be leaving soon to travel to the coast.'

Sophia jumped up, dutifully kissed his cheek and then rushed from the room. She wasn't as tall as her mother but had the same slender build. Her rich honey coloured hair was pinned back in a simple knot at the base of her neck and she had no idea that this style made her violet eyes, unusual in themselves, stand out. Although she was almost at her majority of twenty-five, there was a naivety about her and she had felt dreadfully embarrassed when Papa spoke about needs, especially his and Markus's. And a holiday! She couldn't remember anything like this happening before.

Inside the breakfast room, Lady Constance sat frozen in her seat, staring into space. Lord Willoughby looked at her and then nodded his head. Yes, the bitch was cowed for the moment. Now for the next phase.

'Constance, look at me.' Lady Constance raised her head, flinching at the cold look in his eyes. 'I didn't want to do this. It has made me seriously uncomfortable, my dear, but you did bring it upon yourself. Once you have finished your food, take the slave and give her this morning's dose, then you may begin your own packing. Remember to pack lightly as we will get proper clothing once we arrive.'

Her voice came out as a dry croak as she spoke. 'Where are we bound?'

'I am waiting for some confirmation so I will keep it a surprise for now but we will begin our journey soon as I have already mentioned. Hurry along now.'

Without looking or speaking to him or Markus, she swept out in a rustle of satin skirts and an imperious jerk of her head to the slavey. Samuel turned to follow along but was stopped in his tracks by a command from his Master so he murmured instructions to the slave and watched her as she left the room.

'You heard that we are leaving? Good. Now I want you to get the slave's travelling clothes. Just her decent day wear and a few of the cosmetics. Here is a list for you. You also need to get your things packed too, unless you would prefer to stay behind?' At Samuel's quick shake of his head, Lord Willoughby gave a satisfied grunt.

'You will both begin your journey on the morrow and travel overland to Merino Bay, we will follow along soon after. The ship we are travelling on is the Queen of Light captained by a man called Grigaria. You have four weeks to get there. You will take some of our luggage, as well as that of the slave and yours. I will be hiring some guards to escort you. The distance between ourselves and the slave should calm her Ladyship down a little. Go and begin your work, Keeper.'

Turning away, and ignoring Samuel's short bow, Lord Willoughby held out his hand to his son who took it and both men left for the study. Samuel picked up the list and moved down the passage, hearing the turn of the key in the study door as he passed. After he had gone a few steps, the door unlocked and opened. His Master called out to him.

'Keeper? Get packed quickly enough and you will have time to go and say your goodbyes to your family this evening. Be back by curfew though. The cart will be packed, food and silver provided, along with the slavey's daily doses and gifts for the roadside altars. I want you both to leave as soon as you have broken your fast in the morning. You can give her the morning dose on the road.'

Samuel gave his thanks for the freedom of the evening and then went on his way, hearing the door close and lock behind him.

Chapter Seven

Lady Constance was furious. How dare her husband speak to her as if she was some servant to be chastised! And in front of the children and that bloody slave girl too! Her slippered feet marched swiftly to the drawing room, which was stuffy and stale and already too warm from the fire in the grate. Of course, the stupid girl didn't even have the sense to open the window or not to lay a fire. Watching the slave girl come and stand in front of her, the older woman felt her anger flare even higher. What was it about this damned slave that got her so enraged and caught the eyes of males so easily? Sinking down onto one of the sofas, Lady Constance began to think things out and really try to explain her own emotions to herself.

The few times she had had relations with her husband were fuzzy in her mind. She remembered feeling incredibly hot and having sensations that, admittedly, were not unpleasant and that was all she could recall. Was it because it was unladylike to take pleasure in the marriage bed? Or was it something else?

She stood and began pacing; thoughts, memories and the hundred tiny clues all coming together at long last in her mind. Memories of another time with another man, one who had touched her heart as well as her body. She caught sight of the box of Numb sitting on the table and froze. Could Willoughby have done that? Could he have used some vile concoction on her? She paced more and more as her thoughts racing when, suddenly, she thought about her Father-by-Law. How she loathed that man. The way he had ogled her, smirking as he focused his gaze upon her breasts, the way he spoke so slyly about the family traditions, all of which seemed to consist of perversions based on the men of the family sharing various women.

Then the sickening truth dawned on her. She *had* been drugged. The bastards had bloody *drugged* her! She wasn't having nightmares when she woke with a cry of panic, ice cold yet sweating with fear. It had actually happened. She remembered various times when she had woken up feeling confused and in pain, covered in unexplained bruises and the visit from the physician who told her that the episodes would pass and to take rest whenever she woke up in disarray. The angry, low voiced discourse between the physician and her husband had been too far away for her to hear but she had recognised the seriousness of the conversation. They had never seen him again, a new one was hired any time it was deemed necessary but she hadn't had many more of those episodes, none at all since the death of her husband's father.

Constance tried to remember other specifics but the images slipped through her grasp like water. No matter, she knew now, she knew that her husband hadn't been on his own when he had taken his rights: he had actually shared her with the disgusting lecher who had sired him. Breathing heavily, she clenched her fists and began to plan.

The slave took it all in, watching the tall slim woman, pacing back and forth. Lady Constance was no outstanding beauty but she had a very arresting face. Her hair was braided and pinned firmly, beaded hair ornaments keeping her locks firmly in place. Her blue eyes were cold and slightly unfocused as she stared into her future, her shapely lips pressed tightly together in rage and worry. The silken skirt of her elaborately embroidered dress swung and rustled with every step.

'For the first time since you arrived, I do not attach blame to you, girl. I have placed you in the wrong yet you have never had a choice. Forgive me for my past transgressions. I truly see now that you have had no option in what you do. But I must find a way to make him pay. And you, how much have you had to suffer from his touch? For at least there would be some kind of constraints upon their worst behaviours where I am concerned, purely because of status. If I get hurt, I can turn to the Law in the same way he threatened to. Yet you, my child, what pains have you endured and with no chance to turn for help or to escape. I should have been the one to help you, to stop them but I didn't, too caught up in self-pity and anger. I have done you so much wrong. The *bastard*! I must spoil his games and make him pay for everything he has done to me and to you. What have I become?' She kept her voice in a whisper but the rage was even more obvious for that.

Another turn of the limited floor space and Lady Constance came to her decision. Taking her own face mask, she offered another to the slave, impatiently putting it on her with when the girl ignored the gesture. Taking the ornate box, and moving quickly, she went and stood by the fire. Exhorting the girl to hold her breath before doing the same, Lady Constance then tipped the whole box of Numb into the burning fire. With a noisy '*whoomp*' the flames burned red and green, violet and black as great gusts of smoke billowed into the room as well as up the chimney. Rushing to the window, Lady Constance flung the curtain open and struggled with the sash. When it opened reluctantly, she waved the girl over and reminded her to breathe. Cupping the slave's face in her hands, the lady of the house felt sadness flood her very soul, and anger at her own actions made tears well in her eyes as she spoke.

'Good grief, what have I done? I have killed you, girl. But then, better to be dead then to be at the beck and call of such as us. Slave, if your Master ever asks you, I have given you your dose every day, twice a day as stated. Understand?' Her voice was regaining strength with each word she spoke, yet was still weighed down with emotion. 'You have never missed a dose. Ever. Do you understand? And may Kintrelle receive you with love.' The slave nodded and the Lady of the house sent her on her way. Looking out of the barred window, Constance began planning her future as well as her revenge on Lord Willoughby before closing her eyes, placing one hand over her heart and reaching out with her other to pray for forgiveness.

Walking slowly but steadily back to her room, the slave felt astounded. So many things had happened in such a short time, so many changes. She felt breathless and a strange fluttering under her breast bone gave her pause, until she recognised this unknown sensation. It was hope. Desperately wanting to shout and scream, skip and run, she forced herself to remain numb, continuing to pace down the dark hallway towards her own staircase. Suddenly, Patcher stepped out of the shadows and gave a sly grin.

'You pretend real well, peach, but I know there is something different about you. So remember, I am watching you and that Keeper of yours. One step out of line and the old man will know.'

Without another word, he grabbed the young girl and dragged her forward. His hands squeezed her breasts and the bruises reacted painfully and he pressed his lips against hers, thrusting his tongue deep into her mouth. A split second before she would have screamed, he pushed her away from him with some force and she stumbled a few steps. 'Don't think I've given up on you, peach. I'm still going to have you. Remember, I'll be watching.' There was a pause as he kept looking at her, waiting for a reaction but she continued to stare through him and didn't even wipe the thick trail of spittle he had left on her chin.

'Oh, for void's sake, move! Do exactly what the Mistress told you to do.' The words snapped out and Patcher watched her as she moved towards her stairs at exactly the same measured pace she had always used. He was still sure there was something different but exactly what that was, he couldn't decide.

Samuel opened his mouth to greet the girl as she stepped into the room but snapped it shut as she calmly pushed the door shut before running through to her bathroom where she was violently and noisily sick. With a worried glance towards her, Samuel made sure that the main door had closed properly and heated up some of his own tea on the little spirit stove kept near the fire. When she walked back into the room, pale and shaking with a wet face from washing, all he did was hand her a piece of slightly stale bread and the hot liquid.

'Don't say anything just nibble on this and take small sips of your drink. Sit down and settle your nerves while I tell you what happened when you left the breakfast room.'

So the girl sat chewing carefully on the bread and letting the liquid warm her through, her stomach settling as she listened. Once the Keeper had finished speaking, it was her turn to tell of everything that had gone on out of his sight. She felt a sense of pleasure as he reacted to her story, gasping in surprise at the actions of the mistress of the house then growling in anger at the butler and his words.

'I will kill him.' Samuel spoke quietly and with no particular force but the girl shivered at the dark promise that she heard in his words. 'There are a few things to be sorted before we go tomorrow. I have been given leave for this evening, so I can go out and find Mr Poole, I hope. Now though, I am worried about Patcher; he must have been giving me a sleeping draught for years. If I go to find Mr Poole, Patcher is going to try and have his way with you. There is no way you can fake the Numbness and just let him tup you, right?' A quick glance at her face convinced him of that point. There was a silence while they both pondered the issue before the girl's face lit up and she began to giggle.

'What? Why are you laughing?' Even though his voice was low, she could hear surprise in his voice and she grinned at him, flashing a dimple at the corner of her mouth that he had never noticed before.

'When it is time for you to go, you need to speak with the Master,' she began.

'Are you mad? Void it, girl, I can't tell him about Patcher. That could bring everything out into the open...' his voice tailed off as he saw her continuing to smile at him as she shook her head gently.

'No, Samuel, you don't mention Patcher at all. What you do is go to the Master, acting all embarrassed and awkward. Say something along the lines of you being worried because of so much unrest in the house caused by the travelling plans as well as the fact that I was damaged last night, so you felt that it was sensible to lock his property away safely. Then you hand him the key. If he chooses to believe you're worried about her ladyship but you don't want to speak out of turn, well, that isn't your problem, is it?' she finished triumphantly.

Samuel sat and thought about her plan and then began to grin himself. 'That is perfect. It will pander to his need for power without actually saying anything precise, which also means no comeback on me or you. Even if he does give the key to Patcher, you are still safe because the butler won't dare take the chance of being caught with you. A perfectly elegant solution, my girl.'

The rest of the day was spent in each other's company, packing, cleaning and hiding certain objects within the luggage. By late afternoon all of the slave's property was safely stored in a trunk, leaving plenty of room for food and all of Samuel's belongings. A little more tidying, a few more things hidden away and then they were done. A quick glance at the time and then

Samuel went down the stairs into the kitchen where the cook was busy making an elaborate meal for the family as well as arranging the foodstuffs for the journey. Meat and potato pies were cooking in the oven, as well as fruit tarts and pasties. A side of bacon, a long link of sausages, raw meat and eggs were being packed in straw before being placed into wooden crates. Eight loaves and a bag of oats were added to the box along with a selection of vegetables and fruits. There would be milk, honey, ale, tea and even a selection of herbs added to the box before it was placed in the cool room, ready to put on the cart just before it was time to leave.

Samuel made up a large plate of food stuffs to take to the slave, along with a large jug of milk. The little spirit stove kept in her bedroom would be able to heat it up. The cook raised an eyebrow to see such food and drink being sent just for the girl but Samuel lied about how he preferred eating before he said goodbye to family as his mother was terrible in the kitchen. His comments easily diverted the cook who gave him some of the cake she had baked earlier before she got on with making some cheese scones to add to the travel box. Once he had collected the food and drink onto a tray, Samuel turned to go, almost walking into Patcher. Both men paused as their eyes met but with a slight smile and a brisk nod of his head, the Keeper moved past the butler and took his booty to the top room.

A short time later, Samuel was ready to go and look for Mr Poole. Everything that needed to be packed was in the trunk, including two precious books, although the lid wasn't yet fastened. Samuel had collected the counterfeit Numb that Lady Constance had made from harmless stuff that looked almost the same as the original. Four doses had been left out: two for tomorrow and two for the following day, just in case anyone decided to check the room before he returned. A quick hug to his charge and then he headed for the door. Brandishing the key to her chambers he grinned.

'Wish me luck! Oh, and if you can read, you are welcome to one of the books.'

As he began closing the door, he froze as she quietly called his name. With a quick check to see that Patcher wasn't anywhere near, he stuck his head back round the door and raised a questioning brow.

'What?'

'When you find Mr Poole, tell him that I said hello.'

'I most definitely will...now shush.' He winked then shut the door firmly before locking it. With a shiver, the slave went and looked into the looking glass, examining her features one by one.

'You have a name now, a real name and don't you forget it,' she murmured almost soundlessly.

With that, she changed into her nightwear, selected an apple from the tray still full of food and climbed into bed with one of Samuel's books. Soon she was engrossed in reading about the adventures of a young Mage as he grew and moved through his years in the Academy until he became The Preceptor. Much of it she didn't understand fully, but she found herself enjoying the process of remembering a skill she had not had need to use since she had finished her slave training.

In the meantime, the Keeper walked to the study and knocked on the door gently with his tipstaff. Knowing this door was always locked, he wasn't surprised at the slight delay before it opened. His Master wore his shirt loosely over his breeches and was sweating heavily. This seemed to do with the blazing fire that the Keeper saw Markus adding a few more papers to. Affecting a stammer, Samuel explained that he had locked the slave in her room because of all the upset, just in case there was further trouble. Lord Willoughby gave the Keeper a searching look before giving a grunt of acknowledgement.

'Good idea. Has the slave had her dose? Better she has it too early than too late.' At the other's nod, he gave another grunt, this time of satisfaction. 'Alright, you go and say your goodbyes. Once we have reached our destination you will be able to choose between coming back or staying on, so something to think about that as you travel. Keep the room key, then you can sleep in the slave's boudoir when you get back tonight - easier to get yourselves ready as the sun rises tomorrow. You will need to buy two carts and either horses or giroxes, whichever you can get at short notice. There will also be a few errands to run before you come back and pack the luggage onto the carts. I will see to the hiring of guards and a driver for the second cart. I will write out your final instructions in a letter that I will push under the slave's door, keeping it away from prying eyes. I will also make sure there is enough silver to pay to the road shrines along with food offerings separate from your own. Take these coins to leave with your family and now be off.' With that, he shut the door firmly.

Putting on his short jacket as well as a cloak and his hat, Samuel went out of the front door – a special Keeper privilege – and began his hunt for Mr Poole.

Chapter Eight

The evening was wet and cold and the wind was sharp and cutting as Samuel walked from place to place, hunting for the elusive Mr Poole. The rough, unkempt, pathways told him how far he was moving down into the lower levels of society. He had walked through streets that began as cobbled with broad pavements outside large stone houses set in grounds full of flowers, bushes and trees. The ground had changed slowly to hard packed dirt and smaller dwellings of just one or two storeys and much smaller gardens now full of vegetables and some holding a goat or two. He finally found himself walking along streets of mud and effluence filled with the patched homes of the low dwellers. These were completely different from the previous structures, being made of any scrap that could be scavenged from the piles of rubbish that were collected in one place every few streets. On each floor lived families or crowds of twenty or more, sharing out the rooms between them. Occasionally a smaller hut broke the monotony of the taller wooden buildings. These were of the same patchwork of wood, mud and scavenged parts but were smaller and colder. They could be broken down easily but they gave the illusion of privacy some people craved. Mýste drifted about much more in this part of town so the Keeper kept alert for that and any footpads.

It always amazed the Keeper that just a mile or so away there were empty properties that could be sold to give each of these low dwellers an easier and safer life but they seemed so used to living like rats, none of them moved far from the streets they were born in.

Each pub Samuel entered was the same; full of smoke and wet bodies, with the scent of dirt, mould, sweat and cooking food. Some places had better ale, others had food that wouldn't kill you, very few had both good ale and good food while many more had sour ale and rancid food. As soon as the Keeper walked into each the silence hit as everyone turned to look at the stranger with his smart clothing and his short staff, which acted as a badge of office. The sword strapped to his side and the black throwing stars on the belts crossed over his chest tended to subdue the chatter. In each place he asked that a message be sent to Mr Poole urgently along with the name of the next tavern on his list.

Eventually, he ended up in The Cat and Fiddle. This was a decent enough place with good if plain food, various tasty ales to choose from and an inn keeper very much able to keep the peace. The main tap room was full of smoke and tasty food smells and the noise levels were enough to hurt the ears. Until Samuel walked in, that is. Then the silence hit like sudden death. The people who stood around holding tankards in their hands eyed him up and down. There were working men wearing all manner of cast off and patched clothing, a couple of young toughs in tight trousers and holding polished cudgels as well as two or three bawds, whose clothing was tight enough to emphasise assets but loose enough to lift for access. Samuel walked to the length of counter on which was a jug of ale ready to be poured but before he could say anything, he heard someone speak from the dark shadows at the side of the room.

'Well, well, well, gentlemen, we seem to have got us a shiny penny here!' The voice was high pitched and wet with phlegm. Samuel turned and looked towards the corner but it was wreathed in shadow and smoke with only a vague shape visible, leaning back so as not to be seen.

'I need a runner to go for Mr Poole, if he ain't already on the premises. I have a message for him from a particular friend that he will want to hear as soon as possible.' The Keeper's voice had roughened a little, losing some of the educated drawl as he turned away from the voice to acknowledge the inn keeper.

'Mr Poole? Don't know if I know him. And if this mysterious bloke was wanting to hear from a particular friend, then surely it should be a particular friend standing here talking?' The sneer in the hidden man's tone was obvious and Samuel felt himself growing irritated and wary. He didn't have time for this stupidity. Mentally he began preparing himself for a fight, using his battle-trained senses to plot where people stood around him.

'The particular friend in question cannot travel here, as Mr Poole already understands, which is why I am here with the message.' The Keeper's tone was still calm and polite, giving nothing away. Behind him he heard slight scuffles and the occasional low whisper, which he recognised as someone getting into position and preparing an ambush.

The man leaned forward, his features becoming visible in the lamp light. 'Give me the message an' I will make sure that he gets it.' Samuel had never seen such a grotesque figure. The man was enormously fat. His face was like a moonscape, pitted and hollowed by some disease, probably a pox of some kind, and shining with sweat. What little hair he had was dark with grease and filth and lay lankly across his skull. His features were crammed in the centre of his face – muddy brown eyes, a squashed nose above a tiny rosebud of a mouth and a chin that disappeared into the rolls of fat below. A hard collar stood up, digging into the folds of flesh at his neck and a gigantic shirt billowed down, covered by a delicately embroidered waistcoat that looked to be at least two sizes too small as it could not fasten over the immense belly. Over his shoulders lay a cloak of some undetermined colour. Everything about this man was dirty, grubby and greasy. Sweat trickled down his face as his piggy eyes looked at Samuel in a particularly uncomfortable way.

The Keeper felt his gorge rise at the look before noticing that there was a thin leather lead wrapped around the bully's left hand. Moving just his eyes, Samuel looked to see where it went. Part of his schooling as a Keeper was in not showing emotion or reacting, in any way, to what others did so he was able to keep his face expressionless as he saw the hollowed eyed young boy, sitting in just a pair of short britches, cut to the top of his spindly thighs and with a leather band wrapped around his throat in a poor imitation of a slave collar. The boy could only be eight or so. Sitting, shivering, with cold and hunger, his eyes were hollow and empty of hope but full of pain and despair.

Samuel saw that the bartender gave him the tiniest shake of his head from the corner of his eye. Swallowing his rage Samuel managed to sound almost obsequious. 'My apologies, sir, I dare not pass on any message except to the man himself. If I was able to do so, of course I would.' He spread his arms wide, trying to make himself look vulnerable to the other man and to those behind him. 'As no one here seems to know of Mr Poole, I'd best move on to the Laughing Ram and ask there. Thank you for the hospitality.'

Turning on his heel, Samuel pretended to walk out the door but stopped in simulated surprise when he saw the three men ranged behind him. All three showed a similarity of features – small and rat-like – and held weapons ready in their hands.

'Give me the message, damn you!' All trace of the false friendliness was gone as the fat man clenched his fists and slammed them on the table, jerking on the lead and making the child cry out in pain.

'Sorry, I can't do that. Even if I could, I wouldn't give any information to a fat, slimy pig such as you.' As he spoke, Samuel swept his cloak off his shoulders, wrapping it around his left arm, and moved into a fighting crouch. His eyes locked on the three men even as his ears listened for anyone sneaking behind him.

The fat man screamed out to his henchmen. 'Kill him! Kill the bastard!'

The three men moved forward in a ragged line and Samuel grinned, this wasn't going to be much of a challenge. The man in the centre looked as if he knew what he was doing with his cudgel, though the one to his left was looking less enthusiastic. The one on the right looked eager to get in a hit or more with his own weapon but lacked any true grace in his jerky movements. Snapping a kick out to the tough on the left, the Keeper hit the kneecap with less force than expected. Still it caused the man to stumble and fall with a squeal of exaggerated pain and gave him a chance to stay out of any further fighting. Turning as soon as his foot was back on the floor, and supporting his weight again, Samuel slammed his tipstaff at the man on the right, hitting the ruffian in the throat and causing him to drop and pull at his neck as if that would help him breathe. Hands reached forward from the crowd pulling both fallen men backwards out of the fight completely.

Samuel suddenly bent backwards at the waist, allowing the cudgel aimed at his chin to sail harmlessly past, but felt a punch to his side which made his ribs creak with the power of the blow. Letting out a grunt the Keeper swung around and, quicker than the eye could follow, shot his own fist past the outstretched hand, slamming into the third man's unguarded belly. Sliding swiftly past the groaning, retching creature, he rammed his elbow down on the back of the fallen bruiser's neck, knocking him to the ground. The lout proceeded to land in his own vomit, where he lost all interest in the proceedings. Glancing around quickly, Samuel saw no reason to continue being wary. The other two had gone and no-one else seemed to want to take their places. A glance at the barman gave him even more reassurance. The pitiful lout stood there armed with his own cudgel glaring at the crowd behind Samuel. Seeing all was safe, the Keeper turned back to the greasy man in the corner.

'I came here to pass on a message for my friend, I wasn't looking for trouble.' Samuel's voice was low but held an unmistakeable note of anger. 'I will, however, defend myself and I'll always try to stop trouble at its source. Now, shall we begin this conversation again, in the manner of civilised men? Or shall I just gut you and ask someone else?'

'I'll have you killed... *you'll* be the one who's gutted...' blustered the fat man, his rage and fear causing his words to become more and more incoherent.

'Well then, if that's the way it is going to be, so be it. I hope you have someone better than those were.' The sound of a cudgel tapping a warning on the counter caused Samuel to spin around to face the sound. The bartender just focused on the back of the room and, making another half turn, Samuel saw a man quickly slide his dagger back into its sheath before heading towards the door. Before the scav had managed three steps, the crowd barred his way. Nodding his thanks to the barman, Samuel was just turning back to his quarry when the door to the tap room opened up with a flourish and four men stepped into the already crowded room.

The first one through the door was the biggest man that Samuel had ever seen. Over six and a half feet tall, he had massive shoulders, hands like shovels and a solid barrel of a body sat atop legs like tree trunks. Unlike the big man in the corner, who was just fat, this man was pure muscle. The clothing he wore was clean but well-worn and plentiful to guard him from the freezing, wet conditions. Removing his hat from his bald head and pulling the knitted scarf away from his mouth, he surveyed the scene with a twinkle in his blue eyes.

'Hmmm, I wonder what is going on here?' he mused out loud. 'I was told that someone was wanting to give me a message yet when I get here, I see a mutiny in progress. Who wants to go first in explaining the situation...and you had best be entertaining.'

Before either the fat man or Samuel could begin, the bartender spoke. 'The Keeper came in and asked after you. Wanted to give you a message from a friend of yours who can't come here their-selves. Then Fat Syd put his oar in, trying to get the information instead. The young fella refused to pass it on to any but you so Syd decided to persuade him otherwise. That didn't go so well.' He finished with a grin and a wink to Samuel.

'Aah me, Syd.' There followed a pause as Mr Poole pulled at his lower lip. 'You know, I must be slipping, or getting old or something because this makes it twice in just a few days that someone who is supposed to know better has tried to kick me in the balls. I obviously need to start reminding people of who I am.' As he spoke, he began moving forwards, the crowd melting away from him like snow under a warm sun. Breezing past Samuel, and patting him on the shoulder, Mr Poole held out his hand, palm flat, towards Syd. The fat man, sweating even more profusely now, looked at the hand before raising his eyes in genuine puzzlement.

'The lead, you scav,' came the curt response. , Fat Syd handed over the strip of leather. With a start, he tried to jump back as strong fingers dug deeply and painfully into his face. His eyes were transfixed on the cold blue eyes above him, no longer twinkling but blazing with an icy rage.

'Ask me what I have been doing recently, Syd. Ask me what has happened to your old mate, Weasel.' When there was no response, Mr Poole squeezed his fingers a little tighter. 'I said ask me!' he said in a voice that brooked no defiance.

'Wha-what has h-happened to W-Weasel?' The high voice had lost its petulance and was now muffled and full of pain and fear.

'Well now, I am so *glad* you asked me that!' The fake surprise in Mr Poole's tone had a few in the tavern hanging their heads and heading to the door, only to bump into the three big men who stood in front of the opening and refused to move. Turning in a circle, catching the eye of those in the crowd, Mr Poole continued. 'I gave Weasel fair warning weeks ago but he kept pushing. He kept crossing over the line, the line that stops us becoming animals. He ignored my warnings and then I found him trying something I really don't like. I sent him on his way with the last warning of his life. I gave him till this sun up to leave the city. I promised him that if he hadn't left by then, I would escort him to Mr Thoms, he would be a real draw there, don't you think, Syd? That skinny body of his, him yelling for freedom…yeah, I thought Mr Thoms would be real impressed. So, to cut a long story short I made sure I was waiting when the sun rose and, wouldn't you know it? Weasel was still here. He couldn't really leave, mind you, because he was tied to a chair, but it is the principle of the thing, ain't it? So I took him directly to The Best Show and personally tied him to his own bench. Apart from my name, carved into his shoulders, there isn't a mark on him that shows. Mind you, it won't be my name the blokes will be looking at, will it? He started crying before I had finished securing him and he was screaming by the time I left.'

'As for you, Syd, I am very, very disappointed in you. You know I don't like people bullying and hurting the little ones. I haven't seen or heard about you for months, or I would have shown my displeasure before now. I have been too taken up with other problems, to be fair. I really am unhappy not only to see you here trying to take over on my patch, but you are doing so with a little kid that you have been using, right out on display. I am known for my fairness, for not impeding anyone in their work, unless it is against *my* law. But using kids is totally against MY LAW!'

The last two words were roared into Syd's face, cheeks again being squeezed tightly by the ham like hand of Mr Poole. Syd flinched and squealed in pain, trying to pull his head back as Mr Poole leaned in. 'You will leave this town now. Don't even wait to pack. I heard about little Lizzie and Geordy; how you beat one and raped the other before both were thrown into the gutter and died. Did you know that their da is one of the Night Watch? He's a good bloke, is Derry and as tough as they come. He can call on a hundred men or more with just a whistle. Before I came in here and started this little chat, I sent a runner to his house to let him know where you are. You best get moving. NOW.'

Standing back Mr Poole gave an exaggerated bow as, huffing and wheezing, Syd struggled to get out of his seat and sidle around the big tough without touching him. At a glance from their boss the men who had been guarding the door moved aside and, hobbling as quickly as he was able, Syd disappeared through it. The room was silent, as all of the people inside the tavern held their breaths to listen. There was a whistle and the sound of scurrying followed by cursing, stumbling and crashing as if a heavy object had fallen followed by a high pitched scream. The wailing became muffled before the tramping of many feet passed on by and faded into the distance.

With a sigh of satisfaction, Mr Poole grinned and raised an interrogatory brow at the man behind the bar, who gave a sharp nod. Tugging very gently on the lead to get the young boy moving, the big man jerked his head to Samuel to follow and the three went through into the back room.

This room was spotless and had a large fire burning in the hearth. Two deep chairs and a laying couch were set before the blaze and a table was between them. As the two men settled in the chairs, the youngster looked around him warily. Another door opened and a big, friendly woman bustled in. Carrying a large platter of food, she set it down and handed over some items of clothing. 'For the boy,' she said shyly before backing away.

treated her in the traditional way. I bet you haven't ever even raped her once.'

Samuel had turned a faint pink at the praise but his blush deepened as the comments continued. Sitting up straight and gazing over the shoulder of the older man, he said quietly, 'I haven't touched her for a lot of reasons, one of them being that slaves are prisoners. No-one knows just what they truly feel, what they remember. Being a slave is bad enough I didn't need to add to her burden. It makes me sick to know that being a decent human being is seen as a crime these days and not even for the "glory" of Bisra would I tup anyone in her position.'

There was a pause and then Samuel took a deep breath and looked straight into Mr Poole's eyes. 'I will be honest with you, sir. Even if I didn't have a problem with the thought of having sex with slaves, I still would not have used the girl in that way.'

'Why not? You tell me straight out why not and I will see if there is anything I can do for the girl. No promises mind, the shortness of time makes it more difficult, I may not be able to pull anything together. It could also be that if I don't like what you say, I won't even try, so be warned.'

Samuel stared at the impassive face of the man sitting opposite then raised one side of his mouth in a tiny smile. 'I know that no matter what I say now, you will try and help her. I just wonder what you will think of me after I have spoken. I do know a little about you, Elias Poole. My Mam was a neighbour of yours when you were kids and she told us stories about you as we grew up. You remember Effie of Frank's Pool?'

A grin spread across the homely features of the older man. 'Effie! Effie of the Pool! By all the Gods, I remember her. A little lass, blonde and gorgeous, she was. Loved to sing and knew how to keep us all in line. Ah, there was a time that I thought about asking her to have a kid with me but I would have wanted her to keep it and just be mine, not birth it and send it off to one of the Residences. While I dithered though, she met that Edwin Smith and she only ever saw him after that. I heard she had kids with him and they were allowed Breeder Privileges.'

Samuel burst out laughing. 'First of all, my Mam has always been built like a brick shithouse, her hair used to be brown before the grey, unless you asked my Dad of course, he said it was like polished mahogany. I will have to take your word about her singing because I never heard her do so even once. She always said that instead of having the trilling notes of a song bird, she sounded more like a chicken being boiled alive!'

A quiet laugh came from both men as their memories assailed them. Mr Poole thought of Effie; she had been as big and strong, as Samuel had said, but a real beauty with it. She had been one lass that didn't look like she would break if he had grabbed hold of her. Mind you, she would have thumped him if he had tried anything without getting her permission first. And her singing really was as bad as Samuel intimated. Having only heard it once, Mr Poole had always been grateful for the fact he had never heard it again. Then his thoughts turned to his beloved Charlotte. No, he was content that he and Effie hadn't paired up. Taking a good look at the Keeper, he could see some of his old friend in the younger man. Those dark eyes were definitely Effie's. The Keeper had passed the little test easily.

'How is your Mam these days?' he queried. 'And your Dad, too, of course.'

Samuel became solemn. 'She has the lung sickness. She doesn't have very long now. She is as comfy as I can afford her to be. Her mind has already gone and I am just waiting for her body to catch up and go too. As for my Dad, he went into the Void five years ago. He worked at one of the smithies by the Metal Worker's Market. He did a lot of fancy work so was always in demand. A big order came in and he was worked to exhaustion. There was an accident, hot metal dripped on to his foot and ankle, ate right through to the floor. He died of shock within minutes.'

'Bloody hell, boy, I am so sorry to hear that. Effie should have got in touch when he died, I would have helped her. You got any more family? Do they need anything?'

Samuel shook his head. 'I know you would have helped us. After Dad died, and before she became ill, Mam sat me and my sister down and told us to come to you if we was ever stuck and needed help. She said that you were a decent man. She also said that if you had asked her before she met Dad, she would have said yes but you would have both been miserable together. She met your wifey a couple of times and really liked her. Said she was perfect for you. Mam always said you would keep your word if at all possible. She also said that you had no time for much of the ways of the new laws. And as for my sister, Avra, she lives down south now, she has Breeders Privilege with a good man and they have three children. She doesn't want anything to do with me or Mam or even Harmony. She feels we aren't good enough for her anymore.'

'What? She Breed up or summat?'

'No, he's a labourer, works the land, although he does work for one of the Nobles. He is a good man, our Frith. He keeps in touch and lets us know what is going on in their lives. The reason she won't have anything to do with us is because of me.' Taking a deep breath, Samuel continued, 'See, Mr Poole, I make the perfect Keeper for the safety of female slaves. I am a deviant. I will never want a woman in any way, no matter what. Avra saw me kissing a friend of mine once. A male friend. She said it made her sick. So when Frith stepped forward and asked her to breed with him, she said yes. We all knew he was leaving Harmony so she saw this as the perfect way out. She would have reported me but I think the thought of being questioned by the Watch put her off; as you know, they aren't gentle. Frith told her that if she did report me, he would go to the magistrate and refute her word. That shook her up. He seems such a quiet man but when he riles up, he does a proper job. He knows exactly what she is like and yet he still wants to be the only one who has her. So they left and she has never broken her silence in over twenty years. My Dad guessed about me and he just said that you couldn't help that part of your nature. He was a good man, my Dad. So, there it is. Are you going to report me?'

The two men sized each other up for a moment before Mr Poole shook his head and gave a wry grin. 'I will ignore that last comment, Samuel, my lad. You have a lot of guts, spilling that out. You remind me of your Mam like that. I don't have a problem with most of the deviants just as long as they follow my rules. I have known a lot of different types of people; deviants, Abominations, fey and magikers and it all comes down to what someone is like towards others or when there is a problem needing fixing. If you look after those weaker or in need of you, then I don't care who you share a bed with. Unless it is kids. If it is, know this, Samuel. Son of my friend or not, if you harm a child, I will kill you.' The last sentence was so lacking in any inflection that it took Samuel a minute or so to understand.

'No!' His voice was thick with disgust. 'No, Mr Poole. If I ever do get with someone, I want to know they want to be with me. I am attracted to men, sir, not little kids who aren't given any choice in the matter. If you were to offer me one of any size, I would turn you down. Mind you, I would also gut you too. My Mam always told me that we were supposed to look after those who couldn't look after themselves.

'There was a bloke who decided he wanted me even though he knew how young I was. I fought him off, even broke his jaw, before my Dad heard me yelling.' Samuel couldn't help laughing at the memory. 'I almost felt sorry for the poor bastard once my Dad understood what he had tried to do. He ended up with a broken nose, jaw and ribs, bruised all over and hardly able to walk after a punch to his balls. He was run out of our street with a promise that if he ever tried it again, the bastard would be dead before the next dawn. He would have been, too. As it is, I heard he had been reported a couple of years later and sent to the Punishment Square as a deviant. A bit ironic really. He wasn't burnt for killing a child but because he had raped a male, so being a deviant is worse than the murder of a kid.'

'According to the Law here, that is exactly what it is, son. Breeding more children is the be-all and end-all. Every woman must have at least four children, except poor women will have as many as they can to stop any chance of being forced into Bawdy Houses. All men have to do is spill their seed. I have heard that Breeding Privileges are being allowed less and less nowadays. Unless you have the money and a title, you won't be able to choose one partner for life within the coming year, the most they are going to allow is five years before you have to find another, two years if you don't manage to breed. Don't worry about your Avra and Frith though. Those already granted Privileges won't have them taken away. And now we know where we both stand, tell me what you need from me? I assume you want out?'

Samuel gave a smile at the change of topic before filling in the specific details he had left out of the first narrative, including the fact that guards were being hired to escort the slave and her Keeper as they travelled to reach the ship that would take them to the land across the wide ocean.

'I don't know everything yet, the Master is leaving me a letter with the final arrangements tonight and we are both due to leave early in the morning. I know it doesn't give you any time to do anything but the girl needed you to know that she remembered you.' Samuel looked at the still features of the older man sitting opposite. 'She also has something important she wanted me to tell you.'

Mr Poole looked up and saw that Samuel was trying not to allow his grin to escape, raising his brow in enquiry.

'What is it that is so important, lad?'

'Her name, sir, she remembered her name.'

Mr Poole let a look of surprise cross his usually blank features and his voice shook a little as he prodded Samuel on. 'Well? What is it?'

'She said to say this: she remembered your name as she said she would. You gave her the gift of your name so she will gift you hers. Danielle Wintersborn.'

Again there was silence. The older man found that his voice had choked up on him. The sense he had the night before - that things were changing and he had to change too - was even stronger now. Hearing the emotion in the Keeper's voice as he spoke of the little slave girl really caught him unawares. His eyes became damp and he looked at Samuel, letting the younger man see how much he had been affected.

'That girl of yours holds some magik about her, son. I feel as if you have given me a big slice of the world, telling me this. Thank you. And yes, I did make a promise to help her and I don't break them things ever. You leave it to me, boy. Don't expect me to jump out with all the ideas and instructions for you now. I want you to do exactly what your Master demands. Get on that cart tomorrow and head for the docks. Which ones you going to? Merino Bay? That's alright then. Along the way, I will try and get in touch with you. If not before, definitely by the time you reach there. You take care of our treasure and let me take care of the rest. I have ideas brewing. Do you want me to kill your Master?'

Samuel frowned in thought before shaking his head. 'Not yet, we need him to get us away from here. If the Master and the young bastard find death when we free her, however, I won't cry for them. The thing is, Danielle is alive even though she should be dead. We don't know how long she will survive not being given the Numb anymore. I have promised to get her to the FreeLands so that when death comes, she doesn't die as a slave. That's all I am bothered about. I want to be there, holding her hand when she breathes her last.'

Looking at Samuel's determined face, Mr Poole found himself nodding.

'Ok, my lad. Then we focus on freedom not on death. Let's drink to it.'

Both men drank deeply and then spent some time chatting about Samuel's life and his depression at realising he was a deviant, knowing what troubles he could cause his family. The overwhelming love for his parents as they not only understood him but continued to love him was a precious memory. When he made his choice to become a Keeper, he hadn't understood just how rigorous the training was but he had revelled in all of it. Even having to make his first kill he had coped with. His first sight of Danielle when he collected her from the hospital after her womb had been removed had been a shock though. She had only been twelve and a big eyed waif.

The boy, Bili, began to whimper in his sleep and the two men moved towards him instinctively. Opening his eyes, the youngster cried out in pain and shock. 'I dreamt you left me!'

Seeing the expression on Mr Poole's face, Samuel hid a grin. The boy had decided who he was going to stay with and it looked as if the older man had just recognised the fact as well. Gathering Bili up, still wrapped in his cloak, Mr Poole turned to Samuel.

'That's all for now, son. You get back to our girl and make sure she is safe. Have you seen your Mam?'

Samuel shook his head. 'I couldn't go before as I had to find you. There isn't enough time now to be able to get there and back before we leave in the morning. It isn't a problem though. The last time I saw her, I was told that she would most likely be dead before I saw her again. She hasn't been aware of anything for weeks, so I said all my goodbyes then. I gave some money to the nurses for when the time came. Could you take this and make sure that she is buried properly, please?' Reaching into his waistcoat pocket, he took out the few paltry coins that his Master had given, plus more that he had taken from his savings.

Mr Poole folded the younger man's fingers over the money. 'Don't you fret, boy. I will make sure she is taken care of and she will be sent off with love and proper ceremony. You concentrate on walking that fine line between keeping out of trouble and looking after our little Danielle.'

'I will. Thank you, sir, for everything.' Samuel shrugged into his jacket and cloak before holding his hand out to Mr Poole.

'No lad, not like that with almost family,' said that worthy with a grin. With that, he pulled the Keeper into a rough one-armed embrace which Samuel accepted gladly. Reaching over, he rubbed his hand on the scrubby head of Bili who lay quietly against the big man, before quickly turning and leaving the room.

In the bar he was welcomed with a cheer as they celebrated his fighting prowess. With a laugh and a joke he accepted a glass of ale from one of the crowd, knowing he had to act as if his time with Mr Poole was nothing more than "a bit of business". Looking around at the faces surrounding him, Samuel wondered which ones were the spies that could pass on secrets that could get him killed. With a shrug, he decided that fear of that sort was just wasted emotion. It was time to get back to the house and grab a little sleep, ready for all that needed to be done on the morrow. With one last joke and a quick parting kiss to the bawds, Samuel escaped out into the wet and dreary night.

Chapter Ten

The sun had not long risen as Danielle and her Keeper placed the last few items on the carts the morning they were to begin their travels. There were two of these bulky transports now: one full of small goods, gifts for the roadside shrines or items that could be sold quickly if the need for more money arose, the food hamper as well as the trunk filled with Samuel's and the slave's personal items. The second was full of clothing and larger items that the family deemed important for their journey across the sea but for which there was not enough room on their own elegant travelling coach. Samuel would be driving the first cart with the slave at his side, while the other would be driven by an escort, hired by Lord Willoughby. Both carts would be drawn by a girox each. These huge mammals were taller at the shoulder than Samuel, with wedge shaped heads balanced with forward facing horns that came to a lethal point. Although giroxes ate constantly when they could, they also plodded on for days without food or water quite comfortably. They were steady for the most part but also stubborn. Samuel knew that one of the reasons Lord Willoughby had decided on giroxes was not just stamina but that they were actually cheaper to buy here in Harmony and would sell for a great price at Merino Bay where every part of their bodies would be used for food, clothing, speciality goods and glue.

Samuel and Danielle went upstairs to double check that nothing had been left behind and to give them both a break from Patcher's constant scrutiny. After checking his own room Samuel walked into hers and saw Danielle turning in a circle just looking around her. He held out his arms and she walked into them, resting her head on his chest. They stood motionless for a few moments, both bracing themselves for what was to come. Eventually Samuel leaned back, winked at her and they both turned and left without speaking. Danielle lost more and more of her facial expression with each step. They headed down to the kitchen to eat before beginning the long journey to the Bay.

As they stepped into the room it was lucky that all attention was fixed on the man sitting at the head of the kitchen table because it gave both of them a chance to re-school their stunned features. As the room was ringing with laughter even Patcher wasn't quick enough to see the shock that registered on their faces before it was hidden. He waved a hand in the newcomer's vague direction.

'This gentleman is Mr Poole. Him and his grandson will be driving the carts with you. You will be meeting up with a few more men before you leave the city proper so eat up, for the One's sake! It is time you were off.' With that, he stamped from the room in a fine show of temper, leaving everyone to look after him in surprise. Although he wasn't the most pleasant of men, Patcher rarely allowed himself to show any outward signs of mood changes. This strange tantrum was out of character and surprised all that knew him. There was a general shrugging of shoulders and he was dismissed from their thoughts. If anyone thought about his flash of anger, it would probably have been put down to the stress of knowing he would be travelling with the Family and all the problems that would entail.

The cook bustled about, filling two bowls with the rich, creamy porridge that she felt everyone needed to start the day. Seeing the two newcomers begin eating, she topped up all the other dishes before beginning to fry bacon and slice open warm rolls, fresh from the oven. Within a short time, another large parcel of food had been made for Mr Poole and his "grandson", Bili, plus hot bacon rolls for all. Samuel found a few tears being shed by two of the housemaids, the first intimation he realised he had been held as a figure of romance. Avoiding Danielle's eyes, he gave them both a hug and expressed his sorrow at leaving them but was careful not to respond to the bolder girl's hints that he should promise to come back to her. With a flurry of farewells to everyone else, the travellers left the house, leaving those behind feeling emotionally flat.

The sun shone pale and weak as Samuel climbed up onto his wagon, ready to lead the way. Mr Poole gave a big grin to both Samuel and Danielle before heading for his own cart and throwing the excited youngster dancing around him up onto the seat before climbing up more slowly. Thus began the first day of their journey. Samuel had been given an itinerary that he needed to follow very closely. If they arrived at the port too early, it meant extra risk of robbery, arriving too late meant trouble with Lord Willoughby and the Watch.

Travelling through The city itself wasn't easy as there were crowds that hated to move out of the way but the giroxes stubbornly kept walking forwards. Eventually all moved to the sides, many with bad grace. By mid-morning both carts were nearing the halfway point to the city gates. Samuel gave a slight jump when Bili suddenly appeared at his side, climbing nimbly up onto the cart.

'The Boss says we need to pull into the park just ahead. The guards your old git hired will be waiting there. Hello, miss, you look lovely!' And with a cheeky grin, the boy let himself drop and ran back to his own wagon. Samuel couldn't help but laugh at the impudent little brat. What a difference feeling safe could make. Give that young lad another few weeks and with his looks and confidence he could take over the world. With another snort of laughter and shake of his head, Samuel tugged on the reins, guiding the giroxes in the right direction. The park was just an area of dusty grass with a small bench and filled water troughs along one side. He stepped down and held his hand out to allow Danielle to also stretch her legs. Bili came bouncing up, followed more sedately by Mr Poole. While the giroxes drank, the man spoke quietly.

'The guards are all my men, son, so once we have left this place we should all be able to relax a bit. I hope that once we leave the city proper we will all take turns riding the carts. I want to teach the boy how to ride a horse and it won't hurt our girl to do the same.' Turning to look towards the roadway, he shot a quick glance at the girl. 'The boy was right. You are looking right lovely, Danielle, my sweet.' A tip of his cap and Mr Poole went back to water his own team, leaving the girl blushing rosily.

Samuel grinned at her but before he was able to comment six men rode up. All were dressed smartly in matching clothes that were similar to the garb that Samuel wore. The one riding in front had russet coloured hair tied into a queue under the hard, boiled leather cap. Samuel recognised him and two of the others as the men with Mr Poole the night before and gave a short nod to them. All of the group were well armed and Samuel himself had his staff, daggers and a full-size bow but he thought that he would now be able to use the latter for hunting rather than protection. A quiet comment between Mr Poole and the red haired man had them all dismounting and watering their mounts. Mr Poole and his cohort walked over to where Danielle and Samuel waited.

'This is Luke, he is in charge of the men. Luke, this is Samuel. As I mentioned earlier, nothing must happen to either him or the slave unless we are all dead. I claim them as family along with my boy, Bili. No one speaks out of turn to any of them, understand? After we get to the ship, as long as all has gone well, you will each receive a bonus. And Luke? I am thinking of spending some time at sea with my brother so be ready with an answer regarding what we discussed a few months ago.'

The man named Luke gave a surprised glance to Mr Poole at that comment but said nothing. He stood almost as tall as Samuel, his red hair shining in the sunlight. He examined both of them from a bright blue gaze set in a handsome face. After a moment he shook hands with Samuel, looked closely at Danielle with a slight frown and then grinned at Bili who was eyeing his Bolt Repeater with awe.

'This is a bit too heavy for you, boy, and it has a hair trigger so don't you go touching it without us watching you. No accidents allowed.' to which Bili looked downcast. He glanced at his boss, and quickly added 'We will be doing some hunting on the way, so let's see how you are with the other weapons first. I reckon the boss would want you being able to defend yourself. Come along and meet the lads.'

With a nod of excitement, Bili jumped at the chance and skipped along with Luke. As they reached the group of men, Samuel noticed that Bili slowed up a little and walked slightly behind the red-haired guard. Looking at Mr Poole and Danielle, he realised they had also noticed the change in the boy's behaviour.

'Danielle, I want you to stay in character as a slavey for the time being,' Mr Poole said quietly. 'I have known these lads for years but better safe than sorry. Bili will take messages from me to you but if you need him just whistle. Samuel, and I will send him over to find out what you need. I am feeling a bit wary. Dunno why but my instincts have saved me time and again. All we can do for now is watch and wait so stay in character until I say otherwise. Let's get going now.'

With a shout and a sweep of his arm overhead, he got the men's attention and they came and put their own baggage up onto the carts, got up onto their horses and the group moved on towards the gates.

Moving steadily forward, the carts rumbled along the broken streets while the six men riding on the outer flanks guided them all around the vehicles, clusters of people and patches of the deadly Mýste. Bili again dropped from the cart in front and climbed up onto Samuel's. Crawling over the Keeper, he settled himself between the two seated there. Yawning prodigiously he snuggled up against Danielle and fell asleep within seconds. Raising his eyebrows in surprise at this, Samuel was about to make an unwary comment to the slavey when he saw one of the men, Rook by name, moving in closer to the side of the cart. Samuel turned his neutral gaze to him.

'The Boss wants the mite to stay with you two. Make sure he don't fall off, will ya? That slavey of yours looks right tasty, how much for a tumble later?'

'More than your life,' Samuel snapped back. 'This woman is off limits, didn't you hear? Not only will I hurt you but my Master will kill you if you touch her. Your Boss, however, would only make you wish you were dead!'

'Alright, alright! I was only asking. Some slaves are up for rent, especially the Fireheart ones. I dint know this one weren't.'

'I thought Luke told you that we were off limits?'

'Well, yeah...but I dint think he meant her.'

'Oh, he meant her alright but if you want to argue the point, you go see the bloke ahead on the other cart, go see what he says, ok?'

The pock-marked man looked at the cart in front of them and smirked before he shook his head and then let his horse drop back into its space slightly behind Samuel's shoulder. All the while the short conversation had gone on Danielle had stared blankly ahead, her arm supporting Bili lightly as he slept. Hoping that Danielle could see from the periphery of her eye, Samuel mouthed a warning for her to watch out for Rook before settling more comfortably on the hard seat and allowing his mind to quiet within itself for now. Used as a form of regaining or saving energy, this focused meditation helped the Keeper to take in all around him

94

while resting and seeming to sleep. His trainer used to call it the Alert Sleep but Samuel just thought it was a nice way to pass the time.

Chapter Eleven

Within an hour the group saw the high wooden barricade that ran around Harmony's very outer limits. Close to the gates was a shrine to the Shining One with Servers and a Mage moved slowly along the line of people waiting to leave the city, giving their expensive Blessings for safe travel as well as for health and happiness. A short time after handing over a pouch of silver to the Mage, the carts were in line to go through the heavy gates where they would also be expected to pay more good silver to the guards positioned there.

A group of tumblers who were trying to get into Harmony began showing off some of their skills to prove their tale of being hired as entertainment by a noble house. They scattered, shouting and cursing as a troupe of young men deliberately rode through the precariously balanced group, knocking them in all directions. The yelling and cursing caused the men at the exit gate to walk briskly across to their partners, pikes at the ready, just as a regiment of the Day Watch marched up, shouting their orders to add to the din. While this cacophony of threats continued, the line of people leaving the city began to take advantage of this unexpected opportunity by running through the open gates. All were thankful for being able to save their silver from being spent on hefty bribes now that the guards were otherwise engaged.

The carts and the escort had managed to get through the open gateway and go a short way up the open road before a shout of outrage came from those who had not managed to slip out when the coast was clear, followed by clearly aggravated guards yelling for them to come back. A few seconds later, open fighting was spilling out as some of those who had waited for the guards showed their displeasure at being made to pay for the rule breakers who had nimbly taken their chances. Danielle didn't turn in her seat to watch and guffaw at the sight of grown men rolling around in the dirt like brawling children and Bili continued sleeping peacefully. As the carts trundled on, the noise became fainter.

Now they were out in the open and moving steadily away from the city, the pace picked up a little even with the dreary weather, as the crowds thinned and went their separate ways. Less than an hour away from the gates they reached the first roadside Shrine to the Shining One. These were set up on well-travelled highways in any direction. As Bili was classed as too young to need a blessing, and the slave was beneath the Server's notice, it was only the men who went and knelt down in front of the Shrine. The Server wore a snow white robe with silver and gold stripes randomly stitched upon it. The half circle head-piece with its large rounded front, also striped with silver and gold, was polished to a fine sheen. Privately Samuel thought that the whole outfit looked ridiculous.

The men knelt onto their left knee with their right hand laid flat against their hearts. Their left hands were offered out in supplication as the Server went along the line murmuring a blessing upon each man and their endeavour. They all had a small cut made upon the palm of the left hand before a press of a honey-covered finger touched their closed lips. As always, Samuel felt himself struggling not to shudder at the touch of a Server. He always worried that one of them would somehow sense his less than stellar belief in the Shining One. Although he was grateful that being so close to the city, this man was clean, unlike those they would meet further away. After waving the smoke from burning incense over them, the Server accepted the bag of coins with a smirk and the group went back to the carts to continue on.

Eventually, Mr Poole signalled them by raising his arm and then pulled at the reins, heading towards the first overnight stop. His girox turned off the highway obediently and headed for an open field further on, the second cart and the riders following on behind like ducklings after their mother.

Bili had woken up just after their obeisance at the Shrine and had glared around him as if daring anyone to comment about his nap before jumping off the cart with Danielle and Samuel and jumping up on the cart with Mr Poole. Now all of them worked together, getting the horses unsaddled before rubbing them all down and settling them for the night, hobbled safely and left to munch on nosebags of oats. The giroxes had their harnesses removed and were also loosely hobbled near a patch of thistles, which they chewed though with obvious enjoyment. There was soon a fire blazing away in a temporary fire pit and two of the guards managed to shoot three rabbits. Acting in her slave-like way, Danielle skinned, gutted and boned the fat beasts before putting them into the cast iron pot that sat on the flames, along with barley, vegetables and herbs to make a rich, tasty stew. She also set out loaves of bread, butter and two of the big meat and potato pies with their flaky golden crusts.

By the time the men had come back from relieving themselves and washing away the dirt of the journey, the stew was bubbling away merrily, its scent causing their stomachs to rumble in appreciation. They grabbed hold of plates and utensils before lining up to be served. Samuel was about to do the same when Bili caught his eye. The boy was hovering by Danielle, handing the bread out to the men but he seemed to be trying to get a message to the Keeper. First he looked at the slave dutifully filling up the deep-sided plates of the hungry men and then he would look towards the river before catching Samuel's eye and widening his own. Then he would stare at Danielle again. Realisation hit the Keeper like a blow. Coughing to gain attention, he asked Mr Poole if he would take over the serving of the food as it was time for the slave to get washed also. With a nod, the older man took the spoon from the slave and she moved in Samuel's direction. After receiving a promise from the new cook that plenty would be saved for the two of them, Samuel led the way as the slave followed with downcast eyes.

Moving out of sight from the small group, Danielle walked more quickly before diving behind a bush in desperation. It was only then that Samuel realised that through the day, since the rest of the men had met them, she had been unable to relieve herself. The poor woman must have been close to bursting. As Mr Poole was uneasy, she couldn't just nip off as all the men and the boy had done through the day. Samuel grimaced at himself, annoyed that he was letting his attitude slip too far from his training and grateful that Bili had been more aware. If anything would get them killed it would be this. So instead of apologising or joking about his mistake aloud, he got himself thinking and acting like a Keeper once again. Danielle came back from behind the bush and opened her mouth to speak but recognised from his face that he was wary about onlookers. She gave an infinitesimal nod in his direction before she sank into her slave persona again.

'Go wash yourself, girl,' said Samuel, all his senses alert, not only for ambushers but also for spies.

Turning away, Danielle removed her cloak, her gloves and her dress. Bending over, she washed her arms and face at the river's edge. Knowing that the Keeper would have a reason for acting the way he did, she wasn't surprised when the bushes trembled as Rook stepped through and so was able to keep her slave mask intact.

'Hello, mate,' he said to Samuel. 'I was just keeping my eye on you, make sure you don't get lost, you know.'

'You are a liar and should be very careful. Get dressed, slave and then come here.' Samuel turned to face the small bodyguard. 'You are a fool, Rook, do you think that Mr Poole will allow you to cause any harm to her or me? Be very careful or you might find you cannot handle what happens. Slave, let us go back to the fire. And if this man or any of the others try to touch you, you will scream and keep doing so until Mr Poole or I come to you and kill the man assaulting you. Now come on, we need to eat.' With that, Samuel led Danielle past Rook who took a step back to prevent being knocked over by the Keeper. As Samuel moved ahead, the other shook his head and spoke quietly.

'You are the fool, boy. You have just guaranteed that any man who tries to tup her will now make sure he silences her first. He may only slice at her vocal cords, or he may just slit her throat completely.'

'If that happens, Rook, then no matter who touches her, I will kill them. But know this also – you too, will die. As you are the one who has heard me say what I just have, then if anyone silences her, I will know that it will have been your doing.'

'Really? You think that I was the only one who was out here? Maybe you are a bigger fool than I thought. You think me an enemy. Well, perhaps I am, perhaps I am.'

Samuel walked back to the camp, expecting to see everybody sitting and eating but he only saw Mr Poole, Bili, Luke and one of the other men. He sent Danielle to sit with Bili before filling her plate and handing it to her. 'Eat this slowly. Clear your plate. Once you have done that, wash it.'

He watched as she began to eat her food slowly and as she did, the men began drifting in. First was Rook, a smirk playing across his scarred and pitted face. He could have been a good-looking man of about thirty despite the scars but his attitude and the permanent sneer he had made it hard to see the regular features, the sensual lips and the lean muscled body. The shorter man smirked over at Samuel before getting another plate of stew. As he ate, he stared broodingly at the slave while she studiously ignored him.

Mr Poole now took the time to quietly introduce and discuss each man as they arrived. First there was Varga and Deo, twins who looked at first glance to be completely unlike each other. Samuel realised that part of the reason for this was that Varga had shaved his head completely and wore big gold earrings while his brother had a silver hoop in his nose and hair of the darkest brown that fell down his back in hundreds of tiny braids. Their features, though, were the very copy of the other and although they had a habit of moving and talking slowly, neither were stupid, just cautious and preferred each other's company. As Poole spoke, the two were having a quiet chat about the horses in low tones as they moved their bedrolls slightly away from the others.

A short time later Jasper and Smith came back to camp after checking on the horses. Jasper was in the middle of telling one of his stories so both men halted for him to finish.

'So then he sez...but, but I was only looking!' Whatever the rest of the joke had been, this last comment had both men doubled over with laughter.

There was a strong contrast between these two. Jasper was even smaller than Rook, dwarfish in height. His smiling face disguised the fact his eyes missed nothing. As a member of the group, he was irreplaceable; not only for his acrobatic and fighting skills but because of his ability to raise the men's spirits and see the smallest thing out of place. Smith, however, was medium everything - medium build, medium brown hair, eyes that were of an indeterminate colour, no scars or jewellery – nothing at all to remember him by. As a companion he was as witty and fun as Jasper so the two spent a lot of time together, trying to top the last story in a ceaseless game of one-upmanship. All of the men had worked with Mr Poole on and off for years, so it was difficult to see that any was a spy, yet there was a sense of danger, a faint scent on the air that at least some of the men had noticed.

Once they had all eaten, Danielle was given the crockery to wash and Bili skipped along to "help". Samuel and Mr Poole made a tent-like structure between the two carts for the slave and youngster to share and to protect them from the drizzling rain that had been happening on and off all day. While they did this, Samuel shared his information over what had happened by the river bank with the older man. Samuel spoke of his doubts regarding Rook but Mr Poole could not bring himself to think badly of the scarred man.

'Rook has a chip on his shoulder, lad, I know that. In some ways, that is what has made him a good mercenary. He was due to make a Breeding Contract with a woman of a little village a few miles from Harmony to the North, when he was a Commander of the Watch. Her father owned an inn but Rook having such rank at his age meant he could have bred with one of the younger women of a lesser Noble house but he didn't want anyone else. Loved her, he did, with all his heart and she felt the same about him.

A week before the Contract was signed, he came off patrol and went to see her as planned. He walked in to see her being attacked by a group of nobles who had decided that she was a better choice then what the Bawdy House had to offer. No-one else stepped in to help her so it was just him that went down under a heap of the bastards, beaten until he couldn't move. They tied him to some beams so he was able to see the "show". She, poor lass, was tied to a table and each of the nine men raped her. No matter what they did to her, they couldn't get her to scream - the most was a hoarse grunting sound - so each man tried something worse.

By the time the last one had his turn, he knew he was swiving a corpse but it didn't stop him. Then they finished off by cutting into Rook, using him to practice their sword craft on but there they made a stupid mistake. They didn't kill him.

It took him over six months to recover from the beating and get back up to fighting fitness. Broken ribs, both his arms and a broken leg were the least of it. Although none of the sword wounds were lethal, they did get infected. The barmaid's father asked me to help the man who tried to save his daughter and I knew someone who was a Healer who saw to the worst of the damage. Rook managed to build himself back up to the peak of fitness and skill. Six months from the day it all happened, instead of going back to the Watch as all thought he would do, he disappeared from public view and began hunting down the men who had killed his woman.

Before he killed them, each one was tortured in the way they had harmed his lady. No-one ever heard them cry out. Rook mangled the throat of each man in the same way his beloved's had been damaged when she was just a child. You see, she could never have screamed no matter what they did. The poor lass had no voice to scream with. Twelve months to the day after the attack, the last man died for it. And that was the girl's father.

He had been there and hadn't stopped the rape of his daughter and neither had eight others. In Rook's mind, every one of those seventeen men was guilty. Now he feels that every woman needs to be protected, to be safe. He may try and kill you if you don't let him see you care for her, but he will never, ever harm Danielle.'

Samuel stood in silent thought as he rearranged his thoughts and added the new information. Then he sighed. 'The biggest problem, Elias, is that you think that there is a traitor yet you have worked with all these men for years. They will all have a similar story of pain, I would think. So what do we do?'

'Actually, the only man whose story comes close is Smith's. Luke used to be in the Navy but he had a falling out with his captain. He was flogged and sent to work in one of the slate mines. He escaped after a month and came to Harmony where he set up as a mercenary. He has a good reputation and can afford to pick and choose who he works for. Jasper wants to enrol in the Bardic School but needs to have money for that privilege. Unfortunately he loves roistering, so it is taking time. The twins love to fight and tup but even sex for those two falls far behind the fighting. They always share their women so they pay for bawds from one of the cleaner houses which means money is always needed.'

'And Smith?'

'Hmm, he is another funny bugger. He had a home with a woman on a Breeding Contract. Some of the Watch decided to ignore her Token of Contract and took her to one of their Towers. It took Smith two days to find her and when he did, she was unrecognisable. She had been raped but he expected that - this was the Watch after all – unfortunately, the woman had been shared between both Day and Night Watches so over twenty men in all and she had also been severely beaten. Smith managed to buy her freedom and took her back to his home. He bathed her, remade her Token and promised her she would never have to go through that kind of ordeal again. Then he held her as she screamed and wept. For a week or more he watched her carefully, took care of her needs and rejoiced in her apparent healing. Ten days after he had brought her home he found her hanging from a tree in the garden. It seems that one of the Watch who had stolen her away originally had called to the house while Smith was working. He hadn't hurt the woman but she decided that death was preferable to the fear and shame she felt. The worst thing is that she was pregnant with Smith's first child; they had only known about her pregnancy for a few days before she was taken.'

'I could have had many men in this team who have horror stories similar to the ones I have told but I chose those I thought I could trust most. Now I feel I am going mad. I *know* all is not right, there is a feeling of unease that is new to me in this group. I cannot fully trust these men, which hurts me, but I would rather hurt and keep our girl safe, than I would trust blindly and think that none of these men can been turned. They are all mercenaries, after all. So, we wait and we see. '

'You are right, old man, all we can do is continue to watch. It breaks my heart to do so because I was hoping to give Danielle a taste of freedom before we get to the ship but if we have to wait, we will.' Samuel knew he could trust Mr Poole, not only because of the way the man had stepped in to help Danielle way back at the beginning, but also the way the man had stepped in to help since. He would watch and share all the information with Mr Poole and, hopefully, the traitor would be found. 'I have one question, though. I know you are a good man under that homicidal exterior but why did you pick on a slavey to try and rescue? You must know it is insane to think we can give her much of a life so why her?'

Mr Poole shrugged his massive shoulders. 'I am not sure, Samuel. I had a daughter once, so it could be that. Or maybe it is because the lass reminds me of a woman I knew who I loved beyond all reason. The truth is I just don't know. I don't like slavery and what is done to these poor and helpless buggers. I also like to twist the noses of the people who make the rest of us so bloody miserable. The exact truth is that when I saw Weasel grabbing at her and her just staring into space, it pissed me off, good and proper but seeing a tear roll down her cheek made me snap. O'course, it might have just been rain but even so it looked like she was crying. She has something special about her son. We have to keep her safe.'

Agreeing with the older man completely Samuel walked over to tell the slave to lie down, deliberately not telling her to undress. As she went over to her shelter, he looked around for Bili and was astonished to see the boy sitting on Rook's knee, listening to Jasper telling a story.

'...so Sir Egain and his faithful shadow kat began hunting over the kingdom for the missing pearls. Such huge and magikal jewels,' here Jasper paused to glare at the twins as they sniggered at his last few words. Quickly, they both shut up, not wanting to miss any of the untrained bard's story. *'As I was saying,'* he continued *'Sir Egain went hunting for the necklace with his faithful companion. He walked far and wide, following where the shadow kat led. Closer they moved to the coast and closer to their quarry.'*

By now, everyone was listening as Jasper wove his tale. Luke sat making a fishing pole for Bili. Smith was sitting on his bedroll, sipping tea. Rook had his hands clasped firmly around Bili's middle to stop the boy falling off his knee as the youngster wriggled with excitement. The twins had stopped sniggering and were as captured by the tale as Bili was. Mr Poole sat down and shook his head with a grin as he surveyed them all.

With a nod at Mr Poole, Jasper continued; *'So the knight and his faithful kat reached the coast and there, Flidai, the greatest hunter in all Shadow Katdom, lead Sir Egain down to the beach and then along the coast. Mile after mile they walked, and mile after mile the knight wondered if he was insane to be going to all this trouble. Even if he found the pearls, would he be acclaimed? Or accused? Either way, his life would no longer be dull, so he kept following Flidai.*

'Suddenly the kat gave a yowl and ran into a hidden cave entrance. There stood a startled lady, dressed in strange clothes that were covered in shells and coral. Sir Egain gasped at her beauty before gasping again at the sight of the beautiful pearl jewellery she wore. All at once his hopes for a better life full of horses and gold, died away. How could he hurt this woman? He could not call himself a noble Knight of the Realms if he struck down a woman, no matter how unearthly.

Suddenly the shock drained away from the woman's face and she smiled at Sir Egain. 'Welcome, traveller. You saw and you did not strike or snatch. Why are you here?'

Sir Egain gulped before he spoke. 'I am here, Lady because I have been tasked with finding those pearls you wear so beautifully. I was told they had been stolen from my master.'

'Your Master? I would have thought you had no master, Sir Egain.'

The knight stifled a gasp, wondering how she knew his name. 'I - erm – I have no master as yet, milady but my hope was that by returning the pearls I could receive enough gold to buy back my faithful Spirit, that's my horse, lady. I don't know what I should do now though.'

'You won't demand? Shout? Try and cut me?'

'NO! Of course I won't do any of that! Tell me what you want me to do, lady, and I will do it'

The woman's voice was as soft and as gentle as a breeze as she spoke again. 'You should be careful who and what you bargain with, my brave knight. You may have these baubles on one condition. You will come back here to Mermaid's Cove on the same date every three months. On that day, I will ask a boon and you will do what I wish. Is this a bargain?'

Sir Egain thought about it, then said carefully, 'I would do this happily, lady, but I cannot do anything that would besmirch my honour, so I dare not agree yet.'

The woman laughed gently. 'You are learning caution already, Sir Knight. What if I give my word that no boon will cause you to doubt you honour, what then say you?'

The knight looked down at the huge shadow kat by his side. The kat gave a nod of his head then sneezed. Both the knight *and the lady grinned at this and then the knight said, 'Yes, milady, expect me back in three months.'*

With that, the lady smiled and a chorus of singing filled the Cave like the sound of the sea. Removing the pearls, she poured them into his hand before holding hers out to him. When he looked puzzled, she laughed. 'Kiss it, Sir Egain, and seal our bargain.'

Leaning down, Sir Egain kissed the back of her hand, tasting salt and feeling tiny crustaceans on his lips. Looking up, he was just in time to see the elegant woman leap to the side and dive into the deep water. Her head rose up and she flung back her glorious hair. 'Remember our bargain, Sir Egain, do not forget for your sake!' She then flipped forward head first and dived beneath the waves. As she did, a long sinuous tail in bright blues and greens flipped out and soaked Sir Egain and his shadow kat to the skin. While the kat snarled and spat in irritation, Sir Egain laughed long and loud before turning and beginning his long walk back to the castle he had come from.'

The boy's eyes were wide in wonder and he clung to the hands of the scarred man as they held him. Jasper caught Samuel's eye and brought the exciting episode of the Knight and the Caves of the Mermaid to a close, promising more on the next day. Although protesting, the youngster didn't argue much as his yawns interrupted his words. When Rook picked him up and tickled his ribs, the boy laughed and begged for mercy, promising to be good and go straight to sleep. He carried the youngster over to the tent and, before he even laid the boy down, Bili was fast asleep. Leaning right inside the cloth structure, Rook spoke;

'I see something different with you, lady, and I promise you this. Whether you trust me or not, whether the boss and that Keeper of yours trust me or not, I don't care. Just like the knights of old in one of Jasper's stories, I pledge my life to you. None shall give you harm while I live.' The scarred man leaned close and spoke in a tone so low that no one else heard him apart from the slave girl.

Danielle decided to take a chance, moving her head and looking directly at him. 'Thank you. There may be a spy among us, one who watches to see that I am still under the influence of the drug.'

'Then we will make sure between the three of us that you are fully protected.' He quickly amended the number to four when he saw Bili's sleepy glare.

'Don't do anything to bring harm to yourself.' Danielle whispered in alarm but Rook just gave her a wink and went back to the fire. Samuel took his place holding a hot cup of cocoa with her evening "dose" in it. With difficulty, she choked it down. Cocoa would always remind her of Numb but she said nothing as people were moving about close to the sleeping area. Danielle was determined to let Samuel know as soon as she could that she would not, could not, drink that foul brew again.

The next morning, Bili and Danielle were woken by Mr Poole, laughing at the two slug-a-beds. Once they were both awake, Samuel took them for their morning wash, much to Bili's disgust. Never having been taught much about personal hygiene, he struggled to understand why he had to wash *every* day. Not just every day but two or even three times. It was stupid and he would only get dirty again. He kept these thoughts to himself though, he loved his Mr Poole, so he washed. But he didn't have to like it.

Feeling more revived after their morning ablutions, they ate the breakfast already prepared by Varga. Bacon sliced from the big piece that had been sent from the house, eggs and sausages, bread toasted over the fire and plenty of hot tea. Bili turned his nose up at the tea and enjoyed his cocoa instead. Samuel, having had his ears blistered off by the slave earlier, did her "dose" in a combination of milk, cinnamon and honey that she pronounced later to be very enjoyable. Once breakfast was finished, the slave washed the utensils while the men – with Bili dancing around them in excitement, although he insisted he was helping – struck the camp, saddled and harnessed the horses and the giroxes who grumbled at having to leave the denuded patch of thistles, before they all moved onwards, grateful for the drier weather this day even if it was still cold.

Travelling along the roads wasn't always easy, short detours having to be made around pathways too full of holes to be safe for either wheel or hoof. Trees grew through the remains of old buildings and the occasional broken carcase of a transport vehicle, most of them thankfully free of Mýste, dotted the road side. In comparison to the musty smell of the city Danielle was used to everything here smelled fresh and green. The sun shone with a pale lemon light as fine rain began falling again. Some of the villages they passed by had signs warning away strangers, while others welcomed the new faces and the group were able to barter for fresh foodstuffs and give more offerings to the Servers waiting by their Shrines with open palm.

The slave attracted a lot of attention, sitting so stiffly in her seat and wearing the collar which, by Law, had to be always on display. Some tried to get close to her, talking and offering food or money but she just faced forward without responding to anyone. Luke went off fishing whenever possible and the other men hunted small game, so there was plenty of fresh food. Bili spent most of his time with Mr Poole, Samuel or Rook but was a favourite with them all. They kept at least one of the men standing by the slave seat to prevent people from getting too close and so the first few days passed quickly.

Chapter Twelve

The fourth day began in its usual fashion with the group starting its travels just after sun-up. Samuel was a little worried about Danielle as she seemed much hungrier than was usual and seemed to be running a slight fever. He was sure that this was a side effect from the lack of Numb but daren't let her eat or rest more, after all they still were not certain if there was someone who wanted to betray them among the group. Rook had proved himself to Samuel by this time, having stepped in on one occasion when Varga and Deo had gotten far too close to Danielle. His words would have bitten through metal as he cursed them. Mr Poole frowned at the group at large when he heard the row, gently reminding everyone that both Bili and the slavey were under his protection. Bili had then opted to ride with the angry Rook for an hour or so afterwards and the man calmed down eventually whilst holding the youngster and listening to his bright chatter.

There was a stop about mid-day for rest and refreshment. They had come close to another village so the twins went in to see if anyone had milk to spare and to check on where the next set of shrines were. While they were away, Bili came over to Samuel wearing a frown on his usually happy face.

'What's wrong, trouble?'

'There is something wrong with Butterfly,' Bili looked so worried that the Keeper stopped his thoughts about teasing the youngster and frowned down at him.

'Who's Butterfly?'

'You know,' Bili said impatiently. 'The Boss' girox. There's something really wrong with him.'

Suppressing a smile at the thought of the behemoth being named after something so ephemeral and delicate, Samuel allowed himself to be dragged over to where the two giroxes stood. He noticed what Bili had. While the slightly smaller one chomped at weeds and clover, the bigger one was grunting and beginning to stamp about. There was anger in it but also what Samuel thought was pain. Giving a whistle that brought Jasper and Rook to his side, they all warily unharnessed the beast.

As the harness came off, the girox gave a growl and lunged forward at the men standing around it. Just as swiftly as it began pawing at the ground Samuel and the others could only gape as it suddenly stopped and heaved a huge sigh at the sight of Bili, barely up to its knee, standing in front of the lowered nose telling the animal to stand still so it could be checked over. Quiet as a lamb, the girox settled down and began eating, although not as heartily as its companion.

Putting the child's amazing skill aside for the moment, Rook and Jasper checked over the beast. Both men found sore spots, the size of a man's hand, at particular points where the harness would sit. It took much to damage the skin of a girox, which explained why its leather was so prized, so whatever had caused the damage needed to be investigated. Samuel frowned a moment then gave his orders. Bili ran off to get Danielle, Jasper took the harness to inspect while Rook and the Keeper went to explain to Mr Poole what had happened.

Danielle kept to her slave persona as she walked slowly over to the girox. In her hand was a small earthenware pot, full of a thick green paste. While Bili soothed Butterfly and kept it calm, Danielle spread the paste over the sores. Suddenly she gave a gasp and looked around hurriedly to make sure she hadn't been heard.

'What's up, Dani?' whispered Bili, checking around him.

Danielle grinned down at the boy, loving his habit of shortening or changing everyone's name. All except Mr Poole who stayed resolutely "The Boss".

'It's alright,' she whispered. 'My fingers just started tingling and got really warm. It must be something in the paste, Samuel gave me.'

'Sam wouldn't make anything that could hurt you, would he.' the boy spoke with confidence. He was usually bright and full of chatter, only the occasional nightmare and brooding fit showing that he still remembered his old life. Love, affection, food and boundaries all helped him to feel secure so the fits would become less as time moved on.

'No, sweetheart, Sam wouldn't hurt me. It was just a bit of a surprise to feel my fingers go all pins and needles, that's all.' The slave continued to spread the paste on the large back, stretching to reach some of the sores.

If the boy had been less taken with chatting to his huge friend, he would have noticed the Danielle's eyes had begun to glow as did her hands as she seemed to slip into a trance, only for a few moments, before returning back to herself. Pushing the cork back into the top of the jar, she walked slowly back to camp, Bili dancing and skipping next to her. Neither of them noticed the girox locking his knees and drifting off to sleep, his sores already beginning to dry and close.

Once back in camp, Danielle sat down at her usual spot, close enough to hear what Samuel and Mr Poole were discussing. Jasper came and sat with them, his usually pleasant face now wearing a scowl.

'What is wrong with you?' enquired Mr Poole. 'I haven't seen that expression upon your face for many a moon, Jasper.'

'Someone is playing silly bastards.' The diminutive bard was furious and showed it with his bared teeth.

'What do you mean?' Mr Poole sat up straighter, his attention fixed upon Jasper.

'The harness has been tampered with. In half a dozen places or more there's been an irritant rubbed into the leather. Some of the securing rings have been roughened with a rasp and coated in poison. If Bili hadn't spotted those sores, by the time we settled this evening we would have found the girox sick and vicious. It takes something really dangerous to harm them so the rest of us might have been in trouble too. What is going on, Boss?'

Mr Poole looked at Jasper as he pulled on his bottom lip. 'I am not completely sure, Jasper. Can you save the harness?'

'Sure, Boss. The twins will have the tools needed to sand down the metal and there are plenty of the plants I need to neutralise the irritant and poison. I will take it near to the stream and get it sorted. Just, please, tell me what is going on when you can.'

'We will, old friend, not yet but soon.'

Taking up the harness in his gloved hands, the bard moved away and Mr Poole looked at Samuel. 'Your lot? He asked in an undertone. 'Or mine?'

'Could be either,' Samuel said, 'With one of the giroxes out of play, we would have struggled to keep to Lord Willoughby's timetable. Any delays would have brought down punishments upon Danielle and a chance that I would be sacked. If I was, then Dani would be in a lot of danger from that bloody scavenger, Patcher. He was really angry that he didn't get a chance to tup her before we left and I don't trust his temper. I think if he can't have something, he would happily smash it.'

'That is a problem for when we reach the Bay. For now, son, I want you to keep an even closer eye on our flower as well as the little one. If it is aimed at me, I can deal with it but I need someone I can trust to watch the rest of us.'

With a short nod, Samuel got up and stepped over to the slave. 'Did you hear everything?' When she nodded, he gave a sigh, wiped the jar and replaced it in his bag.

The twins came back a short time later, both of them wearing uncharacteristic frowns.

'Summat's not reet there and I don't want to be relaxing too deep if the neighbours come calling,' was Deo's only comment on the visit. The mid-day meal was cooked and Jasper stood guard while the others ate. Bili murmured quietly to Mr Poole, who decided to forego his tea, leaving it to cool untouched. At his signal, Samuel and Rook followed the big man's lead but the twins and Smith appeared to drink too quickly to be warned. There was a tense silence for a moment before Smith went to relieve Jasper. Collecting the used cups, Samuel saw that Smith's cup had not been touched. Unusual for a man who never turned down a mug of heavily milked tea and for one to pretend to drink it. Jasper returned to camp and reported all was quiet but before he had chance to drink the tea, Samuel dashed it from his hand. Jasper gave a gasp of astonishment at the Keeper but, before he could say anything, Samuel's big hand covered his mouth as he whispered in Jasper's ear.

'Treachery, Jasper. Look at the twins!'

Looking over he saw both men yawning uncontrollably as their eyes closed and they both fell to the ground and began to snore.

'What the hell?' the bard whispered hoarsely.

'We have been set up, boyos,' said Mr Poole, keeping his voice low. 'Reckon we can fight them off?'

'O'course we bloody can, you fool,' Rook replied with a grin, although he too was quiet. 'What about Smithy?'

'Best leave him out there. It looks as if he hasn't drunk any of the drugged stuff so he should be fine. We'd best be acting like them bloody idiots there, I reckon,' Mr Poole nodded towards the loudly snoring twins. Looking at Jasper, he seemed to make his mind up. 'Either I've got this right or I have just signed our death warrants.' Turning away from the puzzled singer, he moved to Danielle, who was sitting next to Samuel as always.

'Here you go, lass. Take this and hide it somewhere. If they do grab you, this will give you a chance to escape them even so.' Poole handed her a small but lethally sharp dagger.

Danielle looked at the tiny thing, not much bigger than her small hand, well suited for a sly cut at an unknowing opponent, or a quick slash to her own arteries if there was no other choice. She nodded her thanks and then leaned against her Keeper, shutting her eyes and breathing heavily. Jasper had to closed his mouth which had dropped open in surprise at both his boss's action as well as the slavey's response. He quickly lay down and feigning sleep immediately with a few realistic snores. 'Good Jasper, that'll give them a nasty shock they won't soon forget' Poole chuckled. Within a few minutes the whole camp was silent apart from heavy breathing, snores and the twins farting loudly.

A little over a quarter of an hour later they heard Smith call out in a low whisper as if he was hurt. Jasper tensed as if to move, but a sign from Mr Poole had him dropping back into his pretend slumber. Another call came, this time a little louder. Again, nobody in the camp stirred. Five slow minutes went by before Smith crept into the camp, quickening his speed, standing more upright as he saw the state of everyone lying about on the ground.

He gave a chuckle as he saw the great man himself, Elias poxy Poole, lying with drool running down his cheek. Smith snorted. No more play acting, no more pretending, no more living this damn lie. Now Smith would get the proper reward he had been working for. For more than five years he had spoken about his poor Breeder love, the damaged Token, the suicide and had been a poor, sad man. Except it was all a lie. Well, not *exactly* a lie. He had actually been part of the Watch patrol who had stolen the smith's wifey. She had been really tasty too and he had been really pissed off when she had been returned. He had gone to find her to let her know she would never be free of him. It wasn't his fault she had then killed herself; a complete waste of a good tup, in his opinion.

He had been able to use the story in his second life though, so nothing was wasted really. Mind you, he had taken part in lots of equally horrific stories that he could have used instead, but he stuck to this one. The suicide gave it a mawkish touch that someone like Poole, who had lost his own wife and child, could not help but be moved by it. The stupid, sentimental fool!

Smith had been asked by a Mage he knew to undermine Mr Poole's business but had not achieved any great success no matter how he tried. When the word had gone out that the bastard immediately needed guards for a special cargo, Smith knew that this was the chance to shut the old man down and earn a substantial fee at last. Then Smith would take the coins showered upon him and retire. Have his own bawd and live like a king, ha! Or maybe he could take on the job as go between, giving instructions on who wanted what type of sex partners in the underground clubs and where to send each specific drug shipment. Either way, Smith would have much more gold than he had ever seen before once the old bastard was dead.

'Remember, the girl goes with us alive. I only need to take Poole's head with me. You can do what you please with the rest of them and take what you want from the carts. Don't touch her stuff though as her Master will want it all back. Once he raises the ransom, that is.'

Smith went straight to Mr Poole and stood over him, revelling in his sense of power. Sliding out his short sword, Smith then prepared to stab the sleeping giant through the heart. He hesitated for a second as he wondered about slicing the big man's belly. It was still a killing blow but was so much more painful and might be due payment for all the time wasted when plans had come to naught because of the sixth sense for trouble the old bastard had. That split second of hesitation cost him his life, for as he looked down, Mr Poole moved faster than lightning and thrust his own long knife into Smith's belly before savagely yanking the blade up as he pulled it free. Even if there had been anyone who wanted to save him, it would have been impossible as this was a killing blow and Smith's intestines clung lovingly around the retreating blade to spill out onto the grass and glisten wetly in the weak sun under his horrified gaze. The younger man sank slowly to his knees and reached for his guts even as Mr Poole rapped him sharply over the head as he ran past. As he began losing consciousness, Smith could see the wifey he had sent to her death standing and looking at him but instead of fear, the only expression he had ever seen on her before, he could now see a smile on her pretty face. As his sight dimmed he saw her smile broaden and then he heard her laugh just before everything went black and his life ended as abruptly as a snuffed out candle.

Not even bothering to waste another glance at the traitor, Mr Poole gave a loud cry that roused his men into battle yet paralysed the invaders for a few seconds in shock. He sent a dagger flying across to the man half turned away from Varga and saw it slice through flesh to give a fatal wound to the thug's neck, the blood pumping out freely.

Jasper rolled over quickly so the blow from the heavy iron-bound cudgel that had been meant to crush his skull missed completely. He hooked a foot around his opponent's ankle and that man toppled over with a shout. Before he could recover, the bard had slit his throat and sprung to his feet, taking a running jump and landing on the back of the man who was beginning to lean down towards Deo. Pulling the man's head back by savagely yanking on his hair, Jasper slit his throat before dropping to the ground.

Rook shot up and grasped his attacker by the throat with an unbreakable pincer grasp. His other hand caught the wrist and stopped the dagger held there from continuing its lethal journey. Still squeezing with both hands, and causing the attacker to send out garbled screams of pain, Rook head-butted him before twisting the dazed, breathless, man's hand sending the knife straight up between the attacker's ribs and into his heart. Dropping the dead man Rook raced towards the carts, Jasper just behind him, ready to tackle the three men who had just begun to rifle through the goods sitting there.

Samuel and Danielle split apart in what seemed a well rehearsed move. Sweeping his legs around in a similar move to Jasper's, Samuel too achieved the desired effect. Crashing down onto his back, the astonished man gave a grunt before Samuel slammed down across his throat with the silver-topped tipstaff, crushing his larynx completely and leaving him to asphyxiate alone as the others got to their feet and also ran for the carts.

Luke came rushing back from the riverbank and slashed across one of the men at the carts with his heavy fishing rod. The wooden shaft whipped across the man's back and the line, with a fat fish sitting on the hook, swung and wrapped itself around the man's face, the flapping tail slapping against his eyes. Rook leapt across some fallen baggage and slashed out with his dagger, slicing through the thug's chest and stomach as he passed. Within a few seconds more, all the attackers were dead bar one. The last remaining thug was standing almost on his toes with Danielle holding her dagger snugly against his balls as she looked at him calmly. When Mr Poole walked up to him, all he did was whimper and continue watching the girl with terrified eyes.

'What's going on here, then, missy?' Mr Poole asked genially.

'I thought you would like to know how and why because we already know who,' she grinned at him, recalling a conversation he had had with Smith the night before when he had said that it was important to get all the facts before sentencing anyone to death. Even knowing he was guilty did not explain how or why he did the things he did. With the extra information provided you could weed out those who were also ready to cause harm or change your own tactics to prevent all out mutiny.

'I would like to know when, who, why, and what the bloody hell is going on!' exploded Luke but Jasper surprised them all by suddenly clutching his stomach, dropping his head and gasping. The others crowded around him, trying to find the wound when he shot upright again and pointed a shaking finger at Mr Poole's second in command.

'Fish!' He managed to croak out before collapsing into a fit of giggles. Luke just looked down his nose at the hysterical man rolling around on the floor before replying.

'Not just "fish", you skinny midget, that was a bloody good perch!' His sense of outrage sent the rest of them into shouts of laughter and bawdy comments flowed thick and fast as each man began checking the pockets of the attackers and placing the contents near the fire before stripping the corpses and dumping them in a pile. In all of this, Danielle hadn't moved, not even when the captive could no longer control his bladder and a wet stain appeared and spread around his groin area.

'So, lad, you are going to tell me everything you know. If you do so without causing me a headache, we can discuss your release. If, however, I feel that you are being evasive in any way, I will tell our little darling there to use that blade to persuade you.' The calm reasonableness of Mr Poole's voice was more frightening than anything the village tough had ever heard before. He gulped and gave another whimper, which he hoped would be taken for assent.

Before any question was asked, Bili suddenly dropped to his knees by the fire. Thrusting the dagger into Mr Poole's hand, Danielle pulled up her skirts and leapt across to him. Ripping open his shirt she found a small but deep tear in the boy's shoulder that had bled freely under his dark coat. The heavy material had soaked up his life's blood, not allowing any to fall so the lad's condition had passed without notice, even by himself. As someone who was used to blows, beatings and other deeper pains, Bili hadn't really felt the thrust hitting home in all the excitement of the short battle. A split second of indecision crossed Danielle's face before she began snapping out orders.

In no time at all Bili was laid upon a pallet with blankets to his waist. Fresh water was being heated over the fire, which had been built up to a fine blaze. Luke and Jasper were rummaging through the carts for Danielle's herb pouch, her surgeon's kit as well as some bandages, thankful that some of the training she had been given under the Numb was finally getting some use.

While scared for the boy Mr Poole had nonetheless taken his captive away to question him and Samuel went along to see if he could help. Rook sat by the youngster, stroking his sweaty head and whispering tall tales and silliness to try and keep the thin thread of life from fraying completely. Danielle wiped away the blood to try and see the wound but even as it cleared away more flowed from the deep cut. Coming to the fire Luke and Jasper opened up the bags and crouched down, ready to react to more orders.

Pressing down with the cloth firmly was still not enough to stop the bleeding and it was soon soaking wet with Bili's blood. A sound that was almost a hum left the girl's throat, causing all three men to look at her in astonishment. What they saw next was even more of a surprise. Danielle's eyes had rolled back in their sockets and her skin had begun to glow with a soft but intense light. An exchange of glances helped to convince them that they were all truly seeing the same thing. Another hum, this time even deeper and it sounded like it was forming the word "no". Luke gave a gasp and the other two followed his gaze to Danielle's hands.

Pressed firmly over the cloth, they were beginning to glow even brighter than her body with a clear, almost blue-white light. Tiny streaks like black lightning began shooting through the brightness and her hands now floated a little above the wound. Her eyes were glowing as strongly as the light on her hands, the same small bolts of lightning streaking across them. On impulse Rook dragged the cloth away from the cut in Bili's shoulder just as a streak of lightning whipped out, catching his hand. He gave a strangled yelp and fell, taking the blood-soaked cloth with him. Landing on his back he continued to look at her in astonishment. Bili had become almost translucent with blood loss but now his colour was slowly creeping back. The cut itself flickered with bolts of black energy, lightning flashes that sizzled in his skin and then began rising to the surface and running over his body, including his damaged throat, still not fully healed from wearing the dog collar. With a last burst of energy, Danielle cried out and collapsed, Luke only just catching her in time.

Bili opened his eyes and smiled sleepily at those surrounding him, before he gave a huge yawn, rolled over and went to sleep. Staring at him in astonishment, the small crowd could see that the youngster was now looking flushed and healthy. Apart from a slight, clotting scratch there was no trace of the fatal stab wound from just moments before. His neck was also better and only carried the faintest of pink marks from the leather collar instead of the sores from just an hour ago. The men gaped at each other in astonishment before placing the unconscious Danielle on to her own pallet between the carts and transporting Bili there before cleaning up the mess of cloths and herbs soundlessly, too overwhelmed with shock and wonder at what had just happened.

When Mr Poole and Samuel eventually returned, looking grim and worried, it was to a clean and quiet camp. When Rook explained about Danielle and the boy, the two men found it hard to believe until they were shown the shallow cut and the faded pink smudges on his throat. Samuel looked closely at the girl and gave a small choking sound.

'I will be damned and sent to the lower hells,' he exclaimed. 'Look at her. She's not only exhausted but she has lost weight. Look at those hollowed cheeks! Not to mention that dress was laced tight this morning but it's hanging loose now. Claiming it loosened through the day won't wash, I always check it as the Master would beat us both if she didn't show her assets enough. She looks like she hasn't had a good meal in weeks!'

'You are right, son,' agreed Mr Poole. 'It seems that she is a magiker, a bloody Healer by all that's holy! That would explain how she has survived so long on Numb.'

At this, Luke shot him a sharp glance. 'I think we should be told what's going on, Boss.'

'You're right, you should be. Let's leave it until later though. In the meantime, put the two youngsters on the carts. We ought to clear out of here, just in case there are any more surprises ahead. We will be deviating off the planned route too, lads. I don't know if Smith had anything else planned so changing how we get to Merino Bay will keep us safe.' With that, he tipped water over the sleeping twins who came awake, cursing and flailing their arms about. It took a few moments to get the basic information into the drug addled brains of the two men but once they understood, they went and ducked their heads in the water of the freezing river before coming back to mount their horses. Jasper harnessed the two giroxes, using rope on Butterfly. Seeing that the open sores from earlier were now just patches of white fur should have surprised him but he just shrugged it off. After seeing the miracle Dani had done for Bili, white patches meant nothing to the bard.

'You sure you are alright to ride, boys? You could sit in the carts if you are still groggy.' suggested Luke when the twins struggled with their horses. With a grunt of acceptance, the two men got off their mounts and threw the reins to Samuel and Mr Poole. Settling onto the carts, still yawning mightily, the men started the vehicles rolling but fell asleep within minutes. The effects of the drug didn't work off completely until the following day, leaving them with foul headaches and even fouler tempers.

Chapter Thirteen

Although the group were no longer on the broad highway, they still found tracks that were easy enough to follow. The people they saw and spoke to on the new route were guarded in their responses but not hostile. By nightfall not only had the group settled comfortably on this less well-used travelling route, but they had also estimated that this would save them at least two days journeying. Apart from being much better for the horses, it also gave the men extra time to teach the youngsters in the group the fighting, hunting and riding skills they had discussed before.

It was only as they pulled up to make camp for the evening that the two sleeping at the back of Vargo's cart began to stir. Bili was the first to sit up, rubbing his head and yawning.

'What happened? When do we eat? I'm hungry,' he said plaintively. His jaw dropped at the shouts of laughter that greeted his comments.

'Oh yes,' guffawed Mr Poole, 'the boy is definitely fine!'

'Why shouldn't I be?' he said, puzzled with the way the men were coming up and hugging him. Not that he minded, like, it was just different. Then he looked around and saw the empty saddle. 'Where's Smith? Has he left us?' The latter was said in such a hopeful tone that Samuel couldn't help laughing.

'Smith has left us. Before you start babbling out more questions, boy, you wake our Danielle up and we will set up camp.'

Bili glared at the Keeper and gave a huff before turning to wake his companion. He immediately felt a spurt of panic when he saw her. The flesh on her face was shrunken in and her skin was dry, her lips cracked and split. She looked starving and ill. Bili began shaking her shoulder and calling her name, fear echoing out into the night. She stirred slightly and then Rook was there, lifting the boy down gently.

'Hey, young 'un, we don't want to frighten her. Come on, let us go find some water and you can have a wash to clean up.' With a sly wink, Rook showed Bili a pear before picking up a bucket and moving off. The young boy stood irresolutely for a moment before the lure of the freckle skinned fruit lured him in. Running after Rook, he caught up quickly and was soon munching away hungrily on the tasty flesh, juice running down his chin.

Danielle sat up groggily. She felt so hungry she was nauseous. Samuel was there, lifting her out of the cart and the twins put down a pallet of straw by a tree so that she could lean back against the torn bark of a silver birch. A piece of bread, fresh and tasty but unadorned, was given to her as Samuel squatted beside her and grinned at her puzzled face.

'Eat that slowly. You know you puke too bloody easily. Everything will be explained later, while we eat the evening meal, ok? Just don't expect answers to everything, we only know a small portion of what is going on.'

Nodding her agreement, Danielle watched as the men efficiently set up camp. Surprise by their awed glances, she also wondered why something was taken away from the cooking fire just before Luke came back from watering and hobbling the horses. Later on, after eating a tasty stew she was even more bemused when the twins presented a plate of fish to Luke, cooked very nicely in lemon and herbs. Immediately, in unison, they cried 'It was a bloody perch!' before bursting into shouts of laughter, which all the other men joined in. They laughed even harder as Danielle and Bili exchanged confused glances and Bili told them all he was "'pletely confuzzled!" that caused even the slave to grin tiredly.

Later, after the slave had talked of what had occurred to her, Samuel and Mr Poole had shared their own parts of the long story which had begun with going to fetch more Numb. The other men told of what had happened while Mr Poole and the Keeper were questioning the surviving thug. Bili bent his head and twisted around, trying to see where he had been cut and scowling at the fact that only a small mark remained, even fainter than earlier in the day. Rook predicted that it would completely disappear by the morning, much to Bili's disgust, which made them all laugh.

'So I am a magiker, Sam? An Abomination?' Danielle asked, fearfully.

'No!' Samuel exploded. 'A magiker, yes but you are no bloody Abomination, any more than I am. Your ability to heal helps to explain why the crappy Numb hasn't killed you yet. It also gives me hope that escaping into the FreeLands doesn't mean sending you to die. Smith was a traitor to Mr Poole. He just wanted all the power that that man possesses, that's what the ambush was about. You, girl, were to be ransomed back to the Willoughbys. That bloody fool thought he could win a game the Master plays in. Now we go on to Merino Bay, we get on that ship and we get to Mertam and then we get you over to the nearest safe place and then to the FreeLands. Hopefully, we will find a gnome or a shadow kat that can send us through some portals which will make the journey both safer and shorter.'

Danielle sat motionless as she tried to come to terms with everything. Her head was spinning and she still felt exhausted trying to understand all that had happened. She couldn't help the tiny bloom of hope stirring within.

'And Smith has done me a favour, damn his eyes,' rumbled the deep voice of Mr Poole. 'He helped me reach a decision that has been bothering me for months. I spoke to Luke a good while ago about this. I am getting old, boys. More than that though, I am getting bloody tired. I hate what is happening here on Bisra and trying to keep the drug dealing, child stealing bastards out of my business is getting more and more difficult. I have been fighting since I was born, it seems to me. Only when I had my Charlotte and wee Amber Rose did I have any rest. Now, it just seems one thing after another. I should have spotted Smith and his bullshit long before this. It was only instinct, and the way Bili here avoided spending time with him, that got me wondering about the bastard in the first place.

'I have enough money to see my life out in comfort and more than enough will be left over to set Bili up for life too. I have discussed with Luke previously about giving him the business reins. Now that we are heading for Merino Bay, I am thinking that maybe I will go on my brother's ship when we get there and go on a trip across the ocean with him before settling down somewhere quiet. So, do you want the business or what, Luke?'

There was stunned silence as the men tried to absorb this life-changing question, trying to figure out what it would mean for them. Danielle and Samuel just gazed around at the others, not really understanding how portentous this was. Bili, however, grinned from ear to ear then burst into tears. Mr Poole pulled the small youngster onto his lap and just held him until the sobbing began to die down a little.

'Am I wrong in thinking you wanted to stay with me, son? Don't you fret, my boy, we can find you a home with whoever you want.' His words, which were meant to soothe, actually had the boy crying even harder as he tried to speak. His distress built up and Mr Poole felt helpless to do anything for him. Danielle came up and simply stroked the hair back from the youngster's hot forehead, wiped his wet and snot-smeared face with a cool, damp cloth and murmured too low for the men to hear. Mr Poole felt the little head moving in response to her words. With a smile and a kiss to the boy's cheek, the woman sat back on her heels and looked at the older man.

'Bili wants to stay with you but felt that it was too much to hope for. You wanting to keep him with you is the best gift he's ever had. It's just too big for him to keep in. He doesn't know how he will ever pay you back and doesn't have the words to be able to express his feelings. He also knows that you will protect him from anyone ever forcing him to do anything like the fat man used to do to him. He is just so happy and too full of emotions that he cannot express.'

Tugging the small head away from his chest, Mr Poole looked into the shining face that stared back at him. 'No-one will ever touch you again in any way you don't want. If I am not there to protect you, there will either be someone else with you who will do the job or you will be big enough to look after yourself. I need you to tell me yourself, son. Do you want to stay with me? Honestly?'

Bili nodded his head vigorously, his black curls bouncing with the movement. Samuel was not the only one to notice that the youngster's hair, shaved close to his scalp just a few days ago, still just a fuzzy covering before the fight, had now grown thick and fast since the Healing of his shoulder.

'Wiv you.' His voice was hoarse and thick with tears still not shed.

'Well then, my boy, stay with me you will!' The big man's voice wasn't as steady or as clear as it usually was either. 'Mind you, I think you may need to train as a cook or hunter just to keep up with your appetite.'

The boy grinned, unabashed. He liked being teased about his hungry stomach and hearing the men around them chuckle too made it even better. Then, without thinking, he raised his hand to cup Mr Poole's cheek and looked solemnly at the man he trusted and was beginning to feel such love for.

'What is it, son?'

'Can I call you something?'

'Tell me what it is you want to call me, son, and we will see if it suits me. I am not going to allow you to call me Cornelius, mind...and definitely not Ebenezer!'

The youngster gave a watery giggle at the reminder of the naming game from the night he had been rescued before leaning up and whispering a word into Mr Poole's ear. The group listening to this exchange were astonished to see tears appear in the man's eyes and he allowed them to run shamelessly down his face. It took a little time before he could speak, coughing as he held the youngster in a tight grip.

'From now on, men, I am not just your Boss but I am also proud to be known as Bili's Grandpa.' He kissed the boy's head and revelled in the cheers raining down on them.

With a smile at them, Danielle gave them both a kiss on the cheek and whispered, 'Well done, this is so very well done!'

Jasper began singing a joyful song. Rook caught the young boy up from Mr Poole and began dancing around; the twins joined in the singing as they took care of the washing up. Danielle sat down next to Mr Poole and leaned against him as he puffed away on his pipe.

'Have I ever said thank you for being willing to help me?' she murmured to him.

'No need, lass. True families never need to say thank you. Besides, I reckon I owe you much more than you owe me. See that boy there? He snuck in and stole my heart the minute I saw him. Thing is, I would never have let him stay near me; too dangerous for him. So helping you actually helped me see what he means to me and just how much I had begun to hate the life I have been living. You have given me the chance of a new life without being lonely and you gave him his life back. No way can I ever repay you, no way.'

'My brother has asked me to go on his ship for years, seems like now is the time to do so. I think Rook might be coming along too as he is as taken with the boy as Bili is with him. Before I met you, lass, I had a lot of people I had to watch my back with, a lot of men who owed me but who I was always wary of trusting. Now? Well, now I have a group here I would trust with my life. Even the twins feel like men I can depend on. It ain't just a group travelling together now. Do you feel it?'

Danielle nodded; it did feel as if every one of them had begun bonding together since the fight earlier. She didn't know if it was the fight itself because the twins had missed that, or the impact of the healing magik or a combination of both. She couldn't hide a grin as she wondered if it might have been the bloody perch that did it. No matter. Danielle knew that she was safe travelling to the ship. The hints dropped meant that she was almost sure that she would be safe on the ship as well, so that just left the landing at Mertam and the planned escape. But many weeks of travelling lay ahead and none of them knew if she would live that long. Mr Poole must have had a little magik himself because he squeezed her to him and kissed her hair, which had also grown since the healing, as he whispered to her.

'You will make it, little Healer, I know you are going to be free.'

With another hug he left her to scoop up his new grandson before throwing the squealing boy at Rook who caught him easily before twirling him around. Danielle laughed and found that she was ravenous again so helped herself to some more of the rabbit stew. The only thing that stopped her eating a third helping was the waves of exhaustion that suddenly hit her. Swiftly, Samuel jumped up as she began swaying in her seat, caught her and laid her in the shelter under her covers. She was already asleep before he pulled a blanket over her and she slept without moving until woken with a hot milky drink and some toast the next morning.

Chapter Fourteen

The next morning set the pattern for the rest of the journey. Once Bili and Danielle were up, washed and dressed, Sam showed them the exercises he did each day. The other men tried to join in but soon fell by the wayside as the Keeper moved from one fluid stance to another. Bili huffed and puffed his way through, determined to become as strong as Sam, although he did trip over his own feet, drop his "sword" which was a stick Mr Poole had given him to practise with. They were all impressed with the boy's focus and stubbornness as he tried over and over to get a movement right. Danielle found she could remember the moves but she was jerky as she changed from one stance to another and got frustrated with herself.

'Relax, Dani,' Sam called out as she gave a growl at her ineptitude. 'You have only just begun to learn. The more times you do this, the easier it will be. You are still half starved and weary, so take it a little at a time. Now, enough! It is time to eat.'

Bili gave a cheer and immediately went to the fire to grab some of the hot travel cake with slices of rabbit. Grabbing a couple of apples, he went over and fed the giroxes their treats as he wolfed down his own food. Danielle moved more slowly but had a heaped plateful of food handed to her. To her amazement, she finished every bite.

The campsite was then broken down and the carts pointed in the right direction. During the morning, both Bili and Danielle were given horse riding lessons. When Bili first got up on Jasper's smaller horse, he looked terrified, but once she began moving, he lost his fear immediately. Danielle was willing to learn but much preferred the cart, although she knew that becoming proficient in riding might be a great help to her after she escaped.

After a few hours travel, they stopped for lunch. Then while the rest of them guided the carts forward to the evening camp-sight, the twins took Danielle and Bili hunting for the evening meal. Here Danielle showed a natural proficiency with a bow, bringing down a small deer on only her fourth attempt. Bili missed every single time with his small bow but Varga decided to give him a slingshot, something Bili had used before. With this, the boy managed to stun half a dozen birds that could be cooked and eaten the following day. Bili gagged a little at the necessary disembowelling and dressing of the beast but as Deo told him, the only option was to dress what he killed, or not be able to eat. Bili decided he preferred eating so took part in slicing open and emptying the insides of the deer, leaving it as an offering to the wood spirits and animals.

The herb hunting didn't go quite as well as Bili seemed to think if it was green, it was alright to eat. After a couple of close encounters the twins and Dani were tasked with herb hunting while Bili swished with his "sword" and danced about impatiently.

'You are going to need to learn patience and how to be quiet unless you want to starve, young 'un,' laughed Deo.

'No, I won't,' the boy shot back. 'You won't let me starve!'

'The worst of it is?' Varga whispered to Danielle. 'The little bugger is right'

When the small group met back up with the others, Danielle sat next to Sam and plucked the birds. She was careful to keep every feather as she knew they could be useful. Bili went to his grandfather and babbled away for a few minutes before accepting some fruit from Rook and then falling into a heavy nap.

Bili woke up when the carts stopped and he got down to begin helping set up camp. He brought firewood to where the twins had set up the fire and then sat glaring at the pile. Deo leaned down and pulled at a stick, only to hear Bili shout in distress. All movement stopped and they all turned to see what was wrong.

'Bili! Bili-boy! What's wrong?' Rook ran over to where the youngster held the stick he had snatched out of Deo's hand.

'I got this mixed up with that lot,' Bili pointed to the pile of firewood. 'It's my sword that Grandpa gave me, I nearly lost it.' Everyone hid their smiles at his woebegone little face and it was only when Mr Poole came and picked him and his sword up and took him over to Butterfly for a fuss, did the boy calm down.

'Is it his "sword"?' asked Rook.

'Doubt it,' answered Deo. 'This is his second lot of stuff. He thinks it is though, so that's all that counts.' With a shared grin, everyone went back to setting up the camp and Bili came back happy now he had fussed over the girox.

After a meal of Danielle's deer, Sam decided to take her through some fight moves. Bili, of course, wanted to join in. Rook stepped forward to be Bili's partner, intending to stop the youngster in his tracks and get the boy resting. Waiting until Sam gave a nod to begin, Rook spun around to Bili's back and crossed his arms, holding onto the boy's hands.

'There ya go, boy,' laughed the man. 'Beaten in two seconds!'

As Rook looked around laughing, Bili bent his neck and bit hard into his captor's arm. As Rook yelled in pain and flung the boy forward, Bili dropped to the floor and kicked out behind him. The mercenary gave a strangled cry and fell, clutching at his groin where Bili had landed a fierce blow. As Rook whimpered in pain, the youngster ran over and grabbed Danielle.

'Quick, Dani, quick. I fink I've hurt him!' Bili was devastated, not having meant to cause his "uncle" any harm but he had reacted to being grabbed with a sense of panic. Danielle looked down at Rook and grinned.

'I call that poetic justice, you silly scav,' she said. 'Fancy thinking you can grab someone like that who has been living in fear for years. And you needn't think I am touching it.' This last comment had them all falling about laughing as she reached down and touched Rook's chest. Immediately they all saw her eyes beginning to glow and streaks of the black lightning play across the man's waist down to his knees. It didn't take long before Rook was able to move and they all sat down for food.

'What did it feel like?' Luke asked.

'Like being in a warm bath but not water, clouds.'

Having no idea how to interpret this, the chat turned to the lessons that had been learned and then Dani went with Luke to wash the plates before the settled down to hear the next part of The Knight and The Mermaid's Cove story.

The Knight and the Mermaid's Cove, Part two

Sir Egain put the beautiful pearls into a soft rag and tied that to the shadow kat, knowing that if anyone attacked, they would not touch the kat.

'Why not?' asked Bili. 'What's so special about a shadow kat?'

'If you hush and listen, I'll tell you,' answered Jasper.

Shadow kats,' Jasper continued, *'are very magikal beings. First, they are really, really big. Standing, most will come up to Sam's waist in height although if they rear up on their back legs, they are even bigger than him. Second, they can fade in and out of sight as well as getting into places without anyone knowing. Lastly, they pick their friends and will always be there to protect them. So when Sir Egain gave the jewels to Flidai, he knew that they were as safe as safe could be.*

The two companions retraced their journey, walking through wind and rain, sunshine and fog, there was even snow at one point. Over hill and down dale, through fields and over bridges they walked.

And walked.

And walked, until they eventually came to the gates of the big city where the knight had first been given his commission. As he walked through the gates he saw groups of men, unshaven and slovenly, wearing gaudy livery. He felt an atmosphere that worried him as he saw people scurrying past with their heads down. The only ones he saw were obviously middle-aged or older, there were no young people out in the open at all. The nearer to the palace Sir Egain went, the more he saw to unsettle him. There was no laughing, no chatting people, no joy. Everyone he saw avoided his eyes and he realised that most were as thin as he was.

Feeling more and more wary he looked down and saw that Flidai was as unsettled as himself and had chosen to become invisible. The knight was relieved and thought about turning around. Then he remembered that he had given his word so he began climbing the marble steps to the palace entrance.

Getting in to see the king wasn't easy and Sir Egain was passed from one snooty official to another until, at last, he was escorted into the Throne Room. There, seated on enormous thrones set on a dais, were the king and his daughter. His throne was gold and covered in firehearts, garnets and rubies. He wore a blue velvet fur trimmed robe and wore rings on every finger as well as other gems dotted about his person. She wore a gown that might have looked lovely if she hadn't had silver and gold thread sewn in dizzying patterns all over it and another cartload of jewels sparkling on hands, throat, head and even feet. Both of the royals were extremely fat and their faces flushed in the heat of the room.

Sir Egain gave a silent groan of dismay. He knew he should have listened to his instincts but he also knew he wanted his horse back. Stepping towards the dais, he gave a sweeping bow, removing his hat to show a respect he didn't feel.

'Your Majesty, your highness,' he said.

'Yes? What do you want? Hurry up, we are busy.' The king took a chocolate off a huge serving tray covered with exotic food and popped it into his mouth.

'You asked me to find the Princess's pearls, sire.'

'Asked you? I think not, peasant. We never ask.'

'I-it was a b-bargain, sire. If I found the pearls I could have my stallion returned and you said you would give me a commission in your army.' Although the knight reminded the king of the latter condition, Sir Egain decided that he would say no.

'Well, it doesn't matter what my daddy said, I don't see any pearls so he doesn't have to give you anything.' The princess spoke in as haughty tone as her father as she sneered at the knight.

'Erm, I have them here, with my shadow kat for safe keeping.' With that, Flidai let his magik go and appeared in front of the royals. The princess gave a loud scream and the king roared for his guards. Sir Egain and Flidai just stood there, astonished at the reaction. Trying to calm the room, the knight removed the pearls and showed them to the king.

'See, sire? I have the pearls. Flidai here has kept them safe on our journey to bring them home.' And then Sir Egain began telling his story, of how Flidai had followed the scent of the magik in the pearls until they found the Mermaid's Cove and the Lady who gave them to him.

The king gave a sly smile as he listened before he burst out with a guffaw. 'Magikal pearls? A mermaid? You are a liar, sir, and a thief! You got the pearls "back" so easily because you never let them go. You stole them! And now you expect us to buy them back? No, sir, you are mistaken.' With a gesture, the king motioned his personal guard forward.

'Take this thief and put him in the jail cell. He will hang tomorrow.'

Stunned, the knight stood frozen to the spot. As the guard surrounded him, the princess ran to him and snatched the pearls back. She looked at them greedily and, with a laugh, skipped back to her seat.

Flidai disappeared and no matter how they tried, he couldn't be found. In the end Sir Egain was dragged off to the jail cell, still in shock over what had happened. As he was dragged away, he made a vow that if he ever escaped, he would get those pearls back, even if it cost him his life.

As he was pushed into the small and dirty cell he heard someone say; 'You are not alone, Sir Knight. Do not worry.'

With that, the cell door slammed shut and Sir Egain was left alone in the dark.

'Ha, looks like our little knight needs his bed,' Jasper broke off the story as Bili tried to protest but was too sleepy to keep his eyes open. Mr Poole took him to the bedding between the carts and he was fast asleep in minutes. It didn't take much longer before everyone else turned in, leaving Luke as first watch.

The remainder of their travel fell into an easy routine. The weather was drier and brighter than it had been recently but the temperature had begun to drop steadily. All woke at dawn, washing and eating before cleaning up the campsite and moving on. Bili complained less and less at the indignity of the cold water when he saw how the grown-ups took personal hygiene seriously. There was a place hollowed out on Mr Poole's cart so anyone could bed down during the day as they still kept a watch throughout the night. The carts set the pace, with the men scattered around and staying alert. Butterfly had completely healed and was devoted to Bili, even letting the excitable youngster ride on its hunched shoulders.

Both Bili and Danielle learnt to love riding lessons after the falls from their first few lessons had healed. Bili's screams of delight the first time he managed a gallop had the whole group laughing. Danielle was now dressed in men's clothing and found it much easier to move around in breeches and a shirt that was buttoned up to her throat to hide the collar. Her hair grew almost as quickly as Bili's had after his healing which made Mr Poole and Sam wonder what healing she was doing subconsciously.

The two of them also learned to hunt, using various weapons. Danielle was amazingly proficient with a bow, whereas Bili preferred the easier option of snares but was getting extremely good with the slingshot. At the end of the day, the twins cooked whatever had been caught earlier while they watched both Bili and Danielle learn more about fighting, each of the men demonstrating a different ability while everyone shouted out helpful – and sometimes not so helpful - advice. At all times there was someone who was on watch in case of unwanted attention and apart from fetching extra milk, bread and eggs, the group managed to avoid all the villages. There were very few shrines with their nosy clerics and even less travellers on these back roads so there was much laughter, joking and camaraderie that went on, only disappearing if strangers were about.

The closer they got to Merino Bay, the quieter and more withdrawn Danielle became. Thankfully she had regained her colour and the weight her healing had cost her. Two days of mostly sleeping and eating had put her right and there seemed to be no side effects from the lack of Numb yet. Bili was put out when he saw the last of his scarring had disappeared and spent days trying to make another one by poking a stick across his shoulder, until his "Grandpa" told him on the last day of travel that really good brigands didn't have scars. After a few moments of thought and of studying the solemn, unmarked faces of Luke, Samuel and Jasper, he gave a heavy sigh before throwing the latest stick away. Then, with a shout, he jumped off the cart and ran to pick it up before letting himself be grabbed by the back of his shirt and whisked up onto a waiting saddle.

'For the fire later!' he grinned at Rook.

'Oh, aye, the fire. That thing will make all the difference!' was the dry response as the others chuckled at the happy lad.

'Where did your scars go, Uncle Rook?' Bili was curious as he looked at the handsome face of his friend. Although they had taken longer to heal, Rook had realised that the pox scars that had marked his face since childhood had mostly faded away, the skin becoming smoother and his expression also becoming lighter.

'A present from our Dani,' he smiled down at the youngster, who gave a satisfied nod and bit into a crisp apple Rook had just handed over.

That night was a party. Even though Danielle would lose her sense of freedom once they reached the gates of Merino Bay, the group decided that Bili needed a birthday celebration. He couldn't remember when his day of birth was so the men decided that this was as the perfect time to choose rather than the customary dates. Those born in the middle six months of the year celebrated their day of birth at Summers End while those born at the turn of the year celebrated at Winters End and those without family took the name of their celebration, which was how a foundling like Danielle gained her surname of Wintersborn.

Stopping early and getting the fire going and making great ceremony about using Bili's stick in the process, the twins began roasting a small pig over the blaze, splitting the skin and pushing herbs beneath, preparing vegetables and tubers to cook on a flat pan greased with some of the hot fat that fell from the cooking meat. Bili was taken off by Samuel and Danielle and bathed with strong soap, his hair trimmed tidily. In his excitement, Bili forgot to even scowl at being cleaned like this. After being thoroughly scrubbed by Samuel, the three of them went back to the fire where he was ceremoniously seated upon a log and wrapped in a shirt.

First he was given some presents, his eyes getting bigger and bigger with amazement at each gift. Under things first, which puzzled him a little. These were followed by a proper set of britches, fitted at his waist and stopping just below his knees, made of moleskin so they moved and stretched with him, so comfortable and hard wearing. A shirt he could simply pull down over his head with a set of ties to tighten or loosen at his neck. Stockings, thick and warm and knitted by Danielle on the journey, were received with some delight but the shining leather boots were clasped to his chest with joy. Allowing the men to help, he dressed in his new under-drawers and vest, followed by the rest of the clothes. Mr Poole made him shut his eyes before placing a small three cornered hat upon the boy's clean head.

'There you go, my boy. Once your hair grows a little more, we will tie it back just like our Samuel's.' Mr Poole found himself grinning broadly at the way the boy kept exclaiming in pleasure at the first clothes he had ever had that were especially for him. Fat Syd gave him nothing but rags, and the first clothes Mr Poole provided had been, by necessity, worn by others, but these! Oh my, these were just Bili's.

The twins and the slave girl had worked on them as they rode and each night as they finished the evening meal. Bili was so used to them sewing and knitting something that he hadn't even thought to ask what they were making. Some of the stitches might be crooked or larger than those of a true seamstress would be, but these clothes were better than gold in the boy's opinion. He looked up at the burly man he now called Grandpa and nodded, too full of emotion to speak. Mr Poole bent down and winked at him, understanding the emotions flooding the boy. The moment was eased when the twins gave a shout and brought out a platter full of bread and fruit, a little cheese and rich butter so everyone began eating, warning the boy not to have too much before the filling pig.

While they ate, Luke came forward with a small fishing rod, complete with extra hooks to "help the boy catch perch", which made him giggle. Jasper gave him his own shiny whistle to play but Bili was speechless with joy as Rook handed over a beautifully decorated dagger, big enough to be used as a short sword. After the boy had excitedly handed the dagger for a moment, Mr Poole gave him a sheath to hold it. This too was a true work of art, with a hunting scene etched along it. Dagger and sheath fitted together perfectly. Then came the best surprise as far as Bili was concerned. A piece of parchment, with elegant writing that had taken Samuel a lot of painstaking work, proclaimed to the world that Biliach Poole was now officially Elias Poole's Grandson. Holding it carefully, Bili stepped down from his special seat and cuddled up on Mr Poole's lap, completely overwhelmed with happiness at all that had been given to him.

The camp itself was quiet for a while, letting the boy calm down before Jasper began singing a ballad in his beautiful tenor voice. It rose with power before whispering with pleasure, suiting the mood perfectly. Before any could become maudlin the twins brought another platter of food, this time the roasted pig with vegetables and potatoes and they all tucked in with fervour.

Dani was less enthusiastic, a feeling of dread building within her, but she ate and sang determined not to spoil the youngster's precious day. Eventually he crawled onto Danielle's lap, yawning hugely, ready for the rest of the tale Jasper had been telling him.

The Knight and the Mermaid's Cove: Part Three

Sir Egain sat in the wet, miserable cell, the walls running with filth. Huddled into himself, trying to keep warm, he cursed the unfaithful king and the others who had gone along with his schemes. His people were starving while the king and his awful progeny ate food shipped halfway around the world. The knight jumped when he felt something warm and furry slide across him.

'Flidai! Oh my word, how good it is to see you. Now, if only I could slide through the bars and escape the way you got in.' Sir Egain felt better immediately. He had been friends with the shadow kat for nearly five years. Wandering around with his horse, Spirit, they had come upon a small kitten that had been badly mauled. With no idea that this was a magikal being, the knight had cleansed the wound and bound it up, staying until the kat was fully healed. Once the shadow kat was well again, the knight rode away, only to find that it followed him no matter where he went. Even crossing the sea didn't stop the courageous and determined kat. In the end, Sir Egain accepted that it was here to stay. Naming the kat seemed natural and he named it Flidai, which meant Silence in Sir Egain's own speech.

The night dragged on and it wasn't until the early hours of the morning that the prisoner heard his cell door click quietly open. There stood the captain of the king's guard, dressed in plain clothes and carrying the knight's sword.

'Come,' the captain said urgently. 'You must hurry, not everyone is with us.'

144

'Us?' queried Sir Egain as he slipped out of the cell and strapped on his sword.

'Rebels. The king is starving his people, yet his favoured few eat plenty off gold plates. I have seen him beat and torture those that have been loyal to him. Yours is not the first hanging of an honourable man that has happened in the last few months. Now, we must away.'

'I thank you for my sword, sirrah, but I cannot leave. My honour tells me I have to get the pearls back, to deliver them to a Lady more worthy. I also need my horse.'

The captain looked at him in astonishment and then chuckled quietly. 'It's a good job I knew you would say that.' Opening his hand, he showed the pearls to the knight, who gasped at their soft glow under the slight moon.

'Wha-ho-wha?' Sir Egain stumbled over his words but remembered to keep his voice down.

'I thought of what I would want to do in your place. I have a friend who works in the royal bedchamber. She saw these thrown into a drawer, put others in their place and brought them to me. Your horse is outside the gates, waiting for you.'

'Come with me,' said the knight. 'The Lady will reward you, I am sure.'

'Perhaps one day, Sir Egain,' said the captain. 'First I have to clear the vermin from my land. Good luck!'

The captain had been moving towards the gates, keeping to the shadows. He slipped down an alley way as they heard a patrol marching close. Not stopping, he led them to a door and tapped twice, then paused before knocking a little harder four times. Immediately the door swung open and they all ducked in quickly. The door closed quickly behind them and Sir Egain saw a tall woman, obviously connected to the captain as he hugged her. She was young and beautiful and the knight felt able to ask what he couldn't before.

'Why didn't I see any young people or children out in the street?'

The lady, who was the captain's wife looked sad as her husband replied. 'We keep all who are young or young looking locked tight away. Those in charge now have no compunction in taking whatever and whoever they wish, understand?'

With a feeling of rage, the knight did. 'I can stay, I can help...' he began.

'No, though we appreciate the offer. All of us who will fight know each other's faces. A new one could get you killed by the wrong side. Go, sir knight, and if you can get any blessings from your Lady for us, we will accept, happily.' With that, the captain pulled up a trapdoor that had been hidden under a rug which the shadow kat and wandering knight stepped down. The captain handed down a small lantern that gave off a golden light, gave a slight nod and then closed the trap.

Although he bumped his head a few times, Sir Egain made good time as he went along. Thankfully, every time there was an intersection a bold cross in the wall showed him which way to go. After an hour of stumbling, he saw that the darkness in front of him didn't seem quite as dense. After a short while he came out of the tunnel at the side of a hill, a little way from the city. There, pulling at some clover, stood his stallion, Spirit.

Grabbing hold of the reins and the pommel, Sir Egain pulled himself up into the saddle, patting the enthusiastic horse on its shiny grey neck. Flidai went and rubbed noses with the animal and then Sir Egain kicked his heels and away they went.

Over hill and through the dales, fording rivers and climbing mountains took much less time with the huge horse under the knight and the supplies the brave captain had supplied. Soon, they could smell the sea and the knight felt excitement in him bubble up into a shout of joy. On down the beach they rode, the kat dancing and diving between the galloping hooves and then they were there.

Stepping down off his horse Sir Egain led it into the Mermaid's Cove. There was the Lady, all sparkling and beautiful. Her beauty was bereft of jewellery or furs or exotic perfumes. She just took the knight's breath away.

'My knight!' she exclaimed. 'I didn't expect you to return so soon.'

Sir Egain knelt down before her and offered up his cupped hands, wherein lay the pearls, still glowing.

'I came to bring you these, milady,' he said. 'Though I was trained to keep my word, it seems some kings don't understand such courtesies.'

'Tell me,' she said with a slight frown. So Sir Egain told her of his arrival at the city and what he had seen. He told of the king, the princess and their greed. Lastly, he spoke of being imprisoned and the good captain.

'What do you ask of me, sir knight?' she said when he had finished.

'If you would still have me, lady, I am yours. Do with me as you will. If, however, you have magik enough to help the poor people in the city, you will have my eternal gratitude.'

'Hmmm,'

After pacing a little she suddenly threw up her hand, the pearls were flung into the air. Some hit the top of the Cove roof.

Some touched on the horse and his master. None, however, touched the kat for shadow kats have their own magik. Then, as the sea came to the shore, a huge wave of magik spilled out of the small cave and ran across the land. In the city, where the rebels had started their fight for fairness and freedom there was a flash of blinding light. Once everyone stopped blinking and had their sight returned, they saw those who had been abusing their power had all been turned into pigs. Big, fat oinking pigs, running around and ripping up their fancy clothing. For many generations the city was known as the fairest and the happiest city of all.

And the knight? Well, when the pearls hit him and his horse, they both shuddered and shivered. Then they struggled to breathe before the mermaid pulled them both into the water where they breathed as easily as they did in the air before. She took them away to a land beneath the ocean where the knight became her adviser and helpmate.

As for Flidai? Well, we all know that shadow kats go where ever they want, so he would go and see them often but he liked roaming the world too much to stay, even for Sir Egain.

As Jasper said the last words, Bili's who had been struggling to stay awake, let his eyes shut for the night. Dani held the boy up for the nightly kisses he adored before she carried him to the bed and cuddled down beside him. Tomorrow they would be in the city itself, heading for the docks. Any freedom she had had was now ended. It made the slave even more determined to be free. As she sank down into sleep she vowed to find a way to live without a collar or die trying.

When Samuel and Mr Poole checked on them later, the Keeper felt his heart break at the sight of tear tracks on her sleeping face. Looking up, he saw the same sorrow on the face of the man he respected above all others. After pulling up the blankets, both men walked quietly away.

'We will save her, lad, we will free her. Get some sleep. Tomorrow is not going to be easy, alright?' The burly man looked down at Samuel with concern.

'I know, I will, Elias, I just hate the bastards that made the world like this.'

'Not the whole world, son...our own gods watch over us. It is man that makes some of the world such as this but keep your eye on getting to the FreeLands and you will both make it. Don't let fear hurt you now.'

Samuel gave the man a hug, surprising both of them before he went and settled down on his own bedding. Mr Poole shook his head and gave a wry smile before going to his own bed. One by one they fell asleep to the crackling of the fire as it slowly died down and the quiet humming from Jasper as he stayed alert for any trouble and finding none.

Chapter Fifteen

The following morning, the group were in a sombre mood. They washed, Bili doing so without complaint for once as he proudly dressed himself in his new clothes and strapped on his "sword" with help from Rook. Danielle was back in a dress of a muddy brown, already regretting the loss of the freedom of wearing britches. Carefully she pulled down the top to the accepted slave level, showing off her creamy breasts as well as the filigree and gems of the collar. Her hair was cut again close to the scalp by Varga who scowled as each piece dropped to the ground. Unseen by Danielle each man, and the boy, took a lock of her hair.

Samuel put on his black, knee length, split panelled coat over a white shirt and fashionable cravat. Next was a black leather waistcoat over the shirt, with straps crossing it, each holding two throwing stars. Around his slim waist he belted his sword on over his grey trousers, the legs tucked into black knee-high boots. He strapped a dagger to his other hip, tying the scabbard snugly to his thigh. Throwing daggers went into the tops of his boots. He walked around, bending his legs and moving his arms, ensuring the open weapons – and those hidden - – moved with him comfortably. Lifting his head, he saw the other men looking at him dumbfounded. He placed his topper with its scarlet band firmly on his head, pulled on his tight leather gloves and grinned at them all.

'No blimmin' wonder you always win yer fights.' Varga's jaw had dropped in shock. Samuel chuckled and then went to do a last check of the carts and baggage while the rest of them finished dressing in their own uniforms, worn for the first time since Smith's end.

An hour later than usual, the group began moving back to the main highway leading to the gates of Merino Bay. Their fighting air and readiness for action made other travellers step back warily and keep to just a nod of acknowledgement rather than any attempted banter or the trading of goods as was usual. At the Shining One's shrine before heading through the gates, the men made their obeisance before the altar and the Server blessed them. This man was clean and sweet-smelling unlike the dirty and sour scented clerics who had blessed them at various places along the journey route. When certain dirty forefingers had pressed the watered down honey onto the men's lips, they all had to fight the gag reflex that rose up. More than once, there had been vomiting after moving away from the Shrine, the men then washing their faces before swigging and spitting water from their mouths in an attempt to get rid of both the stench and the taste that lingered in their nose and on their lips.

The port gates were reached at last and Mr Poole showed his travel charter to the gatekeeper. He explained away the lack of a man in the group due to an attack by bandits, and the group was allowed in with little fuss.

As they had moved further in, the noise and the dirt exploded into their senses. Instead of the drab but respectable muted colours of Harmony: black, white, brown, cream and beige, here was a rainbow of every possible colour and shade. Women walked by in silks, satins and velvets in rich jewel like tones of ruby, gold, scarlet, emerald, sapphire and turquoise, escorted by men in finery just as colourful and decorative. The style for both men and women was looser, more relaxed. No corsets were seen by any of the newcomers, the necklines lower and showing more of the flesh of the bejewelled women, which the travelling men fully appreciated. Men wore lace upon their clothing, delicate embroidery and other adornments unusual to eyes that were used to the plainer varieties.

Apart from the bright colours that seemed to burn the eyes, they were assailed by hundreds of different smells; various varieties of food cooking with unknown but pungent spices while perfumes worn by both men and women clashed and fought to dominate, pomades and hair oils added to the pungent odours of sweat, dirt, rotting food, faeces and urine. Danielle noticed the hidden people: beggars who were starving in nothing but rags, encrusted with dirt and unable to afford any of the sumptuous food offered, waiting until it was discarded as no longer fit to eat. Children scuffled in the dirt for anything that might have been dropped that could still be made use of. Men and women alike, wearing old styles of finery that was dirty, ripped and tawdry, waited for interest from passers-by before disappearing down alleys with their customers. Pickpockets roamed, watching for any likely victim.

Dogs and cats ran around chasing the rats bold enough to move in daylight, excited about the filth, rotting food and other less salubrious offerings of the town. Horses, donkeys, sheep and cows joined to the chaos, their voices adding a raucous tone to the noise surrounding everyone, while their droppings added to the overwhelming stench.

Pulling her attention back to the cart, Danielle focused on her hands. It was impossible to act as a slave, unknowing and uncaring, while taking it all in. Only by concentrating on the shape of her hands, on the way her fingers twined, the colour changes on palm and back, only by doing this could she bring her mind back to her role of a slave, slowly burying any understanding, knowledge and emotion under a heavy weight of emptiness. It took a huge effort but by the time the carts had reached the docks, she was as blank and seemingly unfeeling as any slave should be.

The carts struggled to move through the mass of people who all seemed to want to go in the opposite direction to where the group were heading and there was much pushing, swearing and raised voices. The street boy who thought he could steal from the back of the second cart quickly let go of the small sack of unknown goods. He gulped and wished whoever held the blade to his throat would lower it.

'You go tell all yer mates and any other thievin' bastard you can think of that this stuff and the folks around it all belong to Mr Poole. He may not be of this town but he is big enough to bring the fires of the lower hells down upon you lot. Go on, scram!' Jasper took the dagger away and the boy ran off. Even a lowly member of Merino Bay's criminal fraternity like himself knew of Mr Poole and how the fires of hell would definitely rain down on anyone causing problems for him. Although Mr Poole's brother was not a criminal, he was known here and had a lot of influence.

The group moved towards the docks, pushing aside any attempts at delay. A whispered word in Bili's ear had him dropping off the lead cart to jump up and give Samuel a message. Looking mournfully at Danielle, the boy struggled not to hug her. A gentle word from the Keeper had him nodding before stepping from the cart onto Rook's horse, where the man held him close and murmured comfort into the sad child's ear.

As the carts got to the rendezvous indicated in Lord Willoughby's letter, they could hear the man himself, voice raised in anger. Getting the carts tucked neatly to one side, Mr Poole and Samuel walked up to where Lord Willoughby and a sea captain stood exchanging insults. The Keeper made sure that he stood in his Master's view but didn't try to interrupt.

'Be off with you, scoundrel!' Lord Willoughby shook his fist at the captain who, rather than respond, simply hawked and spat at the ground, very close to the polished tip of the arrogant Lord's boot. He turned and walked between the recent arrivals without expression. Samuel was left wondering if he had actually seen the stranger wink at Mr Poole or had the Keeper got it wrong? Before he could ponder on this, however, he heard the whistle of displaced air as Lord Willoughby slashed his stick around air in rage.

'Impudent bastard, deceiving dog. And you! You are late, you damned scavenger, where the hell is my property? Not that it damned well matters now.'

'My apologies, sir,' said Mr Poole in a respectful tone of voice, ignoring the petulant insults. 'I must have misread your instructions. Your property is just by there and all is hale and hearty. The food you provided did us well and I have even been able to save a little of the travelling silver you let me have. It ain't a lot, sir, but it is something. I see that there is some sort of problem here though. If you would like to tell me what it is, I may be able to find an answer to it for you.'

Mr Poole's respectful demeanor soothed the ego of the bantam-sized Lord. The money purse that was handed over wasn't as light as the burly man had indicated and calmed the older man down.

'Huh, I have been let down most grievously, sir!' Lord Willoughby roared. 'I had hired that thrice-damned scum to take me and my goods west to Mertam and he accepted the commission. Now he tells me I am not able to travel as planned because he has been paid more to travel somewhere to the east. He tells me to get another ship. Just how am I supposed to do that without a long delay, you tell me. I need to leave Bisra as soon as possible. I have business overseas that is important, the damned cheek of it.' The more the short man spoke, the angrier he became, working himself up back into a great rage. Mr Poole made some soothing noises before seeming to sink into deep thought.

Lord Willoughby noticed his pre-occupation and stopped his tirade mid-shout, waiting for some kind of response from the other man. When nothing was forth-coming he glared at Samuel who shrugged his ignorance before launching into the details of the journey. The Keeper mentioned the slave's illness, explaining that he thought it was the travelling and perhaps even the way the food had been prepared. He was careful to stress the fact that the illness had been short lived, consisting of a fever and hungry appetite.

'She is alright now though? No lingering after effects? Strange really, always thought she was as strong as a bloody girox.' Willoughby mused. 'The different food and changes to her routine, you think? Possible, I suppose. You will have to keep an eye on her, boy, make sure she doesn't weaken. If she does there will be no point keeping her. Dammit! A waste of resources if she dies.'

Samuel reassured the old man, saying that as the girl had lived such a rigid life before, it was understandable that she might be affected strongly by all the upheaval and changes around her.

'She has recovered very well, Sir,' the Keeper stated. 'I think that we just need to make sure that if her fever begins again that she gets a little more food and sleep. It might even be because of the slight disarray of her Numb regime. After taking the drug every day without fail for so long, to suddenly have a day of delay where it is wearing off, may have caused some kind of reaction. Should I be giving the powder back to her Ladyship now we are here, Sir?'

Lord Willoughby gave his Keeper a considering look and pulled on his lower lip before abruptly shaking his head.

'No, you will not. You have done well enough these last few weeks. I would prefer to know that the slave has her medicine exactly on time and her Ladyship may just forget again. I, myself, will be too busy trying to sort out another ship to be able to guarantee being free to give her both morning and evening dose so you may as well continue.' Lowering his voice and glancing quickly at the still silent man a short distance away, he continued:

'Were there any problems with him and his men, Keeper?'

'With Mr Poole, you mean, sir? No, no trouble at all. In fact they were very helpful to us. An ambush was planned: a group of villains at one of the villages laid in wait for travellers and attacked us during a rest stop, and if not for the prowess and fighting ability of his men, I would have been overwhelmed and your goods, including the slave, taken. I heard one of them yelling something about holding the girl for ransom. It was a well planned attack, sir, but whether you were the specific target, I cannot say.'

'Helped you, hey?' Lord Willoughby looked at Mr Poole in approval.

'Yes, sir. He also lost one of his men in the attack.' Lowering his voice to a whisper, Samuel continued with the planned story. 'He never mentioned wanting compensation for the man in question. He said it was the chance you take when travelling across the wilds.'

Lord Willoughby nodded sagely. He had travelled in a luxury coach, protected by a troupe of guards equipped with bows, bolts and swords. Stopping every few miles to stretch, sleeping comfortably in the roadside coaching inns, eating the finest food and able to move much more swiftly in the lighter vehicle that held much less weight and four horses rather than the heavier, much slower carts pulled by just one beast, the Willoughby family had very little idea about what the wilds actually were so it seemed a reasonable explanation to him.

Before any further comment was made, Mr Poole cleared his throat and spoke.

'I am not sure about this, sir, but I may – just may – have thought of a way for you to get out of your current difficulties. As I mentioned to you when you hired me, I wanted to come to Merino Bay to meet up with my brother and I wanted to give my grandson some fresh sea air. What I didn't mention is that my brother is the captain of a ship. We were going on a voyage with him, letting the young 'un taste life on the oceans for the first time. We weren't going to be travelling your way but I might be able to get him to agree to also taking you and yours. I hate to say this but it may cost a bit. And there is another problem.'

'What problem?' Lord Willoughby enquired, hope rising in his chest.

'Like most ships that cross the seas, he uses Abominations, sir. Now I don't have a strong opinion on these beings but you might not want the ladies seeing them.'

'Most ships use them? I wasn't told that Captain Grigaria had any on his vessel.' Lord Willoughby sounded more intrigued than annoyed.

'Oh, Grigaria definitely has them. He needs them, in case the winds drop or a leviathan comes to visit. Abominations can call up the wind or make the huge beasts lose interest in the ship. I don't know of any vessel that don't have 'em. Each captain makes his own rules on his own ship, so land laws don't hold sway. If you want me to, I can go see my brother, see if he will be able to take you and for what price. You have a think about whether you are happy to be on board with Abominations and we will go from there. Just out of interest, sir, just how much were you going to pay Grigaria?'

When Lord Willoughby mentioned the sum, Mr Poole snorted in derision. 'Someone is getting a cut out of that money, sir. I dunno who recommended the man but whoever he is, that ain't no friend of yours. D'you want me to see, sir? Gotta be quick to be able to catch the tide.'

As the short man gave his eager assent, Mr Poole gave a slight nod to both of them, turned smartly on his heel and called back to his men to stay and guard the carts for the safety of the goods. Bili scampered down from the wooden seat before running up and slipping his hand into his Grandpa's. Within a few seconds both were out of sight, swallowed by the crowds.

Samuel smiled to himself at the clever way the big man had woven a net to trap Lord Willoughby into doing just what they wanted him to do. The length of time used for "heavy" thinking, the hints dropped about the rich man being cheated, the almost abject worry about Abominations...brilliant!

Walking back to the carts, Lord Willoughby looked at the smartly dressed and heavily armed men grouped around the carts before giving a satisfied grunt. He called sharply to the slave before moving past. Quickly turning back he told Rook where the family would be waiting for news before he spun on his heel and scuttled importantly off. Raising his brow at Samuel, Rook whistled under his breath before turning back to watch the crowd.

The Keeper helped the slavey off the cart and they moved swiftly to catch up with Lord Willoughby. Once at his Master's shoulder Samuel shortened his long stride, slowing down considerably. Sensing the man behind him, Lord Willoughby impatiently thrust something back at Samuel before continuing on. When Samuel saw what it was, he froze. Anger raced through him sending his vision black so that it took the touch of the slave's hand to bring him back to his senses. With a choked apology, Samuel clasped the woven chain around the girl's slim waist before bringing it up around her wrists. Turning, the two again had to rush to catch the self-important man who was their Master. In this, without the two of them realising the fact, the crowd helped. Parting slightly, enough to show the way, they created a clear pathway that meant no jostling or pushing was needed. It also meant that the innocuous looking chain didn't stick its razor-sharp edges into Danielle's flesh as much as it might otherwise have done.

This chain – called a safety chain – had never been used in the Willoughby household before even though it was used by many

Keepers. Whoever was advising the Master didn't have any love for slaves, thought Samuel. A slight gasp from behind had the Keeper gritting his teeth in impotent anger. How many cuts the poor girl would end up with was anyone's guess, the only thing to hope for was that the marred flesh on her wrists and waist would put the two men off touching her. Samuel hoped that the Master and his son would be less interested in the slave with the weariness of travelling done and more yet to come. If, however, they tried to resume their games with her, the story of fever and sickness was there to be used. Every day was to be played by ear, never knowing how others would react.

In a few more moments, Samuel found himself entering a luxurious coaching inn and stared around in wonder. Instead of a small dark and dismal room, lit only by smoky tallow candles with their own peculiar scent and full of noise, drink, laughter and song that he was used to, here was a large, airy space, quiet with very few people within. Big windows with decorative coverings let in a lot of light. Ten or eleven oval tables, all covered in fine white cloths set with flowers and real silver, told him that this was a place for people of true quality. Seated away from the entrance were Lady Constance and her children. Being careful not to be seen studying them, he noticed the expression on Lady Constance's face was still bitter but with a sense of thought behind the glare. Markus lounged back in his chair, his face pulled into a very unattractive sneer, which changed almost instantly as he saw his father. The Keeper gave an inward shudder at the slavish devotion that glowed in the young man's eyes as he straightened up at his father's approach. Lady Sophia sat very quietly, looking almost as expressionless as the slave girl as her hands shredded a fine handkerchief to tiny strips. Lord Willoughby marched up towards the table and began speaking from a distance, his voice carrying to everyone else in the room.

'There may be a slight delay, my dears, but I have everything in hand and we should be getting on board a ship either today or tomorrow. And look who I found at the quay? I am very pleased that you arrived so precipitously, Keeper. If Mr Poole is able to do as he seems to think, by the time the tide turns we will have begun the next part of our adventure!'

Although he spoke in rousing tones, only Markus seemed to be reacting with any enthusiasm, he grinned and clapped his hands in childish delight. Sophia's expression didn't change by even the flicker of an eyelash but her hands tore more fiercely and the lace decorated muslin was now not even worth putting in the rag bag, so tiny were the shreds of material left. Lady Constance glared at her lawful spouse before giving a snort and drinking from her cup and then setting it down with an audible crack.

'Waiter! More tea and make sure that it is hot this time. And slice the lemon rather than hack at it, only peasants would think this debacle as something acceptable. Where are the sandwiches, the cakes? For the One's sake!' Her tone was vitriolic and led Samuel to believe that the combination of Lord Willoughby and his son had done much to worry her and to undermine her authority even more on the journey. With the flickering looks the woman kept sending to both the slave and Samuel, the Keeper also realised that the lady was worried in case the slave had let slip by word, action or illness that the drug was no longer being administered to her. He wondered if she also fretted about him, about whether he had realised that the powder given to him before they left the house in the city was nothing more than harmless herbs. Standing at his Master's shoulder, still holding the safety chain, Samuel stared straight ahead as a good Keeper should do.

'Hush, my dear,' said Lord Willoughby in irritation. 'Why you persist in thinking that the service in such a place as this should be of the standard we have at home, I do not know. Now desist with your prattling, madam! Is everything prepared for leaving as soon as we are given the word?'

Sitting up even straighter, Markus nodded abruptly in a weak imitation of his father's decisive attitude. With an outraged sniff, Lady Constance also nodded, closely followed by a murmur from Sophia that might have meant anything.

'Then yes, I think we do need a little sustenance while I wait for our guard to return. Waiter? Bring some brandy. I would like hot crumpets as well as whatever the ladies have already requested. Keeper? Take the girl to the servants' parlour. Food and drink will be sent to you there.'

Samuel nodded and walked smartly through to the smaller room that led off from the larger. This room was definitely not for the rich travellers. There were benches around three long tables and not a cloth to be seen. Still, it had two large windows and unexpected space. The fire within was the only other source of light and it was small and mean, leaving even a room such as this darker and more dismal than it should be. Danielle took the seat nearest the fire, letting it look as if Samuel was leading her. He gave a muttered curse at the streaks of blood that encircled her wrists and waist. He dare not remove the device without his Lordship's permission, however, so the only thing he could do was ask for clean linen and hot water with some lavender. This arrived quickly, along with two small spiced ciders, bread, cheese and pickles with slices of cold beef. Without comment, both ate as much as they could before wrapping up what wasn't eaten to be hidden for Danielle if she needed it later. In the meantime, Samuel bathed what cuts he was able to from her wrists, biting down on his temper and only looking at her once he had finished. No words were exchanged but the tightness in his features eased a little at the understanding in hers.

Chapter Sixteen

An hour later, the fire had almost died down and the room was beginning to feel damp but both Danielle and Samuel had managed to doze off. It was only when the door briskly opened that they felt the chill in their bones.

'Blimmin' heck, Keeper, it's freezing in 'ere!' Rook stood in the doorway. 'No matter, the boss says it is time to get moving. It has all been arranged with Mr Poole's brother and, if we hurry, we may be lucky enough to hit the tide right this evening. We have already put the luggage we brought on the ship, we just needs you to move your arse and get you both on board. The rest of the lads will bring the other stuff.' He beckoned to them impatiently and only paused when an incautious movement made Danielle gasp in pain.

Seeing the safety chain cutting into her body, Rook had to grind his teeth to stop a shout of anger. Quickly looking behind his shoulder, he stepped into the room and gave the slave a careful hug.

'We really have to kill this miserable piece of slime.' He saw Samuel's fervent nod so, with a sigh, Rook let the girl go. 'Come on Sam, let us get a move on before the dumb bastards think of another way of hurting her.'

Leading Danielle out into the main room, Samuel saw that as well as Mr Poole and some of his men, the family were also waiting. He was satisfied to see a look of revulsion cross Markus's face as he saw the blood on the girl's flesh and rips in her clothing. Lord Willoughby eyed the marks with disfavour. Raising his brow in query, he pointed to them. Samuel gave a deliberately casual shrug, as if it should be obvious to all.

'It's the chain, sir,' he said calmly. 'Even though we tried to keep up with you earlier, the crowd bumped and jostled enough for the razor links to cut into her flesh. Nothing can be done to prevent that from happening. Even a deep breath cuts the skin. I thought that is why you hadn't ever used one before. It does lower performance and worth, I am afraid.'

'Then take it off her, man. I should have known better than to follow Hemingway's advice. Now come on, move! Captain Poole says that it will cost more if we delay travelling until tomorrow morning. There will be far too many ships then, jostling to leave.' The family group moved, following Mr Poole and Bili while Luke and Jasper surged ahead with two handcarts holding the rest of the luggage.

Samuel, Rook and Danielle had delayed for a few moments to remove the safety chain. Both men had gaped at Danielle in astonishment when she deliberately took a couple of links and swiped them over her wrists, causing deeper cuts. Before either could recover from this, she cut down at her sides and front three times before handing the chain back to Samuel, raising her brow and then turning her back and pointing to her back. A split second was all it took before the Keeper understood and gave a low grunt of protest. Another jab of her finger had him cursing but obediently slicing twice.

'What the void are you playing at?' Rook's voice shook with anger as he braced himself to hit the bigger man.

'Trying to keep those perverted bastards from touching her, what do you think I am playing at?' Samuel's voice grated with anger and disgust. Rook took a step back and made himself work through his own temper before nodding his head.

'Sorry, mate,' his voice was calmer and full of contrition. 'I forgot that everything has changed now that we are here with the aristos. Thankfully, you haven't lost your cleverness. Next time I am out of line, just gimme a thump.' Then eyeing the Keeper's big muscles, he added. 'Not a really big thump, mind, just a tap...a very, very little tap...'

Samuel gave him a fleeting grin before heading to the door. 'You're on. Mind you, my last tap is what got me promoted to full Keeper, just so you know.'

Rook stood motionless before giving a very loud gulp and chasing out into the rapidly darkening night after the two he was supposed to escort. Although theatrical, the swallow of fear he made had a dose of real worry in it. Before a trainee Keeper could get his promotion, he had to show that he could beat an opponent using every weapon that he might carry as well as in unarmed combat; sometimes this involved literally beating someone to death.

Deciding to concentrate on his job for now, Rook intercepted the others and guided them to the ship. The crowds had significantly thinned down now it was getting late which allowed Samuel, Rook and Danielle to make up the distance easily.

Stepping briskly along the docks they passed a few men from other ships heading for an evening's drink and play with the local doxies. Samuel and Rook stayed alert. They could see the family just up ahead, moving towards a ship. The vessel was not as large as Samuel expected but it looked nice and trim. It seemed to sit higher in the water than many of the others while not being quite as long, the half dozen sails that were attached to the three tall masts were getting unfurled, ready to move. The mermaid figurehead was painted and gilded beautifully. A row of small windows indicated that the below decks weren't as dark as Samuel had expected, in fact, everywhere was polished, bright and shiny.

The Keeper caught up with the tail end of the family, guiding the slave by placing a hand on her shoulder. Rook slid behind them, joining the twins and Jasper as guards. They trailed up the gang plank, following Mr Poole, Bili and Luke. The burly man stepped forward with a shout of pleasure and pulled the captain of the ship into a warm hug which was returned just as fiercely. The captain was smartly dressed in trousers, boots and long coat and was as big and burly as Mr Poole but instead of bald, he had thinning brown hair tied back in a ribbon. A wide grin flashed out, aimed at the whole group not faltering an inch when he saw the disdain upon Lady Constance's lips. Releasing his brother, the captain got his men jumping into action so as to be ready to leave as soon as possible.

Mr Poole took his own men to one side for last instructions and goodbyes. Luke had to promise Bili that the giroxes wouldn't be taken to a knacker's yard, as Lord Willoughby suggested, but to a breeding farm that Luke knew of. He was very happy with his fee as well as the letters of introduction to people of power here in Merino Bay, and also in Harmony, but he was sad to be saying goodbye to a man he had looked up to for so long. Jasper and the twins, although not given the same levels of responsibility for the future, were feeling the same contradictory emotions. There was pleasure at the gold they were given, which was almost double the amount promised at the beginning of the venture, but also sorrow at the breaking up of the company. The men hated separating from Bili and Danielle too so, even though the main goodbyes had been said the night before, hugs and advice were quietly exchanged again, apart from with the slave. They had to completely ignore her which cut them deeply. Eventually, after they had all repeated murmured oaths of loyalty, the men quickly moved off the ship leaving a tear stained Bili waving after them and holding onto the hand of his Grandpa, whose own eyes had taken on a damp sheen.

Everyone stilled as the Speaker of The Shining One came to bless the ship for the forthcoming journey. After a long discourse on the need to accept the guidance of Kintrelle, and to do all they could to meet His demands, he offered a drink of sweet rose wine to the important men while giving a kiss as benediction to the women. Afterwards he began a long and rambling talk with Lord Willoughby, barely acknowledging anyone else. The captain was careful to hide his displeasure at the way the Speaker and his party lingered and it was only when he mentioned the extra money needed if they were to wait any longer, that Lord Willoughby brought his conversation to an abrupt halt and almost rushed the bemused official away. Only after being handed a heavy purse did the Shining One's representatives eventually left the ship.

Captain Poole led Lord Willoughby and Lady Constance personally to their cabin, his second in command taking Lord Markus and Lady Sophia to their separate accommodations while the ship's surgeon showed Mr Poole, Bili and Rook to their shared quarters before also pointing Patcher, Samuel and the slave to the last tiny rooms, one of which was round the corner from the rest, at the end of the narrow corridor. Before too much time had passed the family, Mr Poole and a scowling Bili had all changed for dinner and were now seated in deep, comfortable bucket chairs in the communal salon. A table was set next to them with little bowls of marzipan sweets for their enjoyment, as well as glasses of very good sherry and milk for Bili.

Lady Constance looked around her, her habitual sneer no longer in evidence as she saw just how beautiful the room was. In fact, if she didn't know different, she would have thought that this was the drawing room of a rich city eccentric. Allowing her expression to relax a little more, she nodded in response to a comment from the captain, who was such a polite man. She passed on her appreciation for the cabin she had been assigned with her husband, mentioning the beautiful furniture and decorative touches.

Bili was overawed by everyone as well as the conversations that made no sense to him so he just leaned against his Grandpa quietly. He kept looking up at the captain before seeking reassurance from his own Grandpa but Mr Poole was pleased to notice that the boy wasn't clinging to him or avoiding contact with his brother. Next to the sofa was one of many chairs, set at an angle, where Markus sat, his legs stretched out before him. Next to Markus, Lady Constance and Lady Sophia sat with a low table between them. Lord Willoughby was a little apart from his family, in a chair with a deeper back and arms in a place that allowed him to take note and keep an eye on his relations and their doings. He would need to have a word with Markus, he decided - the boy was ogling the sailors a little too lasciviously whereas Sophia didn't seem to even notice the handsome men at all. What was wrong with that girl? Looking at Constance, he hid a smirk with his glass of sherry, she was too bloody obvious. Show her money, baubles and any other type of wealth and all of a sudden she was content with life even after acting like a damn fishwife for the short time of the journey so far. At the memory of her voice piercing the stifling air in the coach as they travelled westward from the city he felt his teeth grind before he deliberately relaxed and listened to what Captain Poole was saying.

'It should take between four and six weeks to make the voyage but it all depends upon how the weather favours us. I hope that your accommodations are all satisfactory? I do understand that you are used to much more comfort but, as this is not a luxury vessel, I hope you can all manage for the short time needed. Your luggage, apart from your small cases of necessities, has all been stowed very carefully. The trunks have been settled with packing around so they will be unlikely to tumble, except in the worst seas. We should be able to avoid any leviathans at this time of year but I cannot guarantee this. No one has yet been able to understand what motivates the lone wanderers which could cross our path if we are very unlucky but we have definitely missed the breeding masses - excuse my bluntness, ladies.'

Lady Constance gave a regal nod while Sophia continued to stare down at her shoes, her sherry still untouched.

Captain Poole continued, 'I feel it is important to settle an issue that does need to be spoken about. Thankfully, I understand that you are all intelligent enough to see the necessity of having magikers on the ship. Without them, there would be no travel at all across the oceans, as tides and winds would prevent us moving any distance at all. If you ladies feel you may be offended by the sight of them, we can make sure that they stay out of your way as much as possible but I cannot – and would not even think to – keep them away completely. This is still a working vessel and I still need to be able to move it. Part of my ability to do so depends completely upon these non-humans. If you will have a problem with this, you must let me know now so that I can begin to work out some sort of schedule to avoid unpleasantness. But be warned, I am afraid I will take any insults to my crew very personally indeed.'

The latter was said with just a quick glance at Lord Markus before it slid away, moving to Lord Willoughby where he received a small nod of acknowledgement. Message sent and understood. The captain then looked at each person in the room, beginning with Bili whose eyes were wide with excitement but who was keeping uncharacteristically quiet. Mr Poole just shrugged his shoulders and asked one of the sailors for a brandy instead of sherry. Lord Markus opened his mouth to speak but shut it when his father coughed to attract his attention before shaking his head. Lady Constance frowned and was trying to frame a comment when Lady Sophia surprised them all by speaking.

'Sir, from what I can see, you and your beautiful ship actually rescued my parents from some problems on land as well as saving them unnecessary expense. At the request of your brother, who has already helped my family so much, you have stepped in and solved an awkward situation. So I should hope that breeding as well as good manners would prevent any of us from making a negative, rude or obnoxious comment about any of your crew, be they Abomination or not.' Her voice was clear and surprisingly firm, causing Lord Willoughby to examine her closely. No sense of guile came from her however, just earnest respectability. Looking in her direction, he noticed Lady Constance smooth out her frown. Sophia had managed to stop any problems from that quarter. He wondered if his daughter was quite as innocent as she made out. No matter, he would just take care to watch her over the next few weeks and if the minx was play-acting he would very soon put a stop to that. Murmuring his own acceptance of the situation, he was happy to see his glass being refilled quickly.

'Have you paid off your men, Poole? Will any be travelling with us?' Lord Willoughby was still trying to understand the hierarchy upon the ship. Obviously the captain was completely in charge but surely his brother would not count as highly? Or would he? As for the other members of the crew, there was no telling if they were above or below his own rank. Perhaps he should be more like Constance and assume everyone was below him.

'Rook is staying with us as he wants to travel the ocean. The rest are going back to Harmony tomorrow.' Mr Poole spoke quietly, still a little emotional at meeting his brother again. He didn't mention to Lord Willoughby any of the secret plans that Luke had set in motion.

Rook had decided he wanted a new start and had chosen to throw his lot in with Mr Poole and the boy. Bili himself was sad to see his friends leaving but was overjoyed to be going on an adventure. Not so very long ago, he was a play toy for an evil man, naked, starving and covered in bruises, all of which was mild compared to the emotional and psychological damage within him.

Now he had his grandpa, his Uncle Rook and even grandpa's brother who was captain of a whole ship! Never had Bili expected to feel so safe, so loved or so blessed.

'You may all use this room at any time and the ladies may find it a much more comfortable way to travel than up on deck or stuck in their cabins,' continued the captain. 'My crew can be rough, I am afraid, and the language may be too much for tender ears. I can make sure that morning tea is sent to your cabins but all meals will be taken in here. The food will be in those dishes there, so just fill your plates before sitting at the main table. I will have breakfast, luncheon and dinner served promptly so if you miss them, you will go hungry. I stress again, this is a working boat, not a pleasure cruise. My job is to get you to the dock at Mertam as soon as possible without too much discomfort which I have every intention of achieving. It won't be the level of comfort that you expect, or are used to, however. I do expect your understanding and perhaps even help if necessary.' At Markus's shocked look, the captain laughed and remarked, 'No, Lord Markus, I do not mean steering the ship or scrubbing the decks! As if I would dare. What I mean is simple, I am the mastfuer of this ship so if I give you – any of you – a command, you swear to do what you are asked as quickly and with as little fuss as possible. I have no problems with any of you going up top or asking questions,' the latter comment was said with a sly grin at his newfound family member and the boy grinned back. 'However, if I say you need to get below, you move. It will mean that we have spotted bad weather, or a leviathan, or a magiker needs to be seen or even, may the Light forbid, pirates. I need your agreements for your own safety, rather than my convenience.'

Again, it was Sophia who spoke up first, although everyone gave their word. The door to the salon opened up and Patcher, along with a smartly dressed member of the ship's crew began bringing in the food. It was not served to each individual, as a proper household would, but placed in the deep sided serving dishes screwed to the elegant sideboard running down one part of the room. It felt strange to the members of the Willoughby family to get up and serve themselves, but they followed the captain's lead and found that the food to be very tasty and enjoyable, especially as they could take as much or as little as they chose. A simple consommé to begin with, followed by salmon upon a watercress base with a very tasty dill sauce. Roast mutton was next covered in a mint and honey glaze with tiny roasted potatoes, vegetables and mint jelly. A light lemon mousse was next, decorated with shavings of chocolate. To finish, cheese and biscuits with fruit was handed around on a platter for those who wished to partake. Each course had its own wine which the men drank with great enjoyment.

Once the food had been eaten with varying degrees of pleasure, the captain had one of his men take the ladies back to their cabins while the men had cigars and port. Both Lord Willoughby and Lord Markus found it strange that the boy Bili also stayed but didn't comment about it.

'You say that we won't have the same degree of comforts, Captain, but I assure you that so far you have achieved more than I had hoped for. The food was superb and the wines went with each course perfectly. These cigars are as good as your brandy. Tell me, sir, is all sea travel this good?' There was a faint hint of patronisation in the rich man's tone even though the words were complimentary.

'I am glad you approve, sir, and would say that I find it so.' The captain gave no indication of recognising the Lord's attitude. Looking at the burning end of his own cigar, he smiled and continued, 'I left land many years ago and am very happy to stay on board ship for the rest of my life. My brother means a lot to me, as I do to him, but this is the first time I have met my own grand-nephew, which is why the three of us were taking a lazy trip to nowhere, just to get to know each other properly. As it was Elias that asked for my help, I said yes. We can spend time getting to re-connect as we take you to Mertam before we wander off to somewhere else. The gold you are paying was also a good reason for saying yes.' His tone was perfectly polite yet Lord Willoughby found himself wondering if he was being patronised in his turn. Before he could comment, Elias Poole spoke up after a whispered conversation with his grandson.

'I wonder, Lord Willoughby, if it would be at all possible for my grandson to be allowed to say goodnight to your Keeper? For some reason the lad seems really taken with him. When we were attacked, your servant was a very brave and able man. Not only did he put himself in danger to save your goods but he also saved Bili here. Of course, if you say no, I will try and explain to the boy why...'

'No, no, m'dear sir, there's no reason to be telling him no. As long as your grandson understands that the Keeper is there to make sure no-one interferes with the slave, I don't see why he should be kept away.' Lord Willoughby felt agreeing that Bili could go to see Samuel would get rid of the brat and allow the men to discuss things in a proper adult way. He continued smiling benignly as the youngster gave him a jerky bow and a muttered thank you before disappearing out of the door. As the boy walked past, Lord Willoughby frowned as he saw his own son's gaze upon the child. Looking up and catching sight of his father's look, Markus turned away and quickly took a large swallow of port.

Again, Lord Willoughby made a promise to himself to speak to his son. Being able to enjoy his sensuality was making Markus reckless. Tupping a sailor who never stepped foot on land and was probably desperate for sex in any form wouldn't be too much of a problem but discretion was still important. The Poole's grandson was too young. Even Lord Willoughby had his limits. Besides, if Markus did anything to the lad it could get him killed and might even cause problems for the whole family as well as with Willoughby's personal plans.

Turning to look at the brothers, Lord Willoughby asked if there were any distractions aboard the ship. 'Not that I am expecting anything too much, sir, just if you have card games or anything of that sort at all.'

The captain smiled. 'Here in the salon we do have games of chance but we don't gamble for money, gentlemen. All crew are allowed in here once guests have departed and the day's business is complete. So if you wish to take part you must accept that it won't be what you are used to.'

'So if gold isn't gambled, what is?' Markus was curious at the smile that flickered across the captain's face.

After a slight pause for Captain Poole to think of how to phrase his answer, he said, 'It may be that one of the men has done carving or sewing or painting; most of the crew have artistic skills, these are sometimes used as a stake. Or it may be that a particular job is not enjoyed by anyone, so a man may offer to do that. Some of the magikers may offer something else, even kisses or other sexual favours. The stakes are anything that another may find useful.' The captain then gave a full laugh, keeping the attention on himself when he added, 'I warn you though, sirs, no matter what is exchanged during gambling times, no-one makes any comment about it the following day. It is the easiest way to cause trouble between your crew mates, bringing up bets taken at the table. So, rest assured, gentlemen, no word will be said about what you stake yourselves but make sure that you also keep quiet about the others.'

The men opposite nodded sincerely. Captain Poole spoke to his second in command, sending a message to the crew that the card games would begin as usual the following night one hour after the ladies had retired. The captain then excused himself so that he could take care of his ship and the Willoughbys found themselves yawning deeply.

'It is the sea air, gentlemen,' Mr Poole commented. 'It is best to take to your beds and sleep as much as you are able. Perhaps cross your fingers that you don't succumb to sea sickness too'

They all stood and began moving to their cabins, so the sly grin that flickered across the face of Mr Poole as he rubbed a small glass vial snug in his pocket was missed by the others. The first few days and the last few would have both male Willoughbys drugged and sleeping a lot, giving Danielle some peace from their greedy hands. As the drug couldn't be used constantly, they would have to find something else to do for the rest of the time. Rook, thankfully, had one or two ideas on this. If they could keep her Master and his brat away from her for the voyage, Danielle could use it to build on her new found skills before escaping after the ship docked.

Chapter Seventeen

Bili tapped on the Keeper's door and it was opened by Rook who gave him a grin of welcome. Stepping in, Bili's eyes were big and round as he saw the two hammocks, the open trunk under one of them with a small basket sitting under the other. Danielle was curled up in the hammock farthest from the door, somehow still able to knit despite the swaying of her perch. Samuel sat on the other while Rook went and sat comfortably astride a wooden chair facing them both. Bili went and held his face up for a kiss off both Rook and Danielle before climbing up to lie down behind the Keeper's back. He listened to the quiet conversation around him and dozed a little; letting the voices flow over him as the adults discussed their impressions of the ship and plans to protect Danielle on the way.

'I will have to be strong, for Markus will feel the need for sex, even if the Master doesn't.' Danielle spoke with steely determination.

'No you won't,' said Bili, sleepily. 'That sneery man will want to see if anyone else will do him first. He would like me too but...I'm sorry, Dani, I can't...I won't...' His voice broke and a sob was choked back.

In a flurry of movement, Danielle got off her hammock and exchanged places with Samuel. Climbing up next to Bili, Danielle cuddled up to him just as if they were both back under the tent between two carts.

'Your grandfather promised you that you would never have to do anything like that again, baby, and he meant it. Not only that but it would break my heart if you did. You need to know that proper loving is nothing like what was done to you or me. If I thought that you were doing things that hurt you, things that you hate, just to stop me having to do them, that would make me cry so much. If I do have to let them do these things to me it won't be nice but I can cope. I will just think of being free, of never having to have them do it again once the ship docks. So don't you get upset because you think you are letting me down because it is the opposite, I promise you.'

Bili looked deep into her eyes and felt the intensity and honesty of her words sink into him. Bili sensed that she really meant what she said and finally relaxed against her with a sigh. Sliding his own arms around Danielle's waist, he settled his head on her chest. Quietly he admitted that he was scared of Markus and the way he stared at him and some of the other men.

'Fat Syd used to slobber all over me and get me touching him. He used to hurt me with stuff he did but maybe not as bad as he could have. Most of the time he would just rub himself on me and that was enough. It made me feel sick but it was always over quick. With that Markus though, he really scares me. He will want to do things to make me cry, a'cuz he likes seeing people hurting that way.'

Rubbing her chin gently over his curly head, Danielle agreed with Bili's assessment. Markus did have a sadistic side to him that had previously been kept buried. The man was too much of a coward to let it show before but, now he had been encouraged in his tastes by his father, it was becoming more apparent to everyone just how twisted he was.

'You stay around people you know you can trust and make sure you tell your grandpa and his brother about what we have said here.' Danielle spoke soothingly, cradling the boy close and unknowingly sent healing waves into him. Bili snuggled closer, losing his sense of dread and beginning to doze lightly again. He woke suddenly when Rook spoke.

adulthood but they all felt him to be much older. A beautiful face rather than handsome, he had high cheekbones, full lips and eyes the colour of a summer sky, set on a slender neck and youthful body. The clothing he wore was most formal. A silk shirt with a stand-up collar in a silvery grey that hung down to below his hips and was embroidered with tiny daisy-like flowers in charcoal thread which closely matched the toggles holding it closed. His loose trousers were the darker charcoal grey of his shirt's decorations, with a paler version of the flowers embroidered around the tighter hem of each leg. He wore no shoes or socks and they were all surprised to see that he had wide spaced toes with a little webbing between each. Samuel blinked in astonishment as he realised that the elemental was missing a toe on each foot, his eyes going straight to the hands and finding the same thing, three fingers and a thumb all with the connective webbing. On his forehead, Neera wore a set of goggles, only used when he was flying in his solid form, to keep out dust, insects and other rubbish. Turning slowly, he seemed to enjoy showing off to the company, lifting his shirt and letting them see the fine stitched flowers were sewn into a deep triangle pattern on his trousers with two points wrapping around his waistband and the third curving down his buttocks. Once he faced front again, his weapons had disappeared and his mouth held the slightest hint of a smile.

'I am supposed to be on watch, Captain, so I will go but before I do, you need to know that the young one is close to exhaustion and the female needs sustenance. May I be allowed to take the boy to his bed?' Turning to Bili, Neera gave a formal bow, bending low with his arms crossed at his chest, fingers touching the opposite upper arm.

'It is up to the boy,' Mr Poole responded, 'but he is used to having company at night so might not settle.'

'Perhaps my new kin would allow me to stay linked with him, sir. That way, I can sing to him stories about heroes and battles, love and adventure. A much better way to sleep methinks.' He winked at Bili who leaned against Danielle, thinking hard.

'I am getting big now.' Bili's tone was serious and thoughtful. 'And I ain't a baby and Dani has helped wiv my bad dreams.' Looking up at the fascinating creature smiling down on him, Bili double-checked his information. 'You will come if I need you?' The firm nod in response to his question seemed to satisfy the youngster. With a sigh, he gave Danielle a hug and a kiss before going to each man in confident expectation of a hug or kiss from them all.

Samuel hugged the boy off his feet, telling him that if help was needed, Bili would get it straight away, then with a kiss on the boy's cheek he set him down to go to Rook. Rook also hugged the boy close, breathing in his now much cleaner scent before ruffling his hair and sending him to the captain. All of the travellers watched to see how Bili reacted to the two newcomers to their close knit group. Bili lifted his head automatically for a kiss and was rewarded with one as well as a hug and a whisper from the captain that made the boy grin before he yawned again. His grandpa lifted the worn out child into his strong arms and carried him out of the door with Neera leading the way. A quiet rumble of conversation faded away as the door was shut again.

'That boy is delightful,' the captain commented with a laugh. 'I must learn how to say "no" now before he beggars me!' he spoke to smiles and chuckles from the group.

'Nah,' Rook grinned. 'All you need to do is feed him and you can get him to do anything!' Samuel and Danielle laughed even more, remembering just how much the youngster could pack away in his small frame.

'No wonder he smiled at me!' Levi Poole exclaimed with another laugh. 'I just promised him a snack beside his bed! Tell me, does he shorten everyone's names?'

had her thoughts and feelings more under control, she looked at the two men again, only to find that they had both noticed her battle and approved of her victory.

Neera smiled at the other two and explained what he was there for.

'I am the one who watches all night.' He said in his light voice. 'I will bring you your morning sustenance so that you are awake and ready for them when they call you.' The flicker of distaste that ran over his face told Danielle and Samuel exactly who he meant.

'Bili slept easily for most of the night, I was able to soothe him when his dreams became frightening and I have made sure that milk and cookies sit at his bedside for when he wakes up.' He grinned at Samuel and Danielle's incomprehension. 'Cookies are what you people from Bisra call biscuits. My Captain will find out what Danielle's duties are to be but in the meantime I suggest you prepare yourselves to be ordered to do things that won't necessarily turn out to be what they might seem. Now, I am off to rest a little. I am still "aware" even when sleeping so will still hear any call from you.' With an easy smile, a kiss for Danielle, he faded to smoke, escaping through the tiny gaps between the planks of the ship's pull-down wall.

Samuel shut his mouth with an audible snap, his surprise at the Air Elemental's abilities turning to awe.

'That man is amazing!'

'He is...and now we better do as he suggests.' Danielle agreed.

With that, they got up and worked swiftly. Within a short time, both had washed and dressed. The crockery was stacked neatly on the tray and the hammocks had been stored against the wall, while the bedding was folded upon the small tables. A tap on the wall of the cabin leading to the deck had had them both whirling around only to see Bili's grinning face with Rook standing protectively behind him. Jumping through the gap, Bili landed confidently in Samuel's arms and gave the big man a hug before urging to be let down so that he could greet Danielle. Rook shook his head ruefully as he came through more decorously.

'We have created a demon,' he grinned at them. 'Bili loves being at sea and loves his cabin...and the nets...and the sails...and the cook...have I left anything out, boy?'

Bili had been babbling away at Danielle but with Rook's query he turned and stuck his tongue out at the laughing men. 'I like it here and I think Dani will too.'

The men grinned at that and Danielle hugged the boy before setting him down.

'What should I do now, Rook? At the house I would be clearing the sewage pans or sweeping the stairs. I don't know what I am supposed to do here and the Master won't accept me being idle.'

'That's one reason I am here, lady,' Rook soothed as he stepped to her for his own morning hug. 'The Boss reckons if we get you doing some stuff before serving morning tea at the usual time and they ask Samuel about what you have been up to, he can be honest. Keep this side open and it will be easy enough to come in and out without them knowing. So far, we think that if Neera wakes you with breakfast, enough to keep you going for a bit, that will give you breathing space, won't it?'

'We just have to take it one day at a time, I think. The Boss has made sure that something is sprinkled in the morning and evening drinks that will cause an upset stomach and tiredness for a few days. We can't use it every day of the journey though, as it could kill them. Not that I think that is much of a problem but the Boss says it could cause too much of a scandal for his brother and could even lead to arrests at Mertam. If they think you are working flat out though, we don't think they will find you any crappy jobs to do – especially if the Captain explains there are certain things you ain't allowed to do. The gambling will start tonight and will take the young bastard's attention, we hope. It is the old man we haven't found a distraction for yet.'

Biting her lip, Danielle paced the small room for a moment as she thought. She stopped abruptly, smiling at Rook. 'I think that within a few days, you will find that her Ladyship sleeps alone in the Captain's cabin. Lady Sophia will be in hers while both men will be sharing Markus's room as Lord Willoughby will want to keep an eye upon his son and his antics. I may be wrong, and it is the ladies who stay together and Lord Willoughby who sleeps alone, but either way, his Lordship will still be focusing on his son. It has taken him years to corrupt Markus and he won't want to lose that headway. As long as the family believe me to be busy, and they see me dressed in work clothes, I should be safe from all of them. The one I worry about is Patcher. He can move in so many more places than the family will so I won't be able to hide from him so easily. Why are you two grinning?'

Bili and Rook exchanged a laughing glance before the man explained. 'We have a few days, maybe even weeks to work that out. He's got a genuine case of mouldy mare!'

Danielle gaped at him. 'What on earth is "mouldy mare", Rook?'

'It's what the sea-faring folk call it, when being at sea makes you throw up,' came the gleeful explanation. 'Now we best get moving, before you get a knock on the door. I am told that all these blokes can be trusted, so breathe a bit easier but don't let your guard down completely. Me, Sam, the Boss and the boy will be keeping our eyes peeled out for you at all times. You won't ever be left alone, promise. Now, princess, your first job today is to go to the cook's cabin and help prepare some food.'

The day that followed was busy, different from her usual, and actually fun for Danielle. There was a crew of fifteen, nine of whom were magikers, not counting the captain. The cook had welcomed her into the galley and Danielle had been slightly surprised to find out that the tall, handsome man was a bloodling. Although she knew little of this type of magiker, she had expected someone a little rougher in both attitude and appearance. He was well over six feet tall, which made him the same height as Sam but there the similarities ended. White hair was swept back and tied in a neat plait that began at the base of his skull and fell to his waist. His skin was so pale that it glowed in the light from the lamps as well as the cooking range, while his eyes were of a liquid black where the whites should be with a glowing, elliptical ruby pupil. An elegant goatee beard drew attention to his well shaped mouth and long slender hands moved constantly to give emphasis to his accented words. Danielle found herself dazzled with both his voice and his movements.

'Now, my little one, you will come here every morning and I will find work for you to do. If we can perhaps dampen your beauty with something dirty and smelly before you take morning tea to those peasants, so much the better. Your Keeper must stay by the door for now and keep watch for that sly weasel you call a butler. Today, I want you to prepare some of this fish for later. It is going to take strong muscles and an even stronger stomach, which I am told you have. For such a stinky fish to prepare, this actually has a delicate flavour when cooked in a light butter sauce and served with tiny roasted potatoes and leafy greens. We will be cooking with the fresh ingredients for as long as they last before beginning to use dried and salted ones. With this fish, we take off the head like so before gutting and putting the innards into this bucket here.'

Quickly, and with no extra fuss, the cook sliced and cut slowly enough for Danielle to follow but swiftly enough that, within a minute or two, what had been a surprised looking fish, with elongated jaws within which were hundreds of needle-like teeth, was now just a long dull pink blob of anonymous flesh. 'Now open the body like this... and see? The bones are laid like a pattern leading from the spine like a fan. Pull gently here and the spine and connecting bones will lift cleanly out.' His voice was almost mesmerising. Bass notes flowed from him, flavoured with his slight accent, turning everything he said into a musical experience. Danielle could see that he had deliberately slowed down his movements to demonstrate to her what to do. When he raised a brow in question to see if she understood, the girl nodded before heaving up a fish from the pile next to the board and beginning to prepare it as instructed. Her movements were much slower than the cook's were but he nodded his approval at the way she handled the large fish. Leaving her to do another five fish, he went and began preparing some freshly killed chickens so that they would be ready for lunchtime.

Despite wearing an apron, the timper fish soon proved why it was renamed "stinky" by sailors all over the world. Her hands, clothes and even hair had the stench of rotting flesh about them. Washing did no good in fact it seemed to intensify the smell. Grinning, the bloodling then prepared the morning tea for the family and Keeper and slave set off for the main cabins. By the time both had headed back to the galley sometime later, they were both red-faced with the effort of suppressing their laughter.

Entering the Captain's cabin, they had both been greeted with the sight of Her Ladyship awake and covered from head to toe in fine muslin and delicate lacework, a small sleeping cap on her head and a little book in her hands. Lord Willoughby had slept upon a settee and was in his nightshirt of striped cotton. His nightcap had the same patterning of blue and white. The room wasn't large but had polished walls of the best oak, inlaid with fancy scroll work. Heavy damask curtains in a deep burgundy were hung at the leaded windows, matching the bed covers. There were no ornaments in the room, but a few pictures were screwed to the wall and the furniture was of excellent quality.

Following Samuel's instructions, the slave went over and placed the morning tea-tray upon the bedside table. As she moved, the rotting scent wafted out. Lady Constance's nose twitched before a look of horror appeared on her face and she brought the covers up quickly to cover her nose. Lord Willoughby glared at his wife before his own nose caught the smell.

'Good gad, what is that bloody awful stench?' he roared out.

'My apologies, sir.' Samuel made sure that his tone was deferential even though he could feel laughter already wanting to break out. 'As we had been given no specific instructions regarding the slavey apart from being told to make her useful, I took her down to the galley to help prepare food for everyone. She was given the job of gutting this evening's fish course. It means she has a stronger odour about her than I expected. Should I find something else for her to do? It is difficult to know what is best but I know you hate her to be idle.'

'Hmm, well...erm...we do need to have her earning her keep but we can't have her coming to us smelling like this. I will have a word with the Captain at breakfast and see what he can suggest. In future, while we are upon this vessel, I think we will have Patcher fetching the morning tea. I am sure this lot will taste of this smell...faugh, get going, the whole cabin is beginning to reek... and take that tea with you.'

Moving at her slowest speed, Danielle collected the cups and piled it all back on the tray. Her gaze caught Lady Constance's and she saw puzzlement show briefly in the blue eyes. Keeping her face and eyes blank, the girl moved away and out of the cabin, leaving behind a mumble of voices. They next went into Markus's cabin, much plainer than the captain's but still showing both taste and quality. Here they were greeted with the sound of retching and a thrown boot. Sophia was up and moving about in her cabin when they entered, already dressed and looking forward to the day's adventure. Her eyebrows shot up and her nose wrinkled as the smell reached her and she began giggling even as she waved a dainty scented handkerchief in front of her nose. Nothing was said as Danielle poured out a cup of hot tea and handed it over to the younger girl.

'I assume that my parents won't have you bringing the tea in future.' Lady Sophia said with a smile that included both Keeper and slavey.

Staying expressionless, Samuel responded. 'No, m'lady. I am afraid I have made a mistake in getting the slave working on this ship without checking with the Master first. I think it will be Patcher's job to bring the tea from now on.'

Looking at both of them in turn, Lady Sophia's expression darkened as she shook her head slightly. 'Then I will make sure that I am up, dressed and in the salon by then. I have no wish for that man to come into my room at all. I will deposit my sewing and my reading book in there immediately. The slave's smell has not affected the taste of this excellent tea at all,' she finished with a smile before handing over her cup and saucer. 'If you should need to keep the girl occupied at all, please remember that I have plenty of mending and plain sewing she could help me with. It will be such *hard* work and I am sure that it could take *weeks* to go through all I have brought with me.'

Bowing in acknowledgement of her offer, as well as in understanding of her intonation, the other two left her to pick up her bejewelled embroidery bag and one of the precious books she loved so much before she bustled along to the salon as quickly as she could, narrowly missing Patcher as he left his own quarters and knocked on the door of his Master's.

The butler left his Master's presence a short time later, growling in anger under his breath. Morning bloody tea! Damnation, that meant he couldn't try to tup the slavey first thing like he had hoped. He would be having to rush about making sure he was tidy enough for the Master's gimlet eye first thing, when his lordship's temper was at its worst. A leer appeared on his face as he realised that he would also be serving the younger lady of the household, maybe he would see her in all her disarray if he was early enough. Now then, that was something to look forward to. If only his bloody stomach would settle down, it was making him feel sick the way it was rolling in time with the damn ship. Feeling worse by the minute, the butler went back to his room to vomit before he managed to stagger to the ship's galley for tea things.

Going from room to room, his annoyance only grew, making his stomach even queasier. In the main cabin, his lordship had grumbled about it being late for morning tea now but still managed to drink two cups before telling him to take the tray away, her ladyship staying behind the large screen in the corner and not even acknowledging his presence at all.

Lord Markus was sitting at the edge of his bed as the butler walked into his rooms. With red rimmed eyes and grey skin, the younger man looked extremely ill. Seeing the tray, what little colour was in his face drained away and he rushed to grab the chamber pot and noisily threw up. Patcher's own stomach rebelled at the sound of the splashing within the pot, indicating that this was not the first time it had been used in this way. Clamping his lips shut, the butler felt his gorge rise, hot and sour acid flooding his mouth with saliva. As the young Master of the house sat up straight with a groan, Patcher snatched the pot and added his own stomach contents to the vile brew. A knock on the door and a smartly dressed crew man stuck his head around it to announce breakfast was ready, at the sound of which, both men began emptying their stomachs again. The sailor left, shutting the door and cutting off the disgusting sounds as well as the overpowering stench. Going straight to the captain, he told him what was happening.

After laughing out loud at Lord Markus's predicament for a few minutes, the captain issued his orders. By the time he had gone into breakfast, the doctor had given the younger Willoughby a draught to help settle his stomach and that also sent him into a deep sleep for twenty-four hours. The butler was taken back to his own cabin, groaning with pain and was treated with kindness albeit much rougher and brisker than what the young Master had received. The draught he was given was bitter on the tongue but it quickly eased his stomach and he too dropped into a heavy sleep. The doctor shook his head and then went to report what had happened to his captain.

Chapter Nineteen

At breakfast, Lord Willoughby discussed his slave problem with the amenable captain. After some lively discussion, it was decided that both ladies could get themselves dressed in the morning, helping each other with whatever was necessary. The slave could help prepare the meals during the day, clean each of the cabins, change the bed linen as needed, empty the chamber pots and sweep out each room after the ladies had retired to the salon and the male Willoughbys had moved into what the captain laughingly called his war room; a small office with nothing but two comfortable chairs and a desk. Here the captain dealt with crew problems and plotted journeys as well as keeping his ship's log up to date. This room would give the two men the necessary privacy to plan the next part of their lives once they had landed in Mertam.

The first morning, while Markus slept off the seasickness exacerbated by his heavy drinking the evening before, Lord Willoughby sat deep in thought; making, changing and discarding plans regarding his, and perhaps their, future. Apart from his private plans to make himself both powerful and rich, he knew that Lady Constance would very easily slip into the same, mind-numbingly boring, routine as she had always done. No matter that the country was not Bisra, Enlightened Society had rigid rules which the Lady knew how to use to her own advantage. These brought much comfort to her as well as no little help for Lord Willoughby. Lord Markus would be taught and guided in the ways he needed to step into the elder man's shoes when the time was right. Once all the details had been sorted and learnt the younger man would take over a very lucrative business. The stubborn fly in the ointment for the full success of his plans was the unknown force of Lady Sophia.

'Ah, our little bird,' thought her father. 'She isn't a raving beauty, a bit plain really, but she does have breeding as well as her virginity. Her figure is quite luscious under those shapeless rags she prefers to wear. I can get good money for her. Once we have found a house and settled down I will think about selling her off in a few months.' Looking blankly at the malachite and ivory pen moving between his fingers, he carried on with his musings through what was left of the morning.

Luncheon was kept light, just soup and sandwiches, served by the second officer. Once cleared away, the ladies embroidered or wrote letters before going to their rooms for a nap before dinner. They found the sea air very tiring and Lady Constance insisted on having some time alone for them both. Back in her cabin she removed her dress and boned corset before putting on her much more comfortable dressing gown and lay on the bed. Plans had begun to float gently about in her head of what she wanted to do once they landed but she drifted off into a sleep full of happier memories before anything could properly take shape.

Sophia had also removed her outer garments, more quickly than her mother as she didn't wear a corset, and also put on her dressing gown but instead of lying down she sat looking out of her porthole at the waves curling over the surface of the sea. Words tumbled around in her head until she scribbled them down in her personal diary, smiling as she did so.

Dressing for dinner took less time and much less effort than they were used to but at least two of the Willoughby's appreciated the fact immensely. Markus was still in his heavy drugged sleep so would not be appearing at the evening meal. Sophia revelled in the necessary lack of primping with curling irons and face paints, satisfying herself with just twisting her long hair around into a bun. This was decorated with a diamond and sapphire butterfly, nestled to one side, while her dress was a simple gown of pale blue cotton. A low neck had a deep lace inlay, three quarter length sleeves and a nipped in waist with the long skirts falling almost to the floor. This was a particular favourite of Lady Sophia's as she had made the lace and done the embroidery down the bodice herself. Her father was scornful of "the bloody housekeeper" habits Sophia had but her mother approved of the fact that she wasn't just idly sitting around.

Sophia mused on it as she gazed at herself in the oval mirror screwed into the wall of her cabin. The fact was,, that she enjoyed housekeeping. Cooking, sewing and keeping her own environment neat and tidy was very important to her. Lady Sophia wondered what her family would say if they found out that she could not only do normal housework but could also lay a fire that burnt well, polish silver to a gleam and other "heavy" household necessities that included ironing and laundry. Papa would probably want to disown her. If only she could be that lucky! Leaving her room she broke into a grin which brought out a cheeky attractiveness not usually noticed in her features. She didn't notice the appraising looks sent her way from some of the crew men. This lady seemed so different from the rest of the family and now her clothes and face-paints were less than they had been, she looked truly lovely.

Lady Constance wore a gown of pale gold satin embroidered with tiny flowers around the neck, sleeves and full skirts. Sophia had made this for last Winters End, when personal gifts were given to those born in the coldest time of the year. She was pleased to see it being worn instead of hung up and forgotten in some wardrobe somewhere back in Harmony. Lady Constance's hair had been plaited, swirled and pinned around her head. A delicate diamond and amber tiara with matching earrings, necklace and bracelet lent warmth to her mother's usually austere features. The heavy face paints had also been stopped. A light touch of blacking to her lashes, a tiny stroke of blush and a slick of lip dye had really emphasised the genuine beauty of her features rather than making her look like a painted doll, which had been the fashion.

'Mamma, you look lovely!' Sophia's comment was involuntary but sincere and her mother flushed becomingly at the compliment.

'Thank you, my dear. That dress you have on has long been one of my favourites of yours.' Lady Constance's response was as surprising but also as pleasing and both women went to the salon contented.

The same could not be said of Lord Willoughby. He felt irritated and out of sorts. Getting himself dressed wasn't difficult but it was a bloody bore. He wore beige knee breeches and stockings, a pale cream shirt with a heavily embroidered waistcoat in shades of brown. This item had not been stitched by his daughter's clever hands but by one of his tailor's lackeys. The difference in style and quality could clearly be seen and was not to the tailor's advantage. Putting on his jacket made the gentleman too warm but not wearing it was just not the proper thing to do. His hair seemed to puff out from his head instead of lying flat against his scalp neatly and his shoes weren't as polished as they should be. These little issues made him feel completely out of sorts with everyone. Walking into the salon and seeing the superior effort made by the ladies had lowered his mood even further. Instead of irritation or frustration, he now became angry.

'Damnation, Sophia! That dress should have been discarded months ago; it is embarrassing to see you wearing something that a servant girl would on her day off. I am surprised at you, Constance. I would have thought that you would be more concerned about what our daughter was clothed in when she was out in public.' This was Lord Willoughby's opening salvo as he walked into the room, scowling. Not expecting a response, he walked over to get a glass of apple brandy. He was astonished when his wife answered him.

'My dear Jervis, I am surprised to hear that you know anything of fashion. I personally think that my daughter looks very handsome in this outfit. The fact that it has been her own two hands that have created it would make me proud of her, even if it looked like a sack, which it doesn't. This gown becomes her very well, both on a practical and stylish level. Do get a drink and calm down. You would not want to sound silly, would you?'

Gaping at his wife, Lord Willoughby was further surprised when his daughter also responded.

'Actually, Papa, being a skilled needlewoman and homemaker is something that is highly sought after on Mertam or so I am told. Wearing this dress should be encouraged by you, not condemned. As it is, I have only a few suitable gowns, as per your instructions, this being one of them. Once we have reached our final destination, you can buy me new ones in the local fashion. At the moment, however, I am afraid you must endure. Although I could, if you prefer, remove myself from the room and take food to eat in my cabin?' Her words seemed challenging but the tone was conciliatory. Only her mother knew of the anger coursing through the young girl. The tension was broken by the captain, walking into the room and smiling at the two women.

'My dear ladies, you both look absolutely stunning!' His exclamation of delight seemed to echo around the room and two sets of eyes sent triumphant looks to Lord Willoughby. His sense of discomfort only increased when Mr Poole and the child came in, adding yet more compliments about the ladies and their clothing. Sitting and fuming in the far corner, his evening was then completely spoilt when the surgeon – what was his bloody name again? – came in and joined the party, announced that although Patcher was now awake, he was suffering badly from motion sickness and Lord Markus was still in his drugged sleep and wouldn't waken until the morning.

The meal that followed was enjoyed by all, except Lord Willoughby, who was only able to choke down small amounts of his portion of each course with copious amounts of wine. A slice of melon with an assortment of berries began the meal. The infamous "stinky fish" turned out to be delicious and both of the ladies exclaimed over its delicate taste and were delighted to be informed that it would be served again and again. The story of its preparation and strong smell as told by the captain had the ladies giggling in genuine amusement. The next dish consisted of pieces of beef cooked until tender in red wine before being wrapped in a pastry parcel, accompanied by potatoes creamed with horseradish and honey glazed carrots. This was followed by apples and raisins soaked in rum before being cooked with topping of rolled oats sweetened with honey. This was served with a delicious hot custard and Lady Sophia was emboldened enough to ask if she could speak with the cook and get these recipes for herself. The captain gave a slight frown before he answered her.

'I would think that is possible, in fact, I know Leo will be thrilled that you have enjoyed his creations so much. The only issue I have with you speaking to him is he is, unfortunately,' here the captain gave Lady Constance an apologetic glance, 'one of my magikers.'

With a deliberate glance at her inebriated husband, Lady Constance responded calmly. 'As long as my daughter has someone with her as chaperone, I have no objections to the visit.'

Sophia felt her mouth drop in astonishment. 'Mamma, are you alright? Oh, that was rude of me, please accept my apologies...it is just, well, you seem different from how you usually are and, erm, I would, erm...' her voice trailed off as she became more flustered.

Lady Constance let out a peal of laughter before shaking her head ruefully. 'Don't worry, my dear, I am perfectly alright. All that has happened is that I have looked deeply into a mirror and disliked what I have seen there. So it is time I worked upon prejudices and attitudes that are not of my own making but are those which others have pressed upon me.' A deliberate stare at her husband, by now snoring in his seat, made her lip curl in contempt. 'If you would like to see the cook and speak about some of his quite wonderful meals, please do so. I would just prefer you to have someone with you.' Turning to the captain who looked as dumbfounded as Sophia had been, she continued. 'It is not because the chef is an Abomination; I am sorry, you called him a magiker? Well, my daughter needs a chaperone, Captain, not because he is a magiker but because he is a man.'

There was the slightest pause before the whole table erupted into laughter. Calming down, Mr Poole proposed a toast. 'To the ladies and their hidden depths.'

His eyes caught Lady Constance's and she felt herself flush at the sincere regard she saw there. Looking down at her hands, with her cheeks tinted a delicate pink she couldn't deny the pleasure that filled her at his words. She got herself under control enough to join in the discussion as to who was a good enough chaperone for Lady Sophia to be able to wander anywhere on the ship. Again, Constance surprised them all when she suggested the slave and her Keeper.

'I assume she is allowed to move around the ship?' she queried. At the captain's nod of acquiescence, Constance gave a satisfied nod. 'Then, if she has done her duties, the slave is perfect. Of course, being Sophia's escort could easily be one of her duties, helping to fill her day and give it purpose. Plus, having the Keeper with her would mean that no-one would dare to try and interfere with Sophia, at least, never more than once anyway.'

'I could be a chaperone too,' a small voice from the side of Mr Poole piped up. They all looked at Bili in surprise which made him bridle. 'I mean it. If D – the slave is busy with her duties, I can escort the lady to Mr Leo or where else she wants to be. That way, no one else has to stop doing something. I will just be getting into mischief if I don't have a proper job, missus.'

Sophia drew in her breath and held it, waiting for her mother's explosion at the youngster's, albeit unintentional, cheek. Instead, Lady Constance cocked her head to one side, looking at the boy.

'Hmm, you do seem a steady sort, young man. I think that you will be the perfect solution, in fact, as long as Sophia agrees.' At her daughter's surprised nod, Constance tapped a forefinger against her lips. 'Now comes the bargaining, I suppose. Just how much do you want for this service, young man?'

Bili was stunned at her comment, not expecting to be paid at all and so looked at Elias Poole in panic. His grandpa just grinned down at him and winked before rubbing his hands together as he prepared to drive a hard bargain.

'Well now, milady, as the boy's closest relative, it is up to me to negotiate on his behalf, him being new to the game of ladies escort. Knowing that he needs to begin saving up to be able to provide for me in my old age, how does six pieces of gold for his sterling services sound?'

'Too much, is how it sounds! I want him as a chaperone for her, not to adopt him.'

The next ten minutes had the whole room in fits of laughter as the two wily people sent witty comments back and forth. After hearing that Sophia would be in danger of the boy's lascivious nature if he had a sudden growth spurt countered by the fact that the boy obviously had the bearing of a gentleman because his great, great, great, great grandmother was the by-blow of an *olde worlde* king if the story was true, it was settled on eight pieces of silver with six copper pennies which was all Lady Constance had in her reticule at the time. Bili accepted the coins with a sense of wonder, turning them over in his hands and examining each one carefully. Then he handed them over to his grandpa for safekeeping and wandered around the table to where Lady Constance was sitting and he held his arms up. Without pause, she leaned over and pulled him onto her lap, her expression soft in the light of the lamps.

Watching them a memory, long forgotten, came back to Sophia of when it had been herself that had been held so gently but so lovingly. She also remembered how Markus would fly into a rage and hit and bite her if he saw his mother touch her, despite his wanting nothing to do with either of the females. Along with the memory came the inkling that the ice wall her mother had constructed between them was actually for Sophia's protection. A swell of love filled the young girl as she began to dimly understand why her mother had become the way she was. A song, another loving memory, came flowing quietly out of Sophia's mouth, a gentle melody about love and family. Constance gave a startled glance at her daughter before giving her a smile and then adding her own voice to the tune. The men sat around, listening and enjoying the scene of the two women sitting close together with Bili held gently but firmly in a loving grip. Catching a look on his brother's face that was quickly hidden, the captain hid a smile. Another melody followed the first before Bili gave a huge yawn and turned towards his caring captor.

'You must love your children very much,' he said, solemnly.

'I had forgotten just how much and just how precious they are, Bili. Thank you so much for reminding me.' Bending slightly, she kissed his cheek. The boy gave her his own kiss before sliding down and handing out his good night hugs to all except the snoring

Lord Willoughby. Going back to Lady Constance he slid his hand in hers. 'May I go and say goodnight to the slavey, lady?'

An indrawn breath came from somewhere around the table as they waited for her reaction. Mr Poole couldn't help but frown in confusion. His boy was sharp as they come, why would he make such a mistake as to mention the slave girl and not her escort?

Bili just shrugged and nodded towards where Lord Willoughby sat slumped in his chair. 'We don't need to worry about him, the old man is fast asleep.'

Again, Lady Constance surprised them all. 'Lord Willoughby is in a genuine sleep now, poppet, but he isn't always so. Be careful as to what words pass your lips, alright? And I will say this in front of witnesses: of course you can go and see both slave and Keeper now and at any time, do not feel that you need to ask anyone anymore. Just be wary.'

Giving her a blindingly sweet smile, Bili slipped out of the door and was away. Lady Constance looked at the slightly apprehensive group around her and gave a rueful laugh. Opening her mouth to speak, she suddenly looked to her husband's chair and gave a grimace. Then, reaching for her daughter's hand, she stood up and sent a gentle smile around the room before giving a sharp nod towards the sleeping man and her attitude changed completely. She spoke haughtily.

'Come, Sophia, it is time we left these gentlemen to their cigars and port. You will share my room tonight as you dear Papa is in his cups. We had better check to see that your personal items are packed away in case he vomits.' It was only when she snapped back into the old and bitter personage that she had been before did Sophia realised just how much her mother had buried her true personality to stop her father or her brother hurting either of them. Squeezing the hand she held in acknowledgement, Sophia hoped the men would recognise for themselves the change that had occurred in Willoughby's breathing. Standing up by her mother, she watched the men stand and bow at them politely as Mr Poole went to open the door. His murmured 'Madam,' held a level of warmth that caused Sophia to wonder but they swept past and were heading towards her room before she could comment.

The surprises weren't over for the night as they saw the Keeper and the boy's uncle standing at the other side of the door. Before anything could be said, Samuel spoke.

'The Air Elemental told us that you needed help moving some luggage, Lady Constance.'

With a regal nod of her head, they went into Sophia's room and swiftly packed up the little that had been taken out of her trunk before speedily moving it down the corridor to the main cabin. Without being asked, Lord Willoughby's personal items were then packed and taken to the empty cabin. Before Samuel left the room he was halted by his Mistress's voice.

'Wait,' she commanded before seeming to hesitate a little. When she continued, it was in a much gentler way. 'Is the slave alright? She isn't feeling any pain, I hope?'

Samuel swallowed nervously. Bili had told them that Lady Constance was different but this version was not one he knew how to answer. Was there any danger here of causing Danielle more harm? He had already taken too long to respond so knew that he had definitely caused a problem if Bili was wrong.

'I understand that you have no reason to trust me and also that I've given you many reasons not to. The only thing I can do is to apologise to you and the girl. When one feels as if one is trapped and going insane, it seems that lashing out at others in worse predicaments is the only solution. You must know that the Numb you carry is useless so if the girl needs help and you cannot ease whatever it is, let me know and I will see if I can do something.'

The look on the face of Lady Constance gave Samuel hope that she really was as sincere as Bili seemed to think. Knowing that, for Danielle's sake, he had to be careful he gave a silent nod before beginning to close the door. Seeing her face fall at his silent retreat, the Keeper couldn't help pausing before saying; 'The slave is doing very well, Mistress. So far, the major changes in her routine have not resulted in any problems including a reoccurrence of the sleeping illness she had on the way to the docks. Would you wish me to inform you if things change?'

'Immediately,' she shot out quickly. With surprised understanding, the Keeper took the last of the luggage and placed it in the Master's new room before heading back to Danielle and the amazing news.

Chapter Twenty

Sometime later the captain and his brother entered Danielle's room. This time the hammocks stayed folded against the walls and chairs and a few tables had been scattered about. Coffee was being brewed as was a big pot of water for tea on two spirit stoves. The captain looked around in amazement at the men gathered there.

'And just who is sailing the damn ship?' His words burst out of him in shock as he saw most of his crew sitting at leisure, chatting and laughing with the grey-eyed slave girl.

'Don't worry,' chuckled Neera. 'My birds will tell us if we are going to hit anything! We are just ready to hear about Danielle's day.'

Helping himself to one of the chairs, as well as a large mug of the coffee, Captain Levi Poole grinned and gestured for her to continue. With an answering smile, she did so.

'It has been wonderful! The cabins haven't had chance to become very dirty yet, apart from Lord Markus's, so I found it easy and quick to clean them especially with the help of you magikers and even managed to clean up the vomit in *his* room without becoming ill myself. It does stink in his cabin though so tomorrow will be difficult but I have been offered help from both Zutana and Neera so it won't be as bad as I had been expecting.'

Taking a sip of her tea, she continued. 'First thing I began preparing the fish before morning tea – you all know how that went!' The audience chuckled at the memory. 'Then after cleaning the cabins, I helped to prepare the food you have eaten through the day and Leo managed to keep me in the galley until after I had eaten some lunch. After having a walk around the ship and meeting everyone, I went for my first swimming lesson. I was quite frightened for the sea is a very big place, even with a safety line wrapped around my waist, but I had Zutana with me and she kept close by, keeping the water around the ship becalmed while I began to learn how to move my arms and legs. I have picked it up really quickly, she says. I even spent a little time without the rope holding me to the ship.' At the captain's look of astonishment, Danielle giggled.

'Do not worry, Levi,' Neera commentated. 'I had my eye upon them, Danielle was completely safe.'

'But Zutana...'

'Yes, I was surprised myself,' admitted the Air Elemental. 'It seems as if our child here has worked her magik again.'

They all laughed at the frown that crossed Danielle's face at this comment. As far as she was concerned, if she really had magik, she would never have been made a slave in the first place, would she? Her face relaxed as she let go of her irritation in a moment and continued speaking of her day. 'I was tired after being in the water for an hour, so Leo made sure that I had some soup and bread before I had a little nap. A nap! I can't believe that I had a sleep during the day just like Society do. I then helped put the finishing touches upon the dinner you had through there before we ate ours in the galley. I helped Leo and his assistant, Misha, clean up the dishes before coming back here to everyone.'

Levi Poole enjoyed her enthusiasm just as the rest of the men did. To see this girl thrilled to be able to have a nap, to swim, even washing the dishes seemed to have been something she had enjoyed. Sadness filled him as he thought about how empty her life had been. Abruptly, he spoke up.

'If you change your mind about needing to go to the FreeLands, girl, you have a place here on my ship.'

Danielle stared at him. 'Oh, thank you, but as I have said before, it is a place I *have* to go. I am not even sure where in the FreeLands I need to be but I will follow the little tug I am getting inside. The closer we get to Mertam, the stronger the feeling, so that is my place to start. When I find where I need to be and if I survive, I will send you a message. I will have to anyway.' She gave a little laugh, breaking the tension. At the querying looks, she pointed to Bili. 'I need to see if he has left any fish in all the oceans, with his appetite!'

They all laughed at this and seeing Bili's look of baffled pride helped ease the mood even more. Levi felt the burn of disappointment; having this girl safe meant so much to him and he found himself clenching his fists as he thought of the Willoughbys and the harm they did to her. Just then, a small, calloused hand laid itself over his and Bili gazed at him with large, serious eyes.

'Don't worry, Grandpa Levi. Danielle is going to something good,' the youngster whispered to him, too low to be heard by anyone else.

The effort wasn't easy but Levi Poole managed a smile as he pointed to his brother. 'I thought he was your grandpa?'

'He is,' the boy's voice was louder now and full of confidence. 'He was my first grandpa and you are my second grandpa!'

At the general laugh that went round the room, Elias Poole was heard to advise his brother not to argue with Bili's "logic" especially as he, Poole, needed help in paying for the youngster's food. Another laugh rolled around the room only quietening down when a couple of the men gave Danielle a wink as they left to go to the salon and begin a card game. In ones and twos, more followed until only the Keeper, Bili, the Pooles and the slave girl were left in the cabin, the door firmly shut but the window wall wide open. Working quietly, Levi and Mr Poole stacked and removed the empty chairs and tables while Danielle made sure that the crockery was piled tidily on trays and put outside the "window" where they would be taken to the galley by one of the passing crewmen later that night.

Sitting and chatting quietly, the next few weeks were planned in a general outline, as much as was possible anyway, for both Danielle and Samuel. Knowing that Lady Constance and Lady Sophia understood that something was different with the slave was a help and a worry. Not knowing exactly how much these two could be trusted with all the plans meant that everyone still needed to be wary, despite Bili's insistence that they could be trusted absolutely now.

A little later, Neera arrived with a plate of food for Danielle and ready to escort Bili to bed. After the youngster gave his usual round of hugs and kisses, Rook picked him up and followed in the wake of the Air Elemental. Mr Poole shook his head in wonder at the happy little boy as his tired chatter could be heard before the door closed firmly.

'The night I met Samuel and Bili, that boy was a complete wreck. He was so dirty that his skin was cracked and bleeding, he was crawling with lice and was so bloody fearful of his own shadow. Of course he had a right to be. Gods, Levi, he fair broke my heart.'

'How long ago was that? Must have been awhile,' his brother said thoughtfully.

'Less than two months!'

'Plague take you...you must be trying to wag me, you scav.'

'I swear to you, Levi, it has not been that long since he was a timid and starving animal. Now, I will take some pride in helping to begin his transformation, as should Samuel, but I reckon I know who has really helped him.' At that all eyes turned to Danielle who shook her head vehemently.

'I have done a bit,' she said. 'I can't deny that I must have done something but I think it is all of us and the situation we are in. Bili is a clever boy, with his own magik. Being with all of us has helped him to heal, I think I have just helped him physically, that's all.'

Samuel shook his head and gave his own opinion.

'You do heal us physically, Danielle. No matter how much you would love to deny it, we all know how close we were to losing Bili to that stab wound. It is more than just that, however. You give us hope and the strength to keep fighting, even when we are ready to give up. You are the light at the end of the tunnel. All of us feel lighter now, some of which is Bili and his happiness definitely, but you started the whole process the moment you began coming out the Numb trance. I think that you must be some kind of magiker, like Neera says.'

'Well, whatever I am, without you all helping me, I would still be a real slavey or dead by now, so I will stick to my opinion of it being a combination of us all, thank you!'

There was a slight ripple of surprise at her firm tone before Levi broke the tension with a broad grin.

'Did you know? You look just like the boy every time he gets sulky about losing his scar.' A reluctant laugh broke out of the girl before the captain rose to go.

'Come on, Elias. If we are going to persuade them to give Danielle up as a debt, we need to be seen to gamble. Although the scav, as Rook calls him, isn't there tonight, his father is. Let us leave her in peace. Coming, Sam?' The Keeper gave a surprised start before nodding.

'Thank you, sir, I think I will.' Turning and winking at the girl, he unhooked her hammock and spoke in a mock solicitous tone. 'Don't wait up, my dear as I may be a little late.'

Her own voice was waspish, sounding very similar to that of Lady Constance when she replied. 'As long as you don't come home smelling of alcohol and falling over the cat we don't have. Samuel Keeper...really!'

The men chuckled as they bowed and left, leaving the slave to undress and read a little in peace before she turned the light down low and fell into a sleep so deep she never heard Leo pass by and remove the crockery. She didn't even stir when Samuel staggered back later that evening, smelling slightly of drink and still tasting the lips of the surgeon he had left reluctantly at the door. Looking at the sleeping girl, Samuel shrugged off his faint regret at not going to the other man's cabin as he had been asked to do. Although Samuel was very tempted as well as curious to find out what was between himself and the surgeon, he knew that he wasn't free to do any exploring, not yet anyway, not while there was still the whiff of danger to Danielle.

Whistling under his breath he got ready for bed before settling back in his hammock and replaying the events of the evening, including that surprising kiss that he had felt right to his core. His body hardened the more he thought of the slim, hard body leaning into him, the lips caressing his own. Bending his head closer, he had felt Anatoly's tongue sweep across his lower lip, encouraging Samuel to open up, which he did more than willingly. The passion had flared higher as hands explored each other. It was only when the surgeon began to undo Samuel's buttoned fly that the Keeper stopped him with a gentle hand.

'I would and the Light knows, I want to,' he said, gasping for air and control. 'I cannot, not yet, Anatoly. I have to be there for Danielle, I need to keep her safe.'

'As you wish,' the older man said before abruptly pulling away and stalking quickly back to the card game still in process without a backward glance.

Although annoyed at the surgeon's attitude, Samuel still watched the man walk away, eyes lingering over him.

'Be careful, Keeper,' the cook's voice made the Keeper jump as he appeared silently out of the gloom. 'Our surgeon won't like being turned down.'

Sam shrugged negligently. 'I may find him attractive, Leo - I do, obviously - but Danielle is my first priority and he needs to understand that. If he doesn't or won't, then so be it.'

The cook gave a wry smile before moving off. This time Samuel found his eyes lingering over the bloodling as he walked away before he shook his head and moved to his own room.

Samuel sent up a prayer to his gods that Anatoly wouldn't cause any trouble, that sad Leo would find some happiness and that his own rampant imagination would stop and allow him some much-needed sleep. Turning his back to Danielle, he couldn't help smiling to himself even as he fell asleep, his visions of a sexy surgeon morphing into the body and features of a much paler man. Before he could think of questioning why he was dreaming of the bloodling cook instead of the handsome Anatoly, he was fast asleep and the smile stayed on his lips.

Chapter Twenty-One

The next day set a loose routine for the rest of the voyage. Lord Willoughby woke in a vile temper, a raging hangover and dry mouth adding to his anger at having to dress himself. He was content with the ladies new sleeping arrangements, feeling that Constance and Sophia were more than welcome to share the bigger cabin, leaving him in peace. He was a little disgruntled to not be able to speak to his son in private but the younger man's cabin stank of unwashed body and vomit and it would take a few days for the stench to clear. Markus was, as yet, too enfeebled to come to his father. Lord Willoughby had hoped for a pampered, luxurious voyage but, because of the rush of leaving and his own parsimonious nature, he had decided against paying for a bigger passenger ship and now he reaped the rewards. His temper was volatile for the whole journey, making his family and others extremely wary of him.

Lord Marcus began his second day much happier in both head and stomach although wobbly on his feet. When he eventually left his cabin, his eyes roved around, looking the crew up and down and making more than a few of them uncomfortable under his less than subtle gaze. Both Bili and the slavey kept out of his way as much as they could but the young Lord did not notice their absence as he found himself fascinated by the Air Elemental who didn't seem to mind his regard and served as a distraction for the crewies. Evenings were spent in the salon, gambling with the crewies as well as Rook and Samuel on some nights. The Captain and Mr Poole turned up occasionally, as did Lord Willoughby. Markus was too taken with eyeing up the crew to recognise how often he "lost" the slave girl on the turn of a card. The captain seemed to win every time but as Markus was using the slavey as his stake, the younger Willoughby never counted up these losses. All he was concerned about was the times he won a kiss or more off others there.

Lady Constance and Lady Sophia went about their days in a quiet manner but both were a great hit with the crew. Lady Constance had earned many thanks as she gave a poultice and medicinal draught to one of the younger crewies before lancing a wound in the arm that had become infected. Ignoring the thick, dark blood mixed with yellow pus that burst out to soak into her clothing, she bathed the wound with hot water and heals-all; gently pressing the open sides of the wound until all that came out was red blood, clear of any poison. Once the blood flowed clear Lady Constance sewed the gash with quick, neat stitches, joking that her embroidery had come in useful at last. Later that day, Danielle was quietly asked to check the wound and she praised the job that had been done, emphasising that it could have killed the crewman without Lady Constance's immediate intervention.

An argument between two of the younger crew members was stopped when Lady Sophia began telling a fable that her mother had shared with her many years before. The angry youngsters stopped their shouting and began listening to the quiet voice and soon they were enthralled; loving the romance, the chivalry and the actions of the fictional characters. After checking with the captain at dinner, Sophia planned to have a story time the next and most of the following days, coming up with new tales and adventures each afternoon. By the time they reached Mertam, the story time was a fixed event that many more than just the younger members of the crew enjoyed. As missing the story time was the best punishment the captain could give, the crew was more harmonious and work was done more quickly and with less mistakes.

Captain Poole praised both of the ladies at that second evening's meal and also thanked them profusely; one for saving a life, the other for keeping the crew amused. A comment on how both of them seemed to be blooming in the sea air had them both blushing prettily although Mr Poole scowled at his grinning brother after he had been pushed into making his own comments and he walked away muttering under his breath, confusing the two women and Bili immensely, especially as the captain seemed to find the whole situation hysterically funny.

Samuel and Danielle spent most of the days that followed in a similar way as their first. Samuel mainly walked behind the girl as she went from place to place while Danielle found that many of the really dirty jobs she was used to doing on land were readily taken care of by the crew without thought. Swimming felt so natural to her that she needed little instruction and began working on her endurance.

A small woman, a little less than five feet in height, Zutana held a beauty that was stunning to all senses. Her hair was of a deep turquoise that, when looked at closely, had tiny pearls and shells woven into its long length. It flowed about her head and body as if moving underwater, letting out tiny sparkles of light as it did so, as if sunlight played upon the surface of dancing waves. Her finely drawn features included high cheekbones and deep blue green eyes and a small, almost lipless mouth. On the sides of her neck she had gills which looked just like thin cuts in the skin. Like Neera, she too had one finger and one toe less on her hands and feet but the webbing between her digits was thicker and more solid than that of the Air Elemental. Her clothing was strips of fabric in all shades of blue and green that draped around her, moving and flowing in the same way that her hair did. She never spoke aloud but communicated either with hand signals to most or using mind-speech with a few, but she would sing the most haunting melodies that could chase the dangerous leviathans away from the ship or could draw the happy dolphins to play.

She helped both Danielle and Bili in the water and they all enjoyed this time together immensely, although Bili struggled at first to get his co-ordination. She changed from a shy, quiet and alien-looking woman with two legs into a bright and confident half woman, half fish, with her legs fusing into a luminescent tail once she was in the ocean. Many times various marine creatures swam close to Danielle, thrilling her with their curiosity. She found herself being taken for rides by seawolves, whales and dolphins as well as brushing the long hair of mermaids and mermen as she listened to stories of the sea.

She also learned to swim underwater for great distances, never realising that her endurance was far beyond that of normal human lungs to take. No one mentioned her abilities though; they had all learned how upset she was at the thought of being a magiker who was also a slave. Zutana always kept a close watch on Danielle's undersea adventures and had to call her back more than once when the slave slipped into a trance like state and began to swim towards the FreeLands. A distraction by a seawolf, or one of the merpeople, was enough to bring her back to awareness though.

Danielle really loved her life at sea but occasionally found herself becoming overwhelmed by all the changes and attention she was given, as well as the new faces and different species that she interacted with. Sometimes, especially as the voyage went on, she would slip away and go and sit quietly in her cabin, just sewing or reading. Bili or Samuel occasionally joined her and she enjoyed their quiet company but she was happy to be alone and able to relax fully. Many times, she slipped out of the window space and sat gazing at the mercurial sea, comparing it to the lands of Bisra she had travelled through a few weeks ago. When the sea was smooth, she thought of the fields of grain, hemp and flax whereas when it foamed and thrashed, she was reminded of the woods and the singing of the wind in the trees.

Bili spent his days either by Danielle's side or with his grandfather. He found that the ship's cats as well as some of Neera's birds loved spending time with him if he was quiet and calm, which helped soothe his still volatile nature. He had also made fast friends with Lady Constance and sought her out often. As a result Mr Poole found himself in the company of the titled lady more than he expected. They both found that she was a much warmer, much more caring woman than she had originally seemed and Captain Poole enjoyed seeing his brother emerging from the hard shell of grief after all these years.

Patcher spent most of the rest of the voyage in his cabin, finding that he couldn't stand or move for long without becoming nauseous and light headed. Most of the ship's crew would have to escort the man back to his cabin every time he ventured out. There he lay on his bunk, vomiting up the little he had been able to stomach and too dizzy to move. The ship's surgeon checked with the captain, and with Leo, that no medicines or food were being used that could make the man ill. He eventually decided that it was an imbalance within the butler's ear which Anatoly had heard of but never before seen.

Samuel and the surgeon eventually came to an uneasy pact where Danielle was concerned. They spent a few nights talking and sharing information of their separate lives, with Anatoly wanting to move forward more quickly than Samuel was comfortable with. The Keeper enjoyed being kissed and being able to be honest about his sexuality for the first time but he resented the feeling of being pushed beyond his limits.

One evening had ended with Samuel pulling away from the doctor with a sound of irritation, saying again that he wasn't free to follow his wants as he was still employed by Lord Willoughby. The man would send Samuel to the Punishment Square, quicker than blinking if the old man ever found out that he was a deviant. Pouting, Anatoly stood and then strode across his cabin to pour himself a drink.

'I think you have feelings for this girl,' the surgeon scowled.

'Don't be ridiculous, 'Tolly! You know I prefer the look and feel of men rather than women. The slave is my responsibility, I am her Keeper. Once we get to Mertam, I will be given a choice whether to stay with the family or leave. Until then, however, I am their servant and *must* do as I am told. If you want more from me, then please be patient. If you cannot wait, then stop now, before this goes any further.' Samuel felt his face flame with anger. He wouldn't share Danielle's plans with someone he hardly knew and who had, so far, showed little or no respect for the girl in his charge and whom he loved like a sister. It infuriated the Keeper to see someone who was supposed to care about the welfare of others blinding himself to the terrible conditions that the slave had to live under. The fact that Anatoly didn't realise that Danielle could think for herself now somehow made the situation even worse.

Looking at the sulking man, Samuel gave a sigh. How could he expect the man to understand all the ramifications of the situation, when Anatoly didn't know all of what was happening underneath the surface? Walking over to where the surgeon stood, drink in hand, Samuel took it from him and sipped from the glass.

'Look, I understand that you want more between us, I do myself. But I cannot do anything that will jeopardise the situation with my Master. I am the only thing that keeps the slavey safe from some of the worst things that Lord Markus can think of. At the moment, Lord Willoughby isn't bothering her; or me, for that matter. If, however, he found something he disapproved of, he would punish us both quicker and with less effort than snapping his fingers. Once we get to land, you and I can discuss things between us again, but until then, I can do no more than we have already done. I don't want to promise you things I cannot give,

'Tolly, and I don't want to get used to needing something I may not be able to keep, alright?' Samuel spoke in a quiet tone, hoping that Anatoly would understand.

'I might have changed my mind by then,' snapped the surgeon and Samuel shrugged, keeping a tight hold on his anger.

'It is your choice as well as mine. I will say no more. If you decide to walk away completely, then I will not argue. Goodnight.' With a nod of his head, Samuel walked briskly out of the room and went straight to his own, ignoring the sound of his name being called. Being thoughtful and trying to understand another's feelings should come from both sides he decided as he shut the door to his cabin firmly behind him.

Danielle sat with Bili who was stroking one of the cat's that followed him around, both practising their letters with Neera and Zutana watching over them. The four of them looked at Samuel in surprise but no-one spoke. In total silence he walked through the small room and out of the opened window. He heard quiet sounds behind him as Bili and the Elementals left the room. Danielle came and leaned against him. With a sigh, he pulled her close in a hug and continued to watch the waves as he slowly began to calm down. Eventually both of them turned and got ready for bed, still not speaking but the silence now was companionable rather than full of his frustration and anger.

Chapter Twenty-Two

Towards dawn of the next day, Danielle was woken by a voice quietly calling her name. Looking out on to the deck, she saw Leo smiling down at her and gesturing for her to come out. A quiet murmur from Samuel let them know he was also awake. Exchanging a puzzled glance, both Keeper and slavey got up and stepped through the opening into the open air. There, they saw Captain and Mr Poole, Rook and Bili, as well as the rest of the ship's crew, all standing at the railing and looking to the north, no-one saying a word. Following their gazes, Danielle saw flares of light flashing across the night sky.

'What is that?' Samuel kept his voice low.

'That is the Gryphon Dance, my friends, something rarely seen by humans. It is said that those who see the Dance will receive their hearts desires but not always in expected ways.' After Neera had finished his soft explanation, he fell quiet and they continued to watch in silence.

As the sun began to rise, the crowd at the railings saw figures flying and manoeuvring around each other. Long lines came together before curving around and manoeuvring in circles before breaking apart and making other shapes in the sky with some of the huge figures swooping above while others dived below. As red, orange, yellow and peach lightened the sky even more, the shadows took on better shape and the gryphons came into focus. Danielle felt her lips curve and she grinned until her cheeks ached as she saw them loop and fly higher, weaving in and out of each other. Soon, she could see the flying creatures much more clearly and her heart leaped.

The head and forelegs were of giant birds, eagles or Rocs, with cruel beaks more than able to cut into the bodies of the massive leviathans that were part of their food source, and with fore claws able to grip and carry the largest of prey. The body, rear legs and tail were those of giant cats, with retractable claws ready to rend and tear into whatever they chose. Each gryphon ignored the ship but paid great attention to the smaller flying shapes that played around them. With another smile, Danielle realised that these little beings were not birds, as she had first thought, but were the younglings of the beasts, imitating their parents and resting on whichever body was closest when they tired.

Amazed, she saw a tiny black and silver gryphon weave in and out of a huge couple before landing and settling down on the back of the gigantic male, yawning before curling up to sleep. The expression of resignation on the male's face had Danielle and Bili laughing out loud, both recognising the look as one that Bili received more than once every day from his grandfathers and others.

As the dance continued, the ship crept closer and Neera began whispering what some of the movements meant as well as the deeper meaning behind the dance itself.

'This dance is about two things. The first is that some are flirting, trying to find a mate. For some that do find their mate, it will be just for the thirteen months of the year but others will mate for life, which is another part of the ceremony, a celebration of life partners. Those that move around the outside are not looking for mates but are taking part in the ceremony for Hearthlight. This is when fires are needed by most as the weather turns colder and even dangerous with blizzards and heavy rains; you people from Bisra call it Summer's End. The Gryphon Dance is to ensure that the sun comes back to the world when the season turns.'

'Some gryphons mate for life, but not all. If truly mated for life, magikal beings *cannot* betray their vows. After the death of a true mate, their partner will follow them through the Void immediately, unless there are younglings that still need care. Once the younglings no longer need their parent, then the Void calls and the mate has no choice but to go. All gryphons are Seers, they can see events connected to specific beings or areas of the world. They rarely mix with others now, especially as the followers of The Shining One have been hunting them brutally in recent times, citing them as creatures of evil while incidentally becoming rich from using the fur and feathers in armour and weapons. I am glad to say that this cruel practice has cost humans dearly.'

'How can anyone take the life of such beauty?' Danielle felt her eyes filling with tears as she thought about the waste and slaughter of such noble beasts. Her eyes were glued to a pair of adult gryphons; one with a white eagle's head and wings but with a tawny lion's body and back legs, the other was the male she had first noticed giving the cheeky youngster a bed, he was all black apart from the gold of beak and claws. They truly were magnificent.

Suddenly Neera sucked in a sharp breath before he rapped out a command for everyone to stay perfectly still. Such was the urgency in his voice, no-one even turned to look at him in surprise. Then a concerted gasp rose up and they froze in to position, hardly daring to breathe.

Flying towards the ship was the black gryphon that Danielle had been watching, his head covered in black feathers. His body was sleek and muscled, like a hunting cat. The risen sun revealed a pattern of rosettes set in the pelt along his back. Wide wings flapped lazily and the people at the railings saw how much distance each movement gave the beast.

The huge head of the gryphon moved from side to side as it hovered and looked at those on-board ship out of a swirling orange eye as large as Bili. It moved in closer until its big head was close to Danielle. She found herself looking deeply into the wise eye of a beast she had never known existed until a short while ago. Her breath caught as a roaring filled her ears and her mind filled with words that seemed to blow through her with the force of a hurricane.

'You have no fear of me, little one. How unusual.' the voice said and Danielle knew it was the gryphon who spoke.

'There is no point having fear when I could not survive anything you chose to do to me. I do have respect and wonder though.' The slavey spoke in her mind just as the gryphon was doing.

'I can see your thoughts. I know that you speak the truth and it pleases me. You have magik, little one, but it is hidden from you as yet. Do not fret, you will get where you need to be, you will find more than you lose but there will be a sacrifice that almost breaks you. Do not let it. You are needed. We will come when we are called, never fear. The gryphons are with you.'

With this extraordinary statement, the huge beast rose slightly and gave the sails a breath of wind that sent the ship skimming along, causing Bili to giggle. To the shock of everyone except perhaps the gryphons themselves a tiny obsidian and silver gryphon, the one that had landed on the great gryphon's back earlier, turned to the sound and flew over to hover in front of the boy's face. Bili reached up slowly, his face filled with awe. The small beast landed lightly on his out-stretched arm, climbed along, then settled on his shoulder. The feather covered head snuggled under its wing, one claw slipped inside Bili's shirt and its thick rope of a tail wrapped firmly around the boy's neck.

Neera looked at the ecstatic boy and the stunned expressions of the others before turning back to the obsidian gryphon still moving lazily in time with the ship as its escort flew and played around it.

'You bless us mightily, Great One.' Neera bowed gracefully and then looked up at the beast.

'No, Elemental. You have befriended one who is important to the world of Magik and we show our loyalty and respect. I am known as Scythe and I am pleased that the Gods have given me the chance to meet you all. My time is close and soon I will be on my last flight. I ask a boon of the little Magiker.'

It took a few seconds for Neera to realise Scythe meant Bili, not Danielle, so he gestured to the youngster who stepped closer, careful not to jar his new companion.

'This is Arjannett, one of my line and not long from the egg. It has been many years since one of my kind has chosen a companion. Do you accept her as yours, youngling?'

A short silence ensued then Bili shocked them all. 'No, I can't accept her as mine, she's herself. She ain't a slavey.' He looked heart-broken but determined.

'A wise answer for such a small one.' Scythe looked at him before nodding his head. 'Perhaps then, if she chooses to stay, will you be her friend?'

'Yes!' Bili nodded his head so quickly Arjannett gave a grumble of irritation at being disturbed. This caused the others to laugh and the small creature lifted her head, sending irritated glances around her.

'She will need her hide brushing every day and her feathers smoothed. Feed her as much as she calls for without worry as she won't overeat. If she disappears, do not hunt for her, she will return when she wants to, *if* she wants to. She will be irritating and hard work and sometimes you will curse the day you met her. Do not be afraid though, as she will do the same to you. Have you the patience and skill to be her partner, youngling?'

'I can try my best. An' I reckon she will tell me quick enough if I gets it wrong. So yes, if she wants to stay an' be my friend, I'll do my best to take care of her. Is that alright?'

'Better than alright, youngling. And now it is time for the rest of us to go. The Dance is over for another year, mates have been chosen and the sun will return eventually.' Turning to Danielle again, the huge beast blew on her so gently it caused her shirt to flutter yet didn't reach to any of those standing with her. 'Remember, not all will be as it seems and you will gain more than you lose, though some losses will be severe.' Before the slave could asked for any explanations the gryphon turned and flew off with its entourage, quickly becoming smaller as it moved with great speed.

Arjannett looked over the group and Bili held his breath in case the small beast followed her flock but she just gave a small chirp before settling in around Bili's neck again. Neera looked at the boy then at Danielle.

'I have not known of anyone being so blessed in many years. Bili, you will need to ask Leo to help you to feed the beast. We will save our worry about her getting bigger when she actually does. Danielle? You have been marked by a gryphon. Only magikers can see this but it will give you great protection. For now, we need to move back to where we should be before the Willoughby or the Markus see us.'

Slowly, the group dispersed and went quietly away, still stunned by all that had happened. Watching Bili walk slowly so as not to jolt the sleeping baby, she smiled, pleased at his care. Then she turned to Samuel with a frown.

'It is wonderful that I have been marked, as Neera says. It would have been nicer to have had better information and less riddles though. Blast it, I still don't know where I am going or why or even if we will get free of the Willoughbys.'

'Stop complaining. We will do as we have from the first. We take one day at a time and keep our eyes open for any opportunities. Stop holding on to troubles that might never happen. Come on, time to eat.' With that prosaic remark, the Keeper led the way into the cabin.

Chapter Twenty-Three

As they ate their breakfast, Anatoly knocked quietly on the door of the cabin. Neera whisked the plates of food away and disappeared out of the open wall as Samuel opened the door. When he saw the surgeon standing there, looking downcast, he felt first relief. It was quickly followed by another emotion, not so easily named, that flooded through him.

'I am sorry, Samuel. I was wrong to push you last night,' Anatoly sounded utterly miserable. 'Please forgive me. We can begin again. I was selfish and...'

Before he could continue, Samuel pulled him inside and patted him gently on the shoulder.

'Of course, I accept your apology. I was angry last night but I am glad that you understand that this is not my choice but what I have to do.' Samuel missed the sneer the surgeon sent to the blank eyed slave girl. Danielle saw it and thought that there was going to be a lot more trouble coming from that quarter. No matter what the ship's doctor said, he hadn't changed his mind at all, just a different approach to getting Samuel all for himself. As Anatoly leaned back he kissed Samuel lightly on the lips and left, smirking as he did so.

Samuel turned to Danielle, raising his eyebrows. He grinned at her carefully neutral stare.

'I am not as green as I am cabbage looking, Danielle. He has probably had a sleepless night and now thinks a quick apology will get him what he wants. Maybe, if he is patient, it will get us what we both want. Until then, let's get on with our day, shall we?'

Danielle grinned back, relieved that he wasn't taken in by the doctor's words. She finished off the slice of toasted bread and butter she had hidden behind her back before washing her hands and getting ready to begin her work.

A few slight changes to the ship's routine ensured that Willoughby and Markus remained unaware of what had happened earlier that day. Both were disgruntled about the journey so far which meant that neither caught the silent messages that moved between the crew and the friends of the slavey.

Markus was annoyed that he had had to allow the captain use of the slavey during the voyage and was nervous of his father's reaction if that man ever found out what had happened. He had almost come to the decision not to gamble again, when Neera passed by with a wink and a stroke on his arm. Tingling from the touch, Markus knew that he would be in the salon later to take his chances on cards again.

Lord Willoughby had a raging hangover from the wine he had drunk the night before. His temper was uncertain at the best of times but the pounding of his temples and the dryness of his mouth, made him even more volatile. What made it all worse was knowing that he couldn't blame anyone else for his state. His bloody wife had told him to slow down on his drinking days before, which only made him more determined to quaff the quality liquor that the captain provided. A sudden thought made the portly man hesitate. Could that bitch have understood this? That he would deliberately ignore her and do the opposite? Could she...? With an irritated shake of his head, Lord Willoughby stumped to the salon. Of course she hadn't known, the woman wasn't that bloody clever. Carefully he poured a glass of wine – hair of the dog, he thought grimly – and again went over his plans for when they arrived at Mertam.

Bili stayed below decks in the long cabin that was home to the crew. Most were fascinated by the young gryphon but most stayed prudently away from the sharp beak which flashed out every time anyone got too close. Treb, the truth seeker, showed Bili how to groom the little beast which seemed to find favour with Arjannett. She also fashioned a sling that Bili wore for Arjannett to sleep in as well as putting extra padding upon the shoulder and around one of Bili's forearms. After feeding, grooming and more feeding, Bili had lost a little of the awe at having such a creature wanting to stay. It was beginning to dawn on him that the gryphon would be just as demanding as Scythe had foretold. With a sigh, Bili reached forward and scratched the top of the youngster's head and was rewarded by a contented purr. He knew then, no matter how demanding, he would never want to be parted from the little trouble maker.

The time for the evening meal came but Bili found that he was unable to leave Arjannett. She showed her displeasure very plainly. Sucking on his bleeding finger where she had nipped him, Bili tried to reason with her.

'I have to go for some food for me, an' if any of those Willoughby's sees you, they will want to take you. I want you safe so you stay here an' I will go for food.' He tried again for the door only to have her hiss and squawk at him, flapping her strong wings in his face. Frustration and hunger began to rise up in Bili's body and he opened his mouth to yell when the door behind him opened and Danielle stepped in.

'She won't let me leave,' the small boy was almost sobbing, reminding those that watched just how young he really was. Arjannett glared at him fiercely out of her bright orange eyes before she stepped closer and gave an enquiring hum.

'She doesn't understand why you want to leave her here,' said Danielle, unsure of how she knew the answer but positive she was right. 'Both of you come with me and you shall eat with us. That way you won't starve to death and Arjannett will be happy.'

With a sniff, Bili nodded and held out his arm. The gryphon gave a jump and landed on his arm before walking up to his shoulder and settling down in her preferred place and rubbing her feathered head against his cheek. Following Danielle, both boy and gryphon went swiftly to the slave's cabin where they ate and drank in comfort.

Eventually, the gryphon settled down and became less of a magnet for the crew which allowed Bili chance to get to know her properly. She was a demanding little thing but when Bili explained things, she usually went along with his choices. It was Samuel who had eventually realised the reason for Arjannett's attitude the first evening she was aboard.

'Gryphons protect, that's their job. The fact that Arjannett has chosen you means that you are the one she feels she needs to look after. Being able to read minds, she also knows much about what is going on and what people are really thinking so didn't want you spending time with either Lord Willoughby or Lord Markus. That's why the hissing and such. She likes the ones she saw at the railing when she found you, Bili. When she sees anyone she doesn't know, she looks into them, into their minds, to see if they will cause you any harm. The fact that we are all wary of the male Willoughbys is something she has picked up on. Hence, the reason not to let you dine with them.'

Getting to the end of this explanation, Samuel reached for his mug of ale. Arjannett gave a chirp, landed on his thigh and rubbed her head on his chest before leaping back onto Bili.

'By the gods,' the Keeper gasped before standing up and bowing before the gryphon. With a regal bend of her own head in response, Arjannett settled to sleep while the others laughed at the shock on Samuel's face.

'I forgot she would understand us,' he said sheepishly to Mr Poole, who just grinned back.

'Yes, we will have to mind out language now, we can't have the young 'uns swearing and misbehaving. My, but this is going to be hard work!' Another chuckle went around the room before the party slowly broke up to work, sleep or go and play cards in the salon.

Chapter Twenty-Four

'Bloody Mýste, 'Tolly!' Samuel pushed the slighter man away from him before straightening up his clothing and moving towards the door of the surgeon's room. 'How many times have we gone through this? I thought we had it all settled, so listen for once and for all. I am *not* a free man yet. I have the responsibility of the slave right up until we land. I will not put her in any danger because you want more than I can give. You say you need me desperately yet you are ignoring what I *have* to do, against what you desire. Until the slave is off the ship and I have been cut loose by the Master, I won't be spending my free time with you. Once it is all settled and if you still want me or I want you, we can take it further. Until then, good day, sir.'

Opening the door, the Keeper almost missed the surgeon's murmured words. Suddenly the Anatoly found himself slammed into the wall with the point of a knife pricking his vulnerable throat.

'You best only be saying what you just did in temper, man. For I promise you, if any harm comes to the slave, Bili, Arjannett or anyone else I count as family, I will make you regret every plague blackened syllable that has ever passed your lips. And I promise, before it is over, you will beg for death!' After slamming the surgeon's body against the wall again, Samuel moved towards the door, so angry he felt as if he would explode. So much for Keepers not having emotions, he thought furiously.

'Sam, Samuel! I swear I spoke in temper, nothing else.' Anatoly's voice was imploring as he caught at the Keeper's arm and pulled him round to face him. 'I am just so jealous of her and the others that take you from me. I am even jealous of the Abomination in the galley, for the One's sake. I love you and I want to make love with you and to be with you properly. I swear I will not speak against her any more, I do swear it.' Without softening his stance, Samuel pulled Anatoly's hand off his arm and looked at the tear stained face of his would-be lover.

'I hope you mean that, Anatoly, I really do. For I meant every word I just said to you. How you can feel jealousy and not understand the predicament of a slave when you are a healer, I do not know. I have had almost twenty years to have touched her and never thought of doing so, so why would I start now? I will not keep listening to your petty jealousies and spite, especially now we are getting closer to land.' He closed the door gently but firmly behind him, ignoring Anatoly's muffled pleas, and walked to the cabin he shared with Danielle, stopping and pausing before going in, to compose his face.

The room was almost empty. Danielle was sitting in a comfortably upholstered chair, sewing while she listened to Bili reading a book borrowed from Sophia, Arjannett curled up on his shoulder, looking at the pages intently. Bili's voice was clear and only stumbled over a few words now and then, the gryphon giving a chirp of encouragement every so often. They both looked up as Samuel walked in and made it obvious that they knew something was wrong but also that they wouldn't pry.

'Your reading is coming on amazingly well, Bili.' The Keeper was genuine with his compliment, although his voice was strained. 'What is it you are reading?'

'It is all about people from somewhere long ago who could change shape into dragons and stuff. It is really great! Sophie says I can borrow the next one. Just think of it, Sam, Sophie has eleven books! And she has read so many more. I never knew reading was so good. I think she should write a book and put in all those stories she tells us, she is brilliant,' the youngster enthused. Standing up, he started towards the door.

'Hey, kiddo, her name is Lady Sophia, not Sophie and you don't have to leave just because I am here.' Samuel chastised. Bili looked at him before grinning.

'I just finished this book and want to take it back. Besides, you are angry, sad and want to speak to Danielle. And I *like* saying Sophie better than that Lady stuff.' With that, he went out of the room, making sure the door was properly shut behind him.

'That blasted child picks up too bloody much,' growled the Keeper.

'Perhaps,' murmured Danielle. 'But is he wrong?'

With a heavy sigh, Samuel threw himself down in a chair facing the girl. Leaning forward with his head in his hands, he was quiet for a few minutes. Then he raised his head and grinned ruefully.

'No, he isn't wrong, is he ever?' The Keeper said. 'Anatoly tried pushing me too far again and I have told him for the last time that I will not give in. He threatened you! He makes me so bloody angry so why the hell can't I...' With a groan, Samuel let the words trail off. A few minutes passed and although his mind was still in turmoil, the Keeper felt himself begin to relax within the soothing atmosphere of the cabin. Eventually he sat up and looked at the slave, seeing the concern and the understanding on her face. Raising an eyebrow, he gestured her to speak.

'You have always known that you were an invert, brother mine. But you never believed that others would be attracted to you. You wear your Keeper uniform as if it were armour and just watched men from the corner of your eye, without taking it any further. Living in Harmony and touching a man could have got you killed so you sent your needs and desires deep inside. The danger we are living with is in every breath and knowing that we could die heightens our passions for life. For the very first time you have allowed your own passions free range. I'd imagine you are very confused right now. I think you are right to not step forward into the surgeon's arms. For weeks now he has been seducing you yet you have not succumbed to his erotic blandishments. That, I think, is what you need to be working out. So it isn't "why can't you walk away" but "why haven't you *given* way"?'

Amazement flickered across his features as Samuel thought about what Danielle had said. It was true, having a sensual man like Anatoly who wasn't afraid to show his needs openly, was very exciting and very much added to Samuel's attraction. Having always been so careful to hide his own desires, it did feel liberating to have a man want him with such open fervour. So just why had he been holding back on allowing full consummation of their mutual attraction? Using Danielle as the excuse was not the full answer, it couldn't be. Thinking things over and concentrating heavily Samuel didn't hear Danielle get up and leave the room, smiling at him as she left.

Walking into the corridor, Danielle turned her still smiling face up at Neera who was hovering around in his Air form, close to the their quarters as he often did. All that could be seen was a faint smoke-like substance, there only because of a promise to his captain that he would always give some indication of his presence unless he was spying on the Willoughby's. Danielle knew that the Air Elemental found Samuel attractive but she also knew that his very casual attitude to sex with others would be very painful to the Keeper.

'Please leave him be, Neera. Samuel needs to work things out for himself and you would only confuse him more and probably drive him into the arms of the surgeon.' The girl sounded sharp which was unlike her.

Solidifying in front of her, Neera looked deep into her eyes, puzzled at her unusual show of emotion. Danielle was never judgemental when it came to people and who, or how many, they chose as lovers. The only time she got angry was when force or manipulation was used. As this thought came to him, he found himself nodding in understanding.

'You think Anatoly is manipulating your boy? Perhaps he is. He has no magik he can use though so any manipulation is purely emotional and not to my taste, little cousin. I am open about my desires and your Keeper knows that if he was to make any move to me, I would gladly teach him my way of loving. I agree with your thinking that this would be too much for him though. It is a pity he is not bloodling for I think Leonid would be perfect as Samuel's first lover but, alas, your Keeper is much too human.'

'Why can't Leonid be Samuel's first?' Danielle was surprised, as she had thought that the ship's cook would be a fantastic lover for the Keeper.

'If Leo and Sam make love there is always the chance that Samuel, because of being human, will be turned because of the magik tinged fluid that...erm...' Uncharacteristically Neera blushed and stumbled over the words.

'Oh!' Danielle flushed before she grinned up at the Elemental. 'Any exchange of any fluid can bring on the change, I expect. Even a kiss?'

Neera nodded, relieved that Danielle understood so quickly. 'Kisses are not so much of a problem but other fluids are. Blood exchanges, the release of – erm – other fluids can begin the change from human to bloodling. When they are first turned they are savage and unpredictable. It takes months for the new bloodling to regain control of their senses and to regain full sanity. Not all make it. Many stay in the blood rage and will attack and drain any victim to death, something which isn't actually

necessary. So the movies and books of yesteryear got that wrong.'
He finished with a chuckle.

Danielle continued to stare as she worked her way through
the flood of information before looking at the Elemental before
her. 'What is a movies, Neera?'

'Good grief, the child knows nothing! A movie was
something from before the Breaking of the World. It is
complicated but, to put it simply, it was a play that you would
watch on a screen. A screen could look a little like a pane of glass
or a piece of sail-cloth but more explanations will be too
confusing!' he cried out, throwing his hands in the air before
laughing loudly as he faded. 'Do not worry, little one, I never
chase uncomprehending or unwilling prey.'

With a shake of her head and a rueful grin, Danielle
walked past the all but invisible man and climbed up to the main
deck for fresh air.

Neera smiled to himself as he floated through the lower
ship, unseen by anyone. It had been child's play to seduce Markus
although his own preferred taste in his male lovers was for them to
be more muscular and masculine, just like that Keeper. Marcus
was ready and eager but still very self-absorbed and expected to be
given more enjoyment out of each encounter, compared to the
effort he made on his own part for his lover. He was an extremely
selfish man, in or out of bed. Samuel would definitely be the more
delectable of the two and Neera spent a few moments imagining
what it would be like to seduce someone who would be concerned
with giving fulfilment as well as receiving it. With a sigh, he
decided that Danielle was right and, as gorgeous as the Keeper
was, Neera would become bored quickly, once his conquest was
made, although perhaps not quite as speedily as Danielle thought.

Chapter Twenty-Five

Still thinking about the situation, Neera moved up on deck in his invisible form and caught sight of Bili climbing up the rigging like a monkey. The Captain and Mr Poole kept an eye on him as they chatted quietly to Rook and Benro, the captain's second in command while Arjannett flew overhead, stretching her wings. Neera saw that the youngling had grown a good few inches in just a few days and grinned to himself, wondering how they would cope as the creature grew even larger.

A sudden cry grabbed everyone's attention, eyes shooting up to Bili as he lost his grip and began to fall. There was a loud snap, followed by a piercing scream, as his leg caught in some of the rigging. Bili tumbled over and over as he went down like a rock, ready to smash himself to pieces on the hard oaken decking as Arjannett screamed in terror, soaring down at speed, trying to get beneath the boy as he fell. At the last moment Bili hit an object, much softer than the solid deck, who threw arms around him and slowed his headlong journey downwards.

Neera had sped towards the falling boy faster than the wind and had changed to his physical form to slow the falling boy down. The force of Bili hitting his midriff had hurt Neera more than he expected and, as they landed, he rolled away from the youngster and curled into a ball, wracked with pain. The boy hadn't got off scot-free either, his leg was swollen and obviously broken, the bone sticking out of his skin just below his knee and his face wearing an ugly spreading bruise. Several crewmen shouted for the surgeon as the boy was gently patted, each of the men trying to comfort him. Arjannett swooped and flew around the group, screeching and cawing in panic until Mr Poole grabbed hold of the creature, holding her close to him and murmuring gentling words even as his heart froze in terror.

'Bring him to the surgeon's room,' snapped out the ship's doctor, rushing to get splints, herbs and instruments ready. Following behind at a slower pace, the boy was carried to the infirmary. Every step jerked his poor leg and made him cry out in pain causing the distressed Arjannett to struggle even more.

Entering the open, room, they laid Bili down upon one of the three beds within, kept for any crewie who was suffering and needed to be watched. The boy was cold, though sweating profusely, as his face became greyer by the minute. Mr Poole held his hand in a tight but gentle grip as Arjannett lay quietly at his side, her eye fixed upon the youngster as the surgeon checked out the bruised and battered little body.

'I am going to brew up a tisane. The boy needs to drink every last drop. I cannot set his leg until he is unconscious as the pain will be too much. As it is, the break to his leg is such he may never walk again without some pain. It was foolish of him to be so high above the deck without an Abomination being with him. As far as I can see there are at least two breaks in his leg. You can see the bone here but there is another lower down also as well as severely damaged ligaments. In the worst case I may even have to remove the limb. That creature also needs to leave the room, I cannot work with a vicious animal distracting me'

The cold voice stopped suddenly as the surgeon saw the glares being directed at him and realised just how clinical and harsh he had sounded, not to mention his slip of the tongue regarding his own thoughts about magikers. His voice became more human as he stammered out, 'I-I am so sorry! I have forgotten how to speak in front of a child. My sincere apologies. Erm...I will go and heat the water.'

Mumbling in embarrassment the surgeon turned away through a curtain of white material, moving and clattering about. A tug at his hand made Mr Poole look down at the tear stained face of the boy he loved so much.

'What is it, young 'un?' Keeping his voice quiet and smooth was difficult for the big man as he was screaming in terror deep down inside, but he managed it.

'I don't want his bloody pissann,' Bili's voice was hoarse from his cries of pain and fear. 'I want Dani. Please get my Dani, Grandpa, I know she will help.'

Mr Poole nodded and looked at Rook. 'Can we fix it so she isn't caught?'

'Of course we can. Do you think I dare face her if we don't fetch her?' Turning to Neera, Rook asked. 'Can you keep watch for the bastard and his offspring, Neera? Danielle will be able to heal Bili without herbs or knives.'

With a look to the captain for permission, Neera nodded and both men moved off at a quick march to go and fetch the girl. Within a few minutes, she walked through the door to sit the other side of the boy. The surgeon walked in and frowned at her and the room in general.

'What is going on, gentlemen?'

'The slave is a healer. She will be able to help the boy without having to knock him unconscious. Bili wants her to try and, as he is the one in pain, I say we give the girl space.' Rook's voice sounded harsh to his own ears but he was angry at this puffed up little snot. Talking like that about Bili and frightening the youngster to death was just wrong but sneering at Danielle had made the pugnacious fighting man even angrier.

'I cannot allow this. No, no, gentlemen, if you allow the slave to try anything then I will feel bound to report her to the proper authorities when we dock in Mertam. I will also have to report her to her Master who is upon the ship.' His voice had gone back to being cold and cutting. At his words, voices rang out in confusion and anger, all talking over each other until the voice of Captain Levi Poole cut through everyone else.

'Enough! Am I the only one who remembers that we have a hurt child here?' Turning to the surgeon he spoke quietly but firmly, giving no one any option to ignore his orders.

'You, sir, will comply with ships rules and ships rules say anything I damn well want them to. If my brother wishes our grandson to be treated by a Healer rather than a surgeon, so be it. If, however, you feel it is your duty to report her to the "*authorities*", let me remind you that I am the "*authorities*" upon this ship. Attempt to speak out when we dock and I will deny that anything has happened and will guarantee that you will never work aboard any ship ever again. You are a damn good doctor but you must overcome your fear and hatred of the magikers if you wish to go on working at sea. For now, the girl will work on the boy and you will be quiet!'

Flushing with rage the surgeon opened his mouth to speak only to find the tip of a knife touching the skin under his chin. He froze and gulped as Rook whispered in his ear.

'Be very careful just what you say next, leech. That boy is precious to us; you have no idea just how precious. Keep your mouth shut and if I hear that even a whisper has got back to the scavs on board I will make you pray for death.'

Looking down into the ice-cold eyes glaring into his, the surgeon croaked out vague platitudes that could have meant anything. Rook gave an approving grin that held no warmth at all. 'If I scare you, that is good, mate, but you need to remember summat else. Out of all of us in this room, I am the least of us. Anyone of these could kill you quicker, quieter or draw it out much longer than I could. And the girl? Being raped repeatedly by those posh bastards must have done summat to her brain, don't ya think? My old Ma used to say "what can heal can always harm." So, you still want to open your fat gob? Or do you want to sit down there and watch her work?'

After a frozen moment, the surgeon moved and sat down on a small stool at the back of the room. About to capitulate and give permission for the healing to take place he was annoyed all over again to find that the damn slave had already begun. He sucked in a sharp breath. Samuel was standing guard by the door and casting a long, cold look at the surgeon. Oh, One's breath, had he heard what had been said? Is that why he looked so coldly at him? Before the surgeon could think, or say, anything else he saw something from the corner of his eye and whipped his head round in shock.

The slave girl had placed her hands over Bili's body, one resting lightly on his hip, the other gently on the twisted knee. As had happened before, her skin slowly took on an eerie glow as her face tipped up, her eyes rolling back in her head. Her hands seemed to glow ever brighter and all in the cabin could feel her power beginning to rise as the air became thick and hard to breathe. The sound of thunder could be heard far off in the distance as they all saw the flickers of black lightning appear from the shining light around her hands, beginning to move speedily over and around Bili's leg.

Taking a chance, Rook undid the boy's britches and pulled them off, only wincing slightly when a strand of energy caressed his hands and moved up him before dissipating into his face. With no material to have to work through, the energies flickered even more strongly, striking at the small leg, knee and foot of the boy with stripes of black as fine as thread. The end of the bone that had made such an ugly wound began to sink back into the boy's leg even as his opened flesh began to close up. His face stayed serene as he half sat up and watched the proceedings with immense interest whilst leaning against his grandfather's chest and absently stroking the gryphon's head to keep her calm. Even she too, watched with interest.

The crooked set of the leg began to straighten out and a small pile of splinters and dirt trickled out and off his body. Within minutes, his pale and waxy skin took on a healthy glow even as the young bruises disappeared. No one said anything or made any sound as they saw the energy striking over to his other leg before moving in flickering steps upwards. Jagged streams ran over his hips and torso into his neck and head before moving down and disappearing out of the end of Bili's fingers onto the floor below. There was a stunned silence that lasted a few moments before anyone stirred. The boy relaxed and snuggled up to Arjannett as he fell into sleep even as the last of the energy dissipated and Danielle was caught by the captain as she slumped down, just catching her before she fell face down over the youngster.

'By the One,' whispered an awed voice from the doorway. Spinning around, Samuel froze as he looked into Lady Constance's stunned face. 'She is...'

'An Abomination, yes, we know.' The surgeon was so angry that this chit of a girl had done something that he, even with all his training, could never have achieved. There was also a sense of bitter relief as now all the secrets were out in the open and he hadn't said a word. In fact, it was the Keeper's own lack of sense that had given them away. Caught up in his own sense of righteousness and anger he didn't see, and would not have cared he had, the hatred in Samuel's glance or the disdain in her Ladyship's. Lady Constance moved forward and scooped Bili up into her arms, ignoring the gryphon's squawk of surprise, before turning around to face the room.

'I was actually about to say she is a miracle, Doctor.' And the ice in her tone let the surgeon know just how wrong he had been about the lady.

Chapter Twenty-Six

Carrying the boy from the doctor's room, Lady Constance began firing questions as to the slave's needs. Speaking briskly to find out what was wanted, she headed a small procession to the shared cabin belonging to the Keeper and slave girl, allowing the captain to open the door and Rook to unhook the hammocks. Neera and Zutana appeared quickly, showing no surprise at seeing Lady Constance gently laying the boy down in Samuel's usual sleeping place. They carried a travelling bath between them and Zutana opened the wall to magikally pull up water directly from the ocean to fill it up.

With a growl that cleared away the onlookers, Samuel undressed Danielle completely and set her naked body into the tub. He was stunned to see the way her skin began to absorb the water into herself, sucking up the moisture like a sponge. Zutana kept adding a little more water each time the level in the tub went down too far before she finally nodded her head in satisfaction and silently left, leaving the filled tub behind.

Mr Poole sat near his grandson, back turned to the naked girl and her escort, stroking his big hand gently across the boy's curls. Although Bili insisted on having his head shaved every week, just like Danielle, his healing had caused his hated hair to sprout again. A smile crossed Mr Poole's lips as he wondered at how Bili would react to this. Then he gave a prayer of thankfulness, just grateful that Bili was alive to complain.

After long moments had passed, the unconscious boy opened his eyes smiled sleepily at his grandpa. 'I feel better, grandpa. Too tired to be hungry now but can I have cake when I wake up?'

Elias Poole gave a choked sound before leaning in close and kissing the flushed cheek that only a short while before had carried a deep purple bruise. 'You little chancer. Yes, I will find you some cake but only if you promise to stop scaring me like this.'

His voice stopped as it hit him just how close he had come to losing the boy yet again. He felt Constance come over to them, having left Samuel to wrap the girl in a blanket before placing her on her own hammock. Without conscious thought he found himself leaning into the titled Lady even as her arms slid around his shoulders. A faint press of lips against his scalp had him looking at her in pleased surprise. Ignoring her own actions, Constance moved past him to check on Bili. After a thorough check of the boy for damage and a last word to the hovering gryphon she moved towards the door but stopped as her hand was caught in a large calloused one.

'Don't you want to know what has happened, my lady?' Mr Poole's words were innocuous but the look in his eyes had Constance blushing furiously.

'I already know most of it, sir. I saw the healing the girl did with my own eyes.' All this was calm, almost clinical but Mr Poole could see traces of fear as well as the tear tracks on her face from when she heard the news about Bili's fall. He also saw the wonderment in her features as she remembered the slave girl working her magik.

Ignoring the Keeper, the invalids and every other consideration, Mr Poole then shocked himself and Lady Constance Willoughby, Countess of Brayton, by leaning in close and kissing her gently but thoroughly on her lips in the way he had found himself dreaming of these last few weeks. Straightening up, he waited for her anger to lash out so was stunned when she cupped his cheek and kissed him lightly in return before slipping out of the room. After a moment of astonishment he noticed Samuel looking at him with raised brows and shrugged.

'That lady is something special. Now let's get *our* lady in some night clothes so we can move Bili across to her. They will both rest better together.' With a nod, the Keeper grabbed a shirt of Mr Poole's that Danielle had been mending earlier and slipped it over her head. Elias watched as Samuel laid her onto her hammock, the Keeper blinking in astonishment as he saw that the water that had beaded upon the surface of her skin from the bath had now soaked into her completely, leaving her body as well as the shirt totally dry. Bili was brought over and tucked in next to her and they were both covered over. Inspecting them both, Sam was pleased to see Danielle was not as skeletal as she had looked before when healing Bili for the first time. She was definitely thinner, yes, but without the sharpness of acute starvation. Bili slept deeply and although he, too, looked a little thinner, he wasn't so thin it would worry them for long. With the way the boy ate, it would soon be impossible to notice. Sitting down either side of the hammock, both men let out a sigh of relief before grinning at each other.

'I think that boy is going to scare me to death...or send me bald,' said Mr Poole ruefully. With a pointed glance at the man's hairless head, Sam grunted out a laugh. Catching Mr Poole's eye, he looked the door questioningly.

'What's going on there, Elias?'

'I don't have a bloody clue, Samuel, and that's the truth. Since my Lottie died, I have never thought of another woman. Never crossed my mind that there ever could be a woman for me once she was gone. As for when I first met Lady blimming Constance.' He gave a snort of laughter. 'Well, let's just say I dismissed her as another snob not worth the air she was stealing from me. Blimey, now look at it. I am smitten, I admit. But if she thinks anything of me, son, it is just as a diversion from that perverted scavenger she is married to. I accept that. Once we dock, the family will leave and you two will disappear and I don't expect to see her again. It won't be easy to deal with but then feelings you can't control never are – but you would know more about that than I do.' Settling back comfortably into his chair, the elder man patted himself on the back for turning the tables so neatly upon the Keeper. The wry look that Samuel sent his way showed that he was fully aware of his friend's tactic.

'Mýste take you, old man,' he said. 'As for feelings, mine are all over the place. Yes, I am, or was, attracted physically to Anatoly but his attitude makes me want to punch the man. I also find myself looking at other men. At the card games he got so angry when he realised your brother wasn't actually going to be tupping the slavey, I think because he thought it would make me turn to him, if only because of jealousy. After listening to his tirade against Danielle, I don't want to have anything to do with him at all but we still have to keep things from Willoughby. Bloody Void, it is a mess.' Rubbing his hands over his weary face, Sam gazed at the other man. 'Even if I wasn't going to be getting Danielle away, I wouldn't want that man now. Do you know? I don't even think I ever liked Anatoly really.'

'Well, boy, you only have another few days to pretend. Levi has a plan for getting you both away and we will be helping all we can. You know you are welcome back here, no matter what happens between you and Anatoly, don't you?' At the other's nod, Elias grinned tiredly. 'So let us just work on getting our girl fattened up and Bili back on his feet. Everything else can wait.'

With that statement silence descended on the cabin as life continued as usual elsewhere on the ship.

The evening meal was an almost silent affair. Bili wasn't there as he was still sleeping with Danielle and Arjannett. Markus was flirting madly with the servers as he waited for Neera to arrive. Lord Willoughby drank much less than usual but felt himself becoming tired much more quickly. Lady Constance and Lady Sophia hardly spoke but shared smiles and listened contentedly to the others. The captain and Mr Poole were also quieter than usual, letting Markus' comments float by them. A full hour before their meal usually ended, the company broke up and went their separate ways.

Later in the evening, Markus again gambled Danielle away, as he had done on every night of the journey so far. He, in his turn, won another night with the addictive Air Elemental. Lord Willoughby was in his own cabin, snoring away as he slept heavily. Mr Poole had again added a few drops of the sleeping draught to the old man's brandy.

Lady Constance sat looking out into the velvet black night, overcast with heavy cloud so the stars only sparkled through on rare occasions. Reliving the emotions of the evening, the terror when she overheard Neera calling for Zutana's help and why; the miraculous vision of the slave girl and the healing that took place; followed by the sheer relief that flooded her body when she realised the youngster would be alright. A small inner voice said firmly, don't forget that kiss. Touching her lips gently with her fingers, Constance did think about the kiss, the gentle but firm pressure that had sent thrills through her. She tingled anew at the memory of his lips on hers and his big hands caressing her waist. Thinking of Elias Poole had her truly looking at her own life and what she had now with Willoughby. She saw how Markus had become needlessly cruel and sadistic and how much she loved her daughter who showed more strength than Constance could have imagined back in Harmony. Knowing she could never be happy or even satisfied with the way her life was supposed to continue, Lady Constance began making serious plans about her future.

Sophia watched her mother, not recognising the soft expression on the lady's face. When fingers touched her lips Sophia began to wonder. She knew something momentous had happened that afternoon but she had been down in the cabin, writing in her journal. When her mother had joined her, neither had spoken. Sophia continued defiantly writing while Constance went to the window seat. When she had finished, Sophia slipped into bed and called out a good night. She was pleasantly surprised when her mother came over and slipped into bed before leaning over and kissing her on the forehead as she was wished sweet dreams

Chapter Twenty-Seven

The next few days seemed to be an endless dance as the crew moved around each other in a dizzying pattern, trying to distract the male Willoughbys from noticing the slave's absences. Mr Poole only needed to mention Bili having a cold to satisfy their curiosity regarding the boy not appearing at mealtimes. Not having understood why the young boy had been included in the first place, it didn't cause the aristos any problems not having the youngster there now. On mentioning the fact that the slave hadn't been seen, they were even happier to be informed that Constance had confined the girl to her cabin. She had sewing to do, including a delicate piece of patching needed for a pair of Willoughby's breeches. He missed the flicker of surprise from Sophia, who had already done this particular piece of mending and confined himself with a comment on how she would know proper work fit for a slave again once they landed.

'Damn slavey will be getting soft,' he wheezed before drinking deeply from his glass again. Willoughby found that he hated sea travel with a vengeance and swore it would never be something he willingly took part in again, unless there was no other option. It had turned everything upside down. Constance had changed during this voyage, losing her sneer and her attitude of looking down upon all those she felt was beneath her.

Markus was now both better and worse than before they left Harmony's shores. The younger man had lost his flabbiness, the excess weight previously carried from his drinking, eating and drug use. Since sharing a bed with the Air Abomination, the boy had become too demanding, constantly wanting something new regarding his bed-mates. It promised to be difficult in the future if Markus continued to be so obvious in his needs.

Sophia hadn't changed much, apart from gaining a little confidence; mind you, that would soon be taken care of once they landed. Lord Willoughby had written some important letters to certain men that would soon be visiting to look at the girl once they had settled in a new home. These letters would be sent by the Air Abomination as they got closer to land and the chit would learn her true worth then.

The rest of the party virtually ignored the man as they were used to his drinking, his complaining and his boorishness by now. It was a slightly awkward and mainly silent group that met at mealtimes in the salon. Lady Constance and the crew, as well as the Poole brothers, knew about the slave and had to keep quiet. Anatoly still silently raged about the slave "interfering" with Bili's healing but was too cowed to speak in public after comments made by both Captain Poole and Lady Constance. He sat near Willoughby and glared at everyone impartially. Mr Poole darted glances at Lady Constance when he thought she wasn't looking and ended up being snared by her gaze time and again before both sets of eyes quickly dropped. Markus was becoming irritated at Neera, wanting the Elemental to show more public affection to him. Markus wasn't in love or even particularly in lust any more but he had not yet decided to cut Neera loose and expected the Abomination to show gratification for being chosen at all.

◼️◀◆▶▬

Two nights after Bili had "learnt to fly straight down", as the crewies laughingly put it, they were in the salon eating a dinner. Though artistic in its appearance, and tasting exquisite, it was consumed mechanically as they all wished they were elsewhere. Markus grew bored with the silence. With a sly smile, he decided to stir up some trouble in the quiet room. 'Ah, Captain, will Neera be gambling in here later?'

With a slight frown at the smirking man seated across from him, the captain bit off his words. 'I would presume so, Lord Markus, although I cannot say that he definitely will be. What Neera does in his free time is his own affair.'

'Hmm, he really is delectable even though he is an Abomination. I wonder why that female Abomination never plays a hand? I would like a chance to win her as the prize.'

The silence that followed this extraordinary statement froze everyone in place before Lady Constance spoke. 'Not knowing which lady you mean, Markus, or exactly what you are talking about I would not like to comment. I am, however, displeased that you would speak in such a way, it is so unbecoming for a gentleman.'

Staring directly into the eyes of the captain, Markus threw a bombshell without thought of the consequences. 'The water Abomination. I have seen her behind the ship teaching the boy and some other crew members to swim. She is delectable and well worth tupping, I think.'

A stunned silence greeted this remark before Lady Constance cried out, 'Markus!' in disgust.

The captain stood and threw his napkin down upon his half eaten meal, rage suffusing his features. 'That Water Elemental is called Zutana.' His words were snapped out in fury. 'She is as beautiful as she is kind and she will never play cards in this salon and never be eager for your touch, *boy*. Zutana is also my lady, sir, and I will expect an apology once you sober up. Understand this, you scavenger, it is only because I know you are drunk that I don't break your Plague-ridden head right now'

With that he left the room, closely followed by his brother. Lady Constance and Sophia also stood up and moved towards the door.

'Your manners have been losing ground rapidly over the last few months, Markus,' Constance said coldly, as she moved past. 'I must say though, I didn't expect even you to be quite so crass.'

The door closed with a sharp bang behind them. Markus looked at his father in bafflement. 'What has them so worked up? It isn't as if he is faithful to the freak.'

'Really? And how do you know that, m'boy?' queried Lord Willoughby, not seeming to be much interested. This evening he had drunk a lot less than usual and looked at his son curiously.

With a start, Markus realised he would have to step very warily. As he had been strictly prohibited from gambling the slavey away, he couldn't now say that the captain had taken her into his cabin most nights of the journey so far. 'I have gambled with him, Papa. I know he is enjoys certain favours offered at the table.'

'Remember what he told us back at the beginning of this infernal sea voyage, Markus. Perhaps he settles his conscience by not going too far with one of his wins or by saying it is just a debt of honour. Either way, he obviously doesn't like your commenting about that particular Abomination.'

Understanding that he had better stay quiet about the slave's involvement with the captain, Markus moved closer to his father and filled both their glasses . 'What should I do about this problem, Papa? We still have a little time on the ship.'

After thinking a little, Lord Willoughby looked closely at his son before smiling drily. 'Well, first of all, you do not stay to gamble this evening. Tomorrow morning you will apologise to the captain and say you did not mean any insult but were trying to give a compliment, clumsy as it appeared. As for tonight...' here, his lordship paused significantly in expectation and the younger man leaned forward with eagerness.

'Tonight we will share a cabin and discuss our final plans. I will explain in detail the way we will make the right connections with the right people all over the Coalition. I will also show you some of my own abilities with the Mage power I still have. By this time next year, not only will we be richer and more powerful than we have ever been but we will have removed these Abominations from the world. Finally we'll be free from their sickness and any thought of plague. We, my son, will have everything.'

Chapter Twenty-Eight

As Lord Willoughby led Markus to his room, he prepared to share a little more of future plans. Sitting in the small cabin that had originally been Sophia's, he looked his son up and down. Markus had been exercising more on the advice of Neera, not realising that this was another way to keep him away from Danielle. Consequently, there was hard muscle where there used to be flab, a straighter posture and confidence in his movements that had been lacking. Nothing could change his air of dissatisfaction or the beginnings of dissipation that was showing on his features but Lord Willoughby didn't notice these.

'Now, my boy, it is time to tell you of our plans. As you know, many have tried to make weapons to shoot missiles more quickly and with more accuracy than a bow. No matter how much effort is put into each shooter, they work only once or perhaps twice before exploding. No one has ever found a way to make the bloody things work for longer or more safely, which is why no-one uses them.' Turning away, Lord Willoughby reached into a box and opened it carefully. Markus gasped and pushed back against his chair in fear.

'By the Light, Papa, put the damn thing down before you blow us both to smithereens.'

'Don't be ridiculous, calm down and listen carefully. As you know, I trained as a Mage meaning that I was searched for and then blessed by the Light of the Shining One Himself. Unlike Abominations, Mages are carefully trained and we work within strict guidelines with Masters of the Art who watch over us. I showed great skill in the alchemical arts and was working on perfecting a missile shooter when your uncle died. With permission from the Church, I brought everything with me and have continued to try and get a revolving shooter to work for longer as well as more safely. And now, I have done it! This shooter emits *five* spiked metal balls and it still works again after reloading. Each ball is coated in Mýste. Even if the ball doesn't kill, the Mýste will. This particular piece has been used eleven times so far and is still in working order. A combination of chemicals and magik have succeeded where engineering failed time and again.

'Once we get to Mertam, I will contact certain people through the Church. These are a group who rightly wish to rid the world of Abominations. This group is eager to buy these shooters off me at any price I choose. It takes lots of magik and lots of time, however, so I will need to get more Mages involved with production, which will be so easy to do as the Preceptors of the Faith want every FreeLander dead, whether they are Abominations or not. We will be rich, my boy, richer than your mother ever was. You also have a job to do; you will be making connections with your peers and finding more outlets for our product. Hard work will be needed but also your charm and wit. Are you with me?'

Markus looked at his father for a few heartbeats before breaking into a smile. 'Oh yes, Papa, I am certainly with you. It wasn't just the law changes that had you wanting to leave Harmony, was it?'

'No, it wasn't, although freeing slaves did play a part in my decision. Some of the Council were unhappy with the thought of these shooters, they said it would be inhuman to use them. I say that as we will be ridding the world of vermin, we *need* something inhuman.'

'Well said, Papa. And we will be rich. What will you do with Mamma then?'

'Get rid of her, of course. Now, not a word to anyone, especially on this ship. All of the Abominations here could cause us some inconvenience. I cannot wait to get onto dry land and begin.' Taking up a bottle of port, he poured them both a drink to celebrate before corking it and setting it aside. 'No more frolicking until we reach land, my boy. We have to be extra careful for now.'

Markus heaved a sigh of regret at the loss of his various bed-mates then thought of all the gold he would eventually have to play with. He sipped his drink and smiled at the bright future ahead and then at his father, who was examining him in return. One smug expression was the mirror of the other.

Neera slid out under the door of the cabin in his True Form. He felt sick at what he had heard rushing straight to the captain. After telling all, Captain Poole leaned back in his chair and looked to his brother.

'So, what do we do now? If we kill them, we still won't know who Lord Willoughby has contact with. We don't know how much he has talked about the production of his shooters. So, as much as I want to tear both of them to shreds, I think we must just watch for now and learn all we can, even after they land and are at their new abode.' He turned back to the Air Elemental. 'Neera? Do you have anyone close that you can trust to help?'

Neera thought and then nodded. 'I know of a few that will help. Some Elementals but also Fae and 'shifters. So, we search out all who are involved with this plot to kill magikers...then what?'

'Why then, my friend, then we cut off the head of the snakes.'

The ship's surgeon's whole sense of self belief had taken a severe beating. Being an invert, he knew staying at sea was a safer place for him to be than on land, so had joined this crew with no thought of how different life would be. Finding that he would have to live beside Abominations was a big shock to his system but he had to admit to himself that many of the stories he had been told about their depraved natures had turned out to have no connection to the beings he had reluctantly come to know. To find that his own attitudes regarding the way of the world were treated with pity and condescension by many of those he thought beneath him had hurt his pride. Even after that, Anatoly wasn't sure what to think. He had seen the male Willoughbys in action and didn't exactly find them appealing. Lord Willoughby's disdain for anyone aboard ship, whether Abomination or not, as well as Markus's attitude in thinking that everyone and everything was there for his convenience made Anatoly really question his own attitudes. With a slow understanding, he solemnly decided that he had a lot of making up to do.

Danielle was much restored after two full days of nothing but constant eating and sleeping. She and Samuel were surprised when Anatoly knocked on the cabin door just after dawn the following day. As he stepped into the room, he gave them both a slightly awkward bow.

'I have come to apologise to your slave. I have treated her as less of a person on this voyage, purely because I could not accept that life for her is as bad as you have said. I now know that life been truly terrible for her. Although I cannot make up for my past behaviour, I hope that the few days we have left will be enough to show you, Samuel, that I have accepted the error of my ways.' Anatoly then caressed the Keeper's cheek. 'I know that she doesn't understand me, the Numb takes care of that. After seeing her healing gift, however, I realise that there are more secrets being hidden from me than I thought. No matter, I will wait as long as you need me to, my love. I understand why you seek to protect this woman. If you need my help, just ask.' Placing a gentle kiss on Samuel's lips, he gave another bow to them both before stepping quietly out of the cabin. As he shut the door behind him, Anatoly couldn't help smirking at the thought of the stunned face behind him and he walked away, confident that now Samuel really would be his.

Back in Danielle and Samuel's room, the Keeper was scowling fiercely at the closed door.

'Sam?'

He turned to look at her, trying to relax as he met her questioning look. 'I am as mad as hell now, Dani. I have been telling him for bloody weeks there is a reason for us sneaking around. He says he loves me and that he trusts me yet it is only when he sees something that *he* doesn't like does he feel able to take my word. He'll think that everything is fine between us, because he has been man enough to admit his mistake, *again*! All I feel is anger at the fact that he thinks his attitude, and the pressure he put on me for this whole journey, is forgiven and forgotten so quickly and easily.'

Before Danielle could respond, Neera knocked and entered with the breakfast dishes and fresh brewed coffee. 'Good morning, my loves,' he said brightly. 'What was our esteemed surgeon smirking about as he left here? Did he get lucky at last?'

Too late, the Elemental saw Danielle shake her head as Samuel gave a growl of anger and threw his uneaten toast down.

'I am going to speak to Levi,' was all that the Keeper said before slamming out of the room. With a sigh, Danielle glared at Neera before explaining what had happened.

'The surgeon may be under the impression that Samuel will turn to him but I don't think so. The way Sam feels is that the surgeon should not have needed any outside proof but should have trusted in him. It may just have settled things at last but I doubt if it is in the doctor's favour.'

'Blast it, Danielle, I didn't know, I swear!' Neera sounded almost frantic. 'I was busy getting breakfast sorted. I hadn't heard anything about this. I know that father and son were together last night and shared some of what will happen on land. I was going to tell you both about it now, but I didn't expect Anatoly to come here and...' His voice trailed off as he shook his head in disbelief. 'That man is a bloody menace.'

Danielle nodded her head in agreement and began eating as she listened to what Neera revealed about what had happened the night before. Once breakfast was over, she got on with her usual routine, being careful not to make any comment when Samuel came back to help her sweep and scrub the cabin. Slowly he began to speak and smile but even so, he stayed subdued for the rest of the day.

After lunch, Danielle got changed into the loose shirt and under-drawers combination that she wore for swimming. Knowing that Markus had mistaken her for a crewie had made her smile when she heard it the night before from Mr Poole and she went down to the galley to pick up her drink and snack that Leonid prepared for her. As she stepped in, she saw the bloodling standing there with his head bowed, looking completely exhausted.

'Leo?'

He looked up slowly and smiled at her, his face lined and grey. 'Hello, my little one. Is it time for your snack already?'

Turning away, he reached to lift down a tray of pastries, jumping a little as he moved back and saw her directly in front of him. 'By the Plague, sweeting, you move as fast as the lightning bolts you shoot from your hands!'

As she opened her mouth to speak, Leonid just shook his head at her before calmly wrapping three of the delicacies in a linen cloth and filling a stone-wear bottle with some cold milk. 'No words, my lovely. Everything lives and dies to a natural cycle, hmm?'

Danielle felt her sight and hearing begin to fade out and moving as slowly as if she was still Numbed she stepped closer to the bloodling who was looking puzzled and seemed to be calling her name. Behind her she knew Samuel had stepped into the galley too but she was so caught up in her trance that she couldn't acknowledge him. Reaching down, she opened the blade of the small folding knife that she had hidden on her belt. Taking one of the remaining pastries off the plate, she cut off a piece. Then she dug the tip of the sharp blade of her knife deep into her finger, piercing her skin and allowing the drops of blood to spill onto the small piece of sweetmeat. In a voice completely unlike her own, she demanded that the bloodling eat. Flicking a confused glance at Samuel, Leo bent his head as if he had no choice and opened his mouth to accept the pastry. A few drops of blood from Danielle's cut finger fell into his mouth directly, unadulterated with food.

Breathing deeply, Leonid felt the rush of power hit his system. Gasping involuntarily, he braced his arms on the worktop, letting out a moan of almost orgasmic pleasure as all of his aches, pains and breathing difficulties disappeared in one fell swoop. His head fell back and he cried out again as his body began to shake with the energy rushing through him. A strong set of arms enfolded him in a protective embrace and stopped him hitting the floor as his legs collapsed. It was as if he was caught in a hurricane unable to connect with the earth again and so those arms held him safe and he clung on desperately as he felt himself tossed about in a manic dance. He could hear nothing but a rushing sound as if a hundred mile an hour wind was flying by. He could see nothing but the bolts of black lightning flashing in front of his eyes. They grew and separated, flickering directly through him as well as around him, full of the elemental energy of a true storm.

Unknown moments later he found himself coming to, being cradled in Samuel's arms. He felt wrung out emotionally as well as physically exhausted. Tears had run down his face and he had sweated profusely. His biggest embarrassment was seeing the stain at the front of his britches. It would have been bad enough if it had been urine but this was the pink tinge of semen. Slowly his senses cleared and he saw Danielle leaning against the worktable with tears running down her face, whispering apologies over and over again. Sam's voice rumbled in his ear, fear and worry colouring each query into Leonid's state of health.

'Enough, both of you,' he cried out, surprising them all with the strength of his voice. 'I am alright, I swear. In fact, I am so much better than I have been for a long time. Samuel, help me up. My legs are a little shaky now. Danielle, please stop apologising. You did something I have not seen or heard of in many years. My sweeting, you have given me both new life and new hope.'

Standing up eventually, Leo reluctantly moved away from the Keeper's support. He grimaced at himself as he looked down before shaking his head and taking a deep breath. Refusing to look at the Keeper, he began heading for the door before stopping at Danielle's side. 'Why did you do this, my little one?'

She shook her head in confusion, her face tear stained and her eyes filled with fear. 'I don't know, Leo, I swear. I am not even sure what I have done. I saw you and I knew I had to do something. You have a job to do, you can't go yet...I don't even know why I said that...what am I? What...?'

Ignoring the state of his clothes the bloodling hugged her to him before giving her a little shake. 'Enough of this. You are letting panic affect your mind. No matter what you have been taught in that hell hole you come from, no matter what that piece of trash around your neck says, my lovely, you are one of us; a magiker. So, dry your tears and go and swim. That will heal you and refill your energy. I need a rest just now but later you will have such a feast!'

With a watery smile and a hug, Danielle continued on through to the small platform built at the side of the ship and dived straight down to Zutana who felt the distress coming off the slave in waves. She decided not to ask questions but to get the girl down deeper under the water quickly.

Back in the galley Samuel cleared his throat before asking if there was anything he could do to help the cook. With a shake of his head, Leo grinned at the Keeper. 'Not right now, my friend. All I want to do is get back to my cabin and wash and change. I am a mess. I will have a short sleep to recover my equilibrium before beginning the remainder of tonight's meal. I may need some help then if you still wish to lend a hand.'

'As long as you are going to be alright, I will leave you to some peace and quiet.' Walking to the entranceway of the galley Sam paused, 'If you want anything of me, you only need to say, Leo.'

Leonid blinked as the Keeper went on his way, wondering if he had been reading too much in what Samuel had just said. He grimaced and went into his own cabin, set off from the galley. There he had a full wash before changing completely and sleeping for a full hour.

Leo kept his promise. A feast fit for a king was set before them at dinner. The champagne was opened which was appreciated by all. Lord Willoughby had contrived to cut back on his drinking for the evening and consequently had been a convivial companion, even if some of his comments had made certain people grind their teeth behind fake smiles.

'So, Captain, how much longer before we dock?' he asked, pushing back from the table and moving through to sit in the more comfortable seats. The captain raised an eyebrow at this breach of protocol and, with an apologetic look at the ladies, moved after the obnoxious man. The others followed with Constance rolling her eyes in exasperation.

The captain waited for the others to settle themselves before responding to Lord Willoughby's question. 'Tomorrow evening will be the last one at sea, sir. We will dock a little later than now, giving you the option of staying on board or going to a hotel nearby. Tomorrow the crew will be busy sorting the ship out and I would appreciate it if you could all pack your belongings for yourselves as there won't be anyone free.'

'The slavey can do it. No point asking Patcher, he has hardly stirred from his damn cabin since we left Harmony, it was a complete waste of time bringing him. A choice between staying here or being able to sleep in a big soft bed on land. Hmm, no offence, Captain, but I think a hotel will be just what is needed.' Laughing uproariously at the thought of finally being able to take up his proper position again, he missed the dismay on the faces of many around the room, including his wife and daughter. 'So tonight was a celebration, hey? No wonder the food was so good. I would send compliments to the chef if he wasn't a damned Abomination.'

Lady Constance glared at her husband and with a glance at Mr Poole she stood and left the room, Sophia following close behind, both murmuring quiet apologies. Neither Willoughby nor his son noticed Mr Poole sneak off at the same time as both were too busy sharing stories about Abominations and the punishments they received on Bisra.

Mr Poole collected Bili from Neera's care and, with Arjannett flying about their heads, they both headed below deck. Bili skipped ahead of his grandfather and surprised the man when, instead of heading for Danielle's cabin, the youngster went to the galley instead. An even bigger surprise awaited him as he saw Lady Constance shaking hands with the chef. Sophia was exclaiming at the hand painted tins which held spices and herbs. Constance finished expressing her heartfelt gratitude to the bloodling and turned to the galley entrance, smiling down at Bili, her eyes widening at the sight of the gryphon settled upon his shoulder.

'No wonder this is your favourite place to be, young man,' she said with a twinkle. 'Someone who can keep up with your appetite is a definite genius in my opinion.' Her laughing gaze turned and met Mr Poole's as he grinned at her comment. Whatever she saw in his dark eyes brought a delicate blush to her cheeks. Watching them both, Sophia was pleased to see that someone else could see the beautiful woman her mother really was but she also felt sad that this magical journey was coming to an end. A tug on her hand turned her to look at Bili.

'Don't be sad, Sophie, the adventure ain't over yet, not by half!' With a quick hug around her waist, Bili accepted a cake and some strips of dried meat from the smiling Leonid and went out of the crowded galley to visit "his" Dani. The others grinned at his shortening of the girl's name. For Bili, this was a habit with those he liked and cared about. If he couldn't actually shorten a name, he used an initial instead. If nothing else, this proved how he trusted both the girl and her mother.

Sophia began to follow him before a gentle word from the chef stopped her and her face lit up with pleasure at the thick package of papers he handed over to her.

'Most of my recipes I hold in my head now, my lady. So here is the cookbook I began my apprenticeship with. You use it well, add to it, make changes to suit your own palate and then, when you no longer need it, pass it on to someone else.'

Sophia exclaimed with delight as she began flicking through the pages before pulling herself up with a blushing apology. 'This is wonderful, sir, I am sure that I don't deserve it. Thank you so much, it is, oh...' breaking off before she began to babble, Sophia reached up and kissed the man on his cheek. With another whispered remark of gratitude, she slipped past her mother and Mr Poole to head back to the cabin and begin to look through her treasure.

Lady Constance had watched this all, smiling with pleasure at the gift and the positive energy between the other three. As Sophia left and Leonid ostentatiously turned to the ovens, Mr Poole took her by the arm and they stepped out into the empty corridor.

Lifting his other hand he stroked the back of his fingers down Constance's cheek, looking into her eyes intently. 'A while ago I gave my name to someone and told them if they ever needed help all they had to do was get a message to me. They did and it sent me on an adventure that I could never have predicted. I gave away a business, found new friends as well as a grandson and got reacquainted with a brother. I found that I have enjoyed it all. What I never expected, however, was to find a woman who could fill the emptiness left by my Lottie.

'No, shush now,' his fingers slid lightly across Constance's cheek to caress her lips quiet as she opened them to speak. 'I don't expect you to say anything or do owt either, lass. What I feel is my own and you have a husband and children and a way of life I can never hope to provide. Just know that if you ever need me, get a message to someone at the Wharf Rat inn, it isn't a nice place but Neera reckons that all messages to us will not get lost. As soon as I get it, I will come and find you. Remember, I don't care how long it takes, I will come if you call.'

Constance felt her eyes fill with tears as she listened to this wonderful man. How she wished things were different now but she knew she would have to be very careful and to make the changes in secret for the life she wanted. If she slipped up or rushed too quickly she could lose her very life. Turning her head, she kissed his palm before laying his hand against her cheek again.

'If you had known me in Harmony, you would have been disgusted by me. I'm ashamed and disgusted by who and what I was. This adventure has given me so much I treasure even as it has peeled away some of the dross I had become.' Pausing for a moment, she stepped fully into the strong arms of the man who had begun to mean the world to her. 'I have to think and plan, my dear. My daughter is the one I have to protect, even at the cost of everything I now hold dear. Willoughby and I can never reconcile. I will make sure that I am never in a position where he can use those damn drugs on me again.' At Elias Poole's growl of anger, she kissed him tenderly.

'We cannot change the past but I promise you that once I know that Sophia is safe from his plots and schemes then I will send a message to you. Markus is a lost cause now. Whether it is all his upbringing or whether he has natural tendencies no longer matters to me. I tried to be a good influence when he was younger but I see now that all I have done is give Willoughby more power. Markus enjoys it to the hilt. I hate saying this about my own flesh and blood but he is a nasty, vicious man, in the same way that he was a nasty, vicious boy. There was only ever one person who might have prevented this happening. I promise to tell you all about him, one day.' Kissing him again, neither was prepared for the passion that flared as the kiss deepened in intensity. Breaking it reluctantly, Elias rested his forehead on hers.

'I would make love with you now, sweet, but you would begin fretting about it come morning. Just remember that when you call, I will come. Now let me escort you back to your daughter before she gets the right idea about us... or my will weakens.' With a grin, he leaned in for another kiss, which left them both breathless before they reluctantly began to move to the cabin she shared with Sophia.

'It is a bit late to hide this from Sophie.' She smiled as she used Bili's name for her daughter. 'I think she knew how I felt before I did. Now let me know if there is anything I can do to keep Willoughby and Markus distracted while you and the Keeper get the slave girl away.'

A snort of laughter escaped him before Mr Poole shook his head. 'As always, you amaze me, darlin'. How did you know?'

'Don't be silly, Eli! It is obvious that this whole ship has been protecting her...no, don't look so worried, neither Willoughby nor his son will have noticed. Both are too bloody arrogant. One has spent the journey trying to finish all the wine your brother has on board while the other has spent it trying to swive every crew member that stood still for longer than a minute. They won't have noticed anything and Patcher has spent his time unaware in bed. It is only Sophie and I who have realised anything unexpected is going. I hope you know that you can trust us by now?'

As he opened his mouth to respond, a hissed ''Ware!' sounded in the air around them. Instantly, Mr Poole gave a bow to Her Ladyship who accepted it with a regal nod before turning to open her door and stepped inside. Moving away, angry that his conversation had been cut short, Mr Poole saw Patcher standing just around the corner, trying to stay unseen.

'Yes, Mr Patcher?' Mr Poole looked at the man with distaste.

'Nothing, Mr Poole. I was just coming to check on the ladies, see if they need anything. Seems my belly is settling down now we are near land.' A smirk followed these words and Mr

Poole had to restrain himself from punching the centre of the self-satisfied face , much thinner than the few weeks before.

'Well, that is a good thing then,' was all he said in reply. 'You will be up to doing some of the hard work on the morrow then, won't you? Not even managing the morning tea hasn't pleased his lordship but don't worry too much, we made sure he knew you was ill.' With a short nod, Elias headed towards Danielle's cabin, to let the rest know that Patcher was now awake and on the prowl.

Chapter Twenty-Nine

The following day was a busy one onboard. Patcher was in a sulky mood as he packed for the men of the household. The state of Markus's attire was disgraceful yet the ex-butler couldn't complain that the wretched slavey hadn't done her job. For most of the voyage she had only been allowed to empty the chamber pot before Markus threw her out so that he could sleep or grope one of the crew. The butler's day was therefore filled with cleaning the men's cabins and packing every single thing as Lord Willoughby was determined to sleep on land at an Inn even if it was below his preferred standards, he had had enough of being aboard ship.

The slave did the same for the women but there her work was halved since the two ladies shared one room and had done much of their own packing over the previous two or three days. Danielle stayed in the ladies' cabin until lunchtime, talking quietly with Samuel about possible futures for them, secure in the knowledge that she was there with permission and understanding. In the meantime, the women sat sewing in the salon, talking very little but listening to the raucous noises made by Lord Willoughby and his son as they disparaged the ship, the journey and the crew as they drank wine in the War Room. The men's disgust at sailing with Abominations was loud now that the journey was almost over.

Constance gave a slight start as she was pulled from a very pleasant daydream by her daughter's quiet voice.

'You will leave him eventually, won't you, Mamma?'

'Oh yes, dear, I don't think I have any choice in the matter now,' replied Lady Constance not even pretending to misunderstand her daughter.

'And of course, it has nothing to do with Mr Poole...' Gaping at her daughter's sly comment, Constance saw Sophia's eyes bright with humour and dissolved into a fit of giggles that set her daughter off too. The sudden shocked silence from the two men in the adjacent room struck them as even funnier and they laughed even harder.

In the main cabin Danielle asked Samuel what he now felt he should do about the surgeon. The Keeper shook his head. 'Nothing.'

As she raised her eyebrows, he realised that he wouldn't be allowed to get away with leaving it like that. With a sigh, he elaborated.

'I am attracted to him still, but I don't trust him. He would have had me leave you to the attentions of anyone as long as he got what he wanted. He even threatened to report you to our Master because you saved Bili's leg. I can't ever be comfortable with that level of selfishness. And before you say that he has changed, I agree that he has been showing a better side of himself these last few days but I cannot truly believe that is more than skin deep. My thoughts are only focusing upon getting you to the FreeLands. I have enjoyed being at sea so I may come back and join the ship, as Captain Poole has offered me a place, but for now I am just working out how to get us both free of the port.'

Danielle nodded and said nothing else. She could see that Samuel was upset but if he didn't wish to speak about it, she wouldn't push. Instead she mentioned the changes in the Willoughbys and how surprising some of those had been.

'Lord Willoughby as a sot is a surprise to me as he has always been so much in control of himself. I think that once he is back on land, however, his rigid control will snap back in force. Markus has only surprised me with his stamina. Many of the crewies have avoided the card games and those who have helped divert his attention only chose to do so once. Well, apart from Neera, that is. Did you know that the Captain offered them all a bonus and only a few accepted it?' Shaking her head in wonder, Danielle didn't see the Keeper hide a grin at her expression. 'The real surprise for me has been Lady Constance; don't you think she is a completely different person from the bitter woman we knew in Harmony?'

'That's what happens when a trapped animal feels a sense of freedom coming. And don't forget that Mr Poole may have something to do with this too.'

Both of them chuckled at the memory of the bemused but pleased look on the burly man's face every time he spoke of Lady Constance.

'Sophia has shown herself to be a much more confident woman nearing her majority of twenty-five, rather than the scared rabbit back in Harmony. I found it hard to remember she was not a child when we were there.' Samuel saw Danielle nod her head before she froze in a listening pose and then leapt up, a dull expression in place as she began stripping off the bedclothes. The door swung open suddenly and Patcher stood there, eyeing them both with a scowl. His scowl deepened as he growled out, 'Master wants us both, leave her here.'

Raising one eyebrow at his tone, the Keeper spoke in a slow but clear voice, commanding the girl to finish stripping the bed, fold the top bedding, dust the room and sweep the floor and if she finished before he got back, she should go to her room. He repeated this twice, while Patcher tapped his foot impatiently, and then they left. Danielle completed the few chores in record time and scurried to her cabin in the hopes that she would be able to avoid Patcher on the journey. Reaching it without incident, she shut the door behind her with a sigh of relief and began sorting out what she needed to take and what to leave behind.

Sometime later she was eating lunch with Leonid, Samuel and some of the crew when Patcher appeared in the galley. Benro followed him a minute or so later, wearing a scowl on his usually amiable face.

'What is wrong, my friend?' queried Leo in surprise.

'Complaints about the cuisine, Leo,' was all the reply he got before the servers went out with the next course. Leo grinned and shrugged his shoulders nonchalantly.

'Ah well. All great chefs struggle to find true appreciation among the peasantry!'

At this comment, Samuel choked on a mouthful of soup and the galley erupted with laughter, quickly muffled. Knowing that the lunch was deliberately plain and basic in a bid to encourage Lord Willoughby off the ship added to the mirth.

After helping with the washing up and scouring of pans, Keeper and slave walked back to their cabin, aware of Patcher's scrutiny. Once inside the room, Samuel shut the deceptively flimsy looking door, knowing it would cut out all noise. Patcher wouldn't be able to hear any sound from within. Danielle sat down and looked at him questioningly.

'Couldn't be better, sweetheart,' Samuel hastened to reassure her. 'The family is moving to a hotel once we dock later but we are being told to disembark early tomorrow morning. The downside is that Patcher's staying onboard with us. Lady Constance tried hard to change minds on this but Lord Willoughby wouldn't budge. He said he needed someone to watch the luggage as my job was to keep any dirty hands off you. Not as wonderful as we hoped but not as bad as we feared.'

Feeling her eyes fill with tears, Danielle wasn't surprised to be pulled into a hug. She snuggled into Samuel's chest, feeling warm and safe and loved. Sensing his worry, she raised her head and gave a wry grin, even has her tears continued to flow.

'I have loved being at sea,' she explained. 'Not just the freedom but the way I have been treated by everyone. I may never again see Mr Poole or Bili or...' her voice choked off and Samuel tightened his arms about her.

'I know, sweeting, I know. These people have become our family and I don't want to leave either. Did you know that the Captain has offered us both a place here? I turned him down because Lord Willoughby could cause him too many problems with the ports in all the New Federated World. Being a Lord on Bisra has given him plenty of connections here on Mertam. Don't you give up on seeing everyone again, though. I asked Bili last night why he wasn't more upset and he just grinned at me and said things were going to be just fine.'

'As it is Bili who said it, we had best listen.' Danielle exclaimed with a watery grin. A light tap on the door froze them both before Samuel opened it an inch or so and then stepped back in shock. Danielle gasped out loud as Lady Constance and Sophia hurriedly slipped in.

'Don't worry, my dears,' said Lady Constance quickly. 'Patcher has gone to help Willoughby pack some neck ties. We must still not tarry too long though.'

She turned to the slave girl and looked at the real Danielle properly for the first time. The slavey was so stunned she didn't even attempt to try to achieve her usual blank expression.

'Hello, my name is Constance Fenchurch,' the Lady said in a parody of politeness and held out her hand for it to be shaken. Her eyes twinkled at the bemused expressions on the faces of both slave and Keeper at the mention of her maiden name. A look at the proffered hand was all the slave needed before she straightened up and clasped her former mistress's hand in hers. 'This is my daughter, Sophie; we are pleased to make your acquaintance, my dear.'

'I am Danielle Wintersborn, Goody Fenchurch, and I am very pleased to meet you both.' She responded formally and with a curtsey. Constance felt a smile bloom and let out a sigh of relief.

'So I was right. You are a real person,' she said, happy to be vindicated. 'We have come to give you some things to help your journey. First though, I am here to beg your forgiveness, though goodness knows, I don't deserve it. I have no excuse for acting like a harridan so I won't give any. All I can hope is that you understand that I am no longer that person.' She turned to Sophia who handed a parcel to Danielle. 'Inside this is a set of male clothing to help to disguise you. They will also make travelling much easier once you get used to them.'

Unwrapping the parcel, Danielle found a pair of strong canvas trousers and a loose shirt of a softer but equally hard-wearing material as well as a set of underwear, more practical than any she had worn before. Lifting the short-legged knickers and the camisole and looking amused, Danielle frowned as she realised that each item of clothing was much heavier than it should be. Lady Constance answered the unasked question.

'Sophia has sewn gold, silver and a few gems into hidden pockets of each item. This will help with necessary bribes and to help you begin your new life. I have also written a letter that gives you your freedom, not that it means anything while you wear the collar. I have tried to get the control mechanism for it, but Willoughby always keeps it on his person. I think he may give control over to your Keeper or Patcher before we go.'

Sophia looked as dubious as her mother to the last comment before taking a small leather wallet from her own hidden pocket.

'I am so glad you have had some life,' the younger woman said. 'The gift of your name humbles me and I will pray that you get where you are aiming for. Here is a tool wallet, similar to one I have myself. Inside you can see needles and thread, a fish hook and strong twine plus a few other bits and pieces to help you. May the Gods be with you both.'

The two were shocked by this comment, which would have had her executed on the spot if heard on Bisra. Sophia stepped forward and hugged both of the dumbfounded servants. As the women turned to leave, Danielle managed to speak past the lump in her throat.

'Thank you both. For the gifts of clothing and tools but also for what you have done for me. I don't need to forgive anything, La – I mean Constance. As I have said to Samuel, we had to do things in certain ways or die.' As Constance opened her mouth to argue, Danielle grinned and held her hand up. 'I saw a lot in my drugged haze and have had time to think about what I saw about the household than I could at the time. Constance, every time you fought against Willoughby – and you did do that a lot in the beginning when I had first arrived – I saw you with bruises. When that didn't stop you, he began to beat Sophia. I would have been disgusted if you hadn't chosen to protect her. Then he began drugging you to keep you compliant; yes, I noticed him sprinkling powders into your drinks and on your food. You have tried to keep Markus as an ally and as a gentleman, you have failed in this more because of his own tendencies than your own efforts. You don't need my "forgiveness" but you do have it, nonetheless, and you have my respect. I do have a serious question now though. May I ask it?'

Constance felt her eyes fill with tears as she looked at the smiling woman in front of her and nodded.

'Are your intentions toward Elias Poole honourable?'

A stunned silence greeted this outrageous query before Constance muffled her face with a handkerchief. Danielle felt worried for an instant before she met the laughing gaze of her former mistress. It took a few minutes for the giggling to subside, during which time the others had found themselves grinning like fools. Mopping her flushed face with the damp scrap of cloth, Constance shook her head at Danielle.

'To answer your impertinent question, Danielle...my intentions are most certainly not honourable! I intend to work out a way that I can have that man in my life and most certainly in my bed. But don't worry, I will be free when it happens and I intend to stay with him permanently.' With a last chuckle before straightening their faces, both the visitors left, wearing haughty masks. As Samuel closed the door, he heard Constance, in full Ladyship mode, demand to know why Patcher was lurking outside the door before demanding his help in moving some luggage up on deck, to be ready to take with them when they left the ship in a few hours. Patcher's response was cut off as the door shut completely.

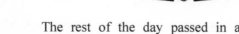

The rest of the day passed in a blur of secret visits, goodbyes, tears and presents. Samuel was given new clothing and boots from the crewies. Bili presented him with a new knife that strapped to the Keeper's forearm but a twist of his wrist would set the blade in his hand. Mr Poole handed him a pouch of small money to pay their way to the place Danielle was drawn to, as well as a pouch of gems to help set up in business or whatever they aimed to do once they had found it. Rook had added some carved runes to Samuel's tipstaff and also some elegant metal arrow heads for his bolts. The captain handed over a book, knowing that this

sleep. Nothing like the butler has had, this is just to help you to relax and let go. It may even help a little with the sorrow.' Handing the drinks over, he nodded to Danielle's hammock and the curled-up figures of Bili and the gryphon. 'He found that when the moment came, it has been more upsetting than he thought it would be. So go and hold him as you sleep, little one.' Smiling at both of them, Leo walked to the door and only raised an enquiring eyebrow when Samuel followed him out. Danielle grinned and swiftly undressed before drinking the hot milk, spiced with cinnamon, honey and something she couldn't quite catch before she settled down and soon fell into a restful sleep.

Touching Leo on the shoulder, just the other side of the door, Sam asked him. 'Don't you want to know why I was cursing, Leo?'

Silently leading the way back to the galley, the cook didn't respond at first. He just began making another set of drinks. Sam watched him moving about the galley, feeling his emotions begin to settle and his own sorrow at leaving becoming less of a burden. Only when the hot coffee with a dash of rum had been set down on the table did the bloodling ask. Hearing the anger building again as Samuel repeated what the surgeon had said Leo reached across and clasped the Keeper's hand.

'Calm down, my friend,' he soothed. 'You are angry and rightfully so, I think, but letting this foolish man affect you so strongly is not helping. So, maybe you were attracted to him but think. His own actions have caused the breach between you. The fact that he does not even recognise the depths of your anger at him frustrates you. You need to stop wishing he was something he is not. He will never understand you. He has a completely different personality. Accept that you are lucky to have realised all of this now, rather than returning to the ship and finding it all out then.'

Thinking over the last comment, Sam examined the slender fingers grasping his own much broader ones. When Leo went to pull his hand back, Samuel gripped a little harder and looked into the dark gaze opposite.

'You're right, Leo,' he acknowledged. 'That man turned my head at first. The more I saw of him though, the less I have found myself liking him. The arrogant way he has spoken about you and the rest of the magikers pisses me off too. The trouble is I have no bloody idea how to cope with attraction or what lust or love is or anything like that. I have hidden away from these emotions all of my life up but now they are out in the open, I am more confused than ever.'

'Drink, my friend.' Leo nodded towards Sam's mug and the big man reached for it with his free hand, keeping hold of Leonid's fingers, absent-mindedly stroking them with his thumb. Taking up his own mug and sipping thoughtfully, Leo eventually spoke.

'First of all, even if you feel that you love another you must *never* feel that your own wants, needs and desires are worth less than theirs. If the surgeon had accepted that you had to support our little Danielle and done what he could to help you both, you would have given way to him before we were far from Bisra. As it is, his habit of trying to force you beyond your comfort levels just made you re-think your connection to him every time.

'You called him arrogant and I agree, he is arrogant but mainly he is just unseeing. He cannot accept that you do not feel exactly the same way as he does whereas you see that you are attracted to him but you also feel the responsibilities to Danielle, your old Master and loyalty to both of the Poole's. He just sees the attraction and wants you to stop wasting time, so he pushes, perhaps thinking that if he touches you at the right time in the right place you will succumb to his blandishments. You could never treat another like this so your anger is in finding out that a man who might have become your first lover is actually not someone you like very much.'

Sam nodded, still studying Leo's hand before frowning slightly, looking up and saying simply; 'Was.'

At Leo's puzzled look, Sam explained. 'I *was* attracted to him, not am attracted.' Sighing gustily, Sam finished his drink and stood up. 'I better get some sleep if I am going to be of any use tomorrow. Thank you, Leo, for the drink, your wise words but most of all, for your friendship.' Stepping around the table, Sam tipped Leo's face up and kissed him gently. Samuel gave himself up to the thrill and the sensation of sharing a kiss with the cook and any last stray feelings for the surgeon disappeared between one breath and the next. Too soon, Leo broke the kiss and wrapped his arms around the Keeper. Tucking his head into Sam's neck, he kissed him there before licking along the skin, feeling a shudder of desire run through them both. Raising his head and looking into the blue eyes that gazed longingly into his own, Leo smiled ruefully.

'I have wanted to kiss you ever since we began this journey. But even if I could do more, I won't.'

Sam frowned and began to speak but Leo interrupted him. 'I want you so much, my friend, but as our Danielle knows, I cannot do more. I am entering into the last stage of my life. I could, without meaning to, turn you into a bloodling if we made love. Only very little of the virus can be passed on through saliva so unless we kissed constantly for days, your immune system would cope with it and kill the little that got through. Semen and blood, however...ah, we have a much bigger problem there. You go now, keep our girl safe. If you come back and I am not yet lost to the sun, we will talk more about this.'

Sam stroked Leo's cheek before pressing a kiss upon his lips. 'I will see her safe. And then I will be back to you.' With another brief kiss, the men reluctantly let each other go and Sam walked back to the cabin where he settled himself and fell asleep quickly, his last thoughts lingering on the bloodling.

Leo finished tidying the little galley kitchen before he too settled to sleep. He found it much more difficult to relax as he kept replaying the first touch of Sam's lips upon his own in his head. He regretted his own hesitation for a brief moment before accepting he could never change anyone just for his own needs. Once a bloodling entered the last stage of his life, there was a compulsion to make another bloodling to take his place, just like humans felt the need to procreate. Leo had decided many years before that he would resist the impulse if he could. He loved being what he was but he chose not to leave a legacy. Snarling in frustration, he prepared himself for a long and restless night.

Chapter Thirty-One

Morning arrived before anyone felt ready for it. The weather was wet, grey and miserable with pouring rain and a cold wind cutting through clothing like a sharp knife. Patcher tried staying in his cabin until the work was done but Neera kept knocking until he got a response. After that, both Patcher and Samuel helped the crewies move the luggage down the gangway and the slave girl carried some of the lighter bags. By breakfast time all the luggage was in a neat pile sitting on the docks and hidden at the far side of it were the two packs that Samuel and Danielle would be carrying when they ran. Samuel was in full Keeper clothing, including his hat, gloves and weapons. He had taken his heavy coat off now as he was sweating from the exertion of the last couple of hours.

Eating heartily, he looked across at Danielle and caught himself before he smiled. Patcher was still watching them both intently. Samuel nodded his head at the ex-butler before reminding Danielle to eat up as they were going soon. Patcher continued to glare at them both. After finishing up, the slave girl began to wash the dishes before Sam told her to stop.

'Time to go,' he said, sounding brusque. Looking at Patcher he asked him. 'Are you coming with us?'

'No, the Master has released me from his service. The tight bastard hasn't even paid my passage back to bloody Bisra. I have had to pay it myself because I was sick all the way here. Don't you be expecting anything extra when you take her to them at the hotel,' he sneered.

'I never expect anything. Come on, slavey, time we were off if I don't want to be in trouble.' With a casual nod of his head Samuel led the way off the ship, forcing himself to keep facing forward even as he wanted to keep a wary eye behind him.

Walking down the slipway carefully, Sam got soaked through very quickly. By the time he stood by the small hill of luggage, he decided not to bother putting his coat on. Once they began running the damn thing would only be in the way, it was so heavy. Danielle was so cold he could hear her teeth chattering. Unlike his own thick clothing, which was warm even when wet, Willoughby had ordered her to wear one of her "special" dresses today. This was thin and flimsy with a very low neck line and no sleeves. Her boots didn't match this delicate dress, being sturdy and dry, but her feet were the only warm things about her. Her head had been freshly shorn and she had no bonnet or hat, neither did she have scarf or gloves. Gritting his teeth, Samuel promised himself that he would make sure that she had something warm and dry to wear as soon as possible. Risking a swift glance up to the ship, he saw Leo watching from one of the galley windows. He smiled and then moved his head to see Patcher glaring at him from the top of the gangway. Masking his mouth with his hand, Samuel warned Danielle about the ex-butler between coughs.

A few moments later Danielle began to casually inch around the luggage towards the packs. They were waiting for Neera's contact to arrive, knowing that a cart from the Master was also due. Sam felt his heart beginning to beat faster and he swallowed, trying to calm himself. He found himself suddenly thinking about Patcher being let go before the slave had been delivered and it suddenly hit him; the control mechanism for the slave collar hadn't been handed over.

A shout of anger interrupted Sam's train of thought. Spinning around he saw Patcher running and slipping down the gangway, waving the box-like controller wildly in his hand all the time spitting and screaming garbled curses out into the pouring rain. Sam lashed out with his stick and caught the butler on the arm but it wasn't enough for the man to drop the box.

'Traitor, you dirty, stinking traitor,' Patcher screamed, still waving the control around. Sam grappled him, trying desperately to reach the box just as a large catlike figure sidled up to Danielle and began pulling at her clothing. Danielle was frozen in place with shock. The insane way that Patcher was screaming and yelling, clinging on to the control box made her think that he had lost his mind completely. She felt a scream building up inside her as she saw Sam's shirt, already wet with rain, soaked with a much darker liquid. The hand that Patcher was repeatedly punching him with held a sharp dagger, slamming into Samuel's flesh again and again. All strength seemed to be leaving him as Sam continued trying to grab hold of the little gold decorated box. He felt his knees begin to buckle and he growled out as loud as he could. 'Run, Danielle, damn you, run!'

He sank to his knees, almost all strength gone, blood pouring from his mouth and his side. Dimly Samuel could hear Danielle screaming "*nahooli*" even as Patcher began laughing maniacally. It began to get dark as his vision blurred and he laboured to draw breath. He could still vaguely hear Patcher but it was difficult to understand what was being said past the roaring in his ears.

'I knew there was somefing different, you doxy! I fucking knew!' Still laughing, with a twisted expression of glee on his lips, Patcher took the time to point the box directly at the stunned slave girl. He could hear people yelling and running towards him from all directions but he was going to savour this moment. The old bastard Willoughby would reward him handsomely. Still grinning, he placed his thumb over the button and began gently pressing. 'You shunt 'ave stopped my fun, you daft git. If you 'adn't stopped my fun, I wunt 'ave 'ad to kill you.'

The button began to depress slowly. In a flash Patcher stiffened in pain and surprise as Sam made a herculean effort. He twisted his wrist as he pushed up from his heels where he had been dazedly watching his life's blood slowly surround his knees with a bright swirl of colour. The hideaway knife, on its first outing, sprang forward and swept up into the black heart of Patcher, slicing it in two. The control box began to fall but Neera, flying off the ship where he had been sleeping just a few moments before, caught it on a cushion of air, preventing the fail-safe of explosive powders from detonating. Samuel fell back onto his heels before toppling slowly over onto his side, his back twisting so that his face looked up at the black clouds above them. His mouth kept moving although nothing could be heard. Danielle rushed towards him, kneeling in a bloody puddle at his side.

'I can heal you; I can heal...' her babbling voice trailed away as he gave a tiny shake of his head.

'Control?' he murmured.

'Neera has it,' she sobbed.

'Then run, Danielle. Run...Danielle, please run...ru...' His voice, quiet as it had been, now faded away altogether. His mouth moved once or twice more but made no sound, before it stopped moving at all. Danielle scrubbed away the tears falling from her eyes to be able to look at her best friend, her brother, her family. As her vision briefly cleared, she saw raindrops hitting his half open eyes. He didn't blink. He didn't move. The only movement now was the ever-widening pool of blood beneath him. Turning her face upwards, she saw some of the crew rushing down towards her while shouts and sounds of battle surrounded her as men on the docks ran in to try and take her. She looked again at the dead face of her brother and her tears stopped as she felt her heart freeze within her breast.

Suddenly she was hauled up in a bruising grip. Mr Poole was there, shouting something at her and shaking her. She just looked at him dazedly.

'Danielle, c'mon girl, focus!' With another fierce shake, Mr Poole saw a spark of anger light in her eyes as she pushed against him. 'Oh no, you don't. For void's sake, get out before the Watch get here and press that bloody button. Samuel gave his life for you so you could escape, don't you dare let him have died in vain.'

Danielle reared back in shock, her eyes filling with tears again and she felt stung by the big man's anger. 'I can't leave him alone,' she cried, her heart a heavy weight within.

'You aren't leaving him alone, are you? You're leaving him with family. Now run, lassie, we'll take good care of him.' His voice was husky with sorrow as she wiped her hands over her face before giving a last glance down at the man she adored. She looked at Mr Poole and gave a short nod before turning on her heel and moving swiftly after the large catlike creature who was now dancing with impatience. As she moved past them, she picked up both packs without pausing and disappeared into the darkness.

Mr Poole looked at Neera who gave the big man the control mechanism before surrounding the Keeper on a cushion of air. The brawny man turned his back on the chaos behind him as sailors and Watch clashed, fought and yelled at each other. He walked up the gangway back onto the ship. His step was as slow and steady as the beat of his grieving, sorrowful, heart.

Chapter Thirty-Two

Lord Willoughby returned to the ship with two men later that afternoon, determined to get the truth behind what had happened earlier. One of his escorts was a dark-skinned man, standing straight and tall in the blue uniform of a Commander of the Port Watch while the other was short and slight, seemingly all grey from his hair to his skin, his suit and highly polished shoes and was a representative of the Council of Mertam. The aristocrat pushed his way into the War Room, grunting with annoyance seeing the brat there with the captain of the ship and his brother, his young face swollen with tears. Both men stayed seated at his precipitate entrance, leaving nowhere for himself to sit down, fuelling his irritation. The captain looked at him enquiringly but didn't speak. It was left to the Commander to begin proceedings. Holding out his hand, he introduced himself.

'Hello, Captain Poole. I am Captain Daventry. We have met once before, I think.'

Without a flicker of expression, Captain Poole half rose and shook hands with the man. He had known Daventry very well over the last twenty years, even having been best man at the Watch Captain's unofficial and unsanctioned wedding to a magiker. 'Captain Daventry. What is going on here?'

'Lord Willoughby has made a serious allegation against you and your crew, sir.'

'Really? And just what does this "serious allegation" consist of?' Captain Poole had not yet formally acknowledged anyone else except the Watch Commander and Willoughby felt his temper beginning to burn.

'You have stolen my property, sirrah, and killed my man.' Lord Willoughby cut through the diplomatic approach and waved his fist at the ship's captain.

'If you are talking about what I think you are, Lord Willoughby, you might prefer to rephrase that. If, however, you persist with the matter I will sue you for slander. You may find things becoming public knowledge that you might otherwise prefer to keep silent about when it comes out in court'

This gave the little man pause for thought. Not only was the captain refusing to be intimidated but there seemed to be something else going on which needed an explanation. Into the quiet, Captain Poole stood up and waved his hand to the main room.

'Gentlemen, if you will follow me through into the salon, I will explain all. Bili, could you go and ask Benro for coffee and pastries for us, please? Check the sick room and sit with our patients after. Good boy.' Watching the youngster as he left the room, Captain Poole allowed himself to relax as he went to settle himself into one of the big armchairs.

Heaving a sigh, he turned to face Lord Willoughby as he spoke. 'As you can imagine, Willoughby, the boy is devastated about the Keeper's death. They got very close with all the travelling they have done together. Bili has had a sheltered life, the death of a friend has hit him hard. It has hit all of us very hard. Your Keeper was a good man and to die in such a way, at the hands of a madman, is almost beyond my understanding.'

Mr Poole would have laughed at any other time, not only at his brother's funereal tones but also at anyone thinking that Bili had ever had a sheltered upbringing. Before the smile came anywhere near his lips, he grimly remembered the events of the day and the impulse to grin faded away before it had begun.

'Now, to answer your comments, sir. I have no idea where your property is. Lying dead in some alley way if the number of times that ex-butler of yours hit the switch on the control mechanism is any indication.' The captain began weaving his version of the events on the wharf, casting doubts upon whatever Willoughby had been told.

The Council's aide spoke up quickly. 'Control mechanism?'

'For the slave,' said the captain, not missing the look of distaste that flickered across the thin man's face. 'What did you think it was for? In fact, gentlemen, exactly what have you been told and who has told you?'

After intense discussion, the coffee arrived and was offered around and everyone helped themselves to the bite-sized pastries. Once the pleasantries were over Lord Willoughby told his story of murdered men and a kidnapped servant, neatly avoiding mentioning the servant was actually a slave. The two brothers listened with growing anger, both fighting for control over their emotions. Once Lord Willoughby had finished his version of events, the captain began to speak.

'Hmm, much of what you have said is correct in itself but a very different and untruthful twist has been put upon it, perhaps by someone wanting a reward, perhaps? I see that you haven't mentioned that the girl who ran off is actually a slave. No matter what happens she will soon be dead from her Numb withdrawal.

'Now as to what really happened. Patcher has been a problem the whole journey. In fact, with my permission, he has occasionally been given a sleeping potion.' Holding his hand up to stem the protests bursting from Lord Willoughby, the captain waited for quiet before he continued. 'I don't mean that that the man was permanently drugged or even that we had anything to do with his sickness. At the beginning of the voyage the Keeper was getting anxious about Patcher's behaviour. He had been caught looking at certain items of clothing belonging to the slavey. Samuel warned him, thinking it might be a simple case of theft. That is when the butler told the Keeper that he knew secrets that could get his master, meaning you my Lord, arrested. When the Keeper asked for clarification, Patcher just laughed and walked away. Sometime later, he was seen touching the slave girl inappropriately. Still he laughed at Samuel's warning.'

'He kept dropping hints about secrets Lord Markus had let slip and how he would be a rich man in the end. When Samuel caught him going through Lady Sophia's undergarments, well, that was the last straw. Not wanting to cause trouble for Lord Markus and not being willing to let the bastard get away with what he was doing, Samuel came to me. He told me he had tried to speak with you but, well, you were a little distracted at the time by my wine cellar and didn't seem to understand the importance of what the Keeper was saying. That is when we added a little sleeping powder occasionally to Patcher's evening drink.'

The captain paused here, obviously waiting for some comment from Willoughby but he appeared uncomfortable, trying to remember when the Keeper had spoken but unable to dredge up anything specific. He vaguely remembered something about a concern but, no, it had gone. With a cough, Lord Willoughby just waved the captain to go on with his story.

'Patcher seemed to become bitter, for whatever reason. He began watching your daughter closely, following her down corridors and knocking on her door. He was constantly spotted by members of the crew, touching Lady Sophia's under garments and also touching himself. Once your daughter had left the ship yesterday, he began trying to touch the slavey again. When the Keeper warned him off and sent the slavey down to wait by the luggage, Patcher started screaming obscenities and pressing the button on the mechanism. The Keeper protected her, as was his job but Patcher seemed to be completely insane and began stabbing out with a knife. So you see, Lord Willoughby, it was your own butler who began the whole thing and caused the deaths of himself, the Keeper and, ultimately, the slave.'

Finishing his narrative, Captain Poole rang for Benro to fetch the surgeon before drinking his own coffee, much cooled now. The surgeon came in a few minutes later, looking tired. A swift look at his captain and he confirmed that both of Willoughby's men were dead from stab wounds. The girl's fate was unknown. He was subdued and spoke in an empty, defeated tone of voice. Staying in the background, listening quietly, Mr Poole felt eyes upon him and looked up to see the captain of the Watch looking at him closely.

After another thirty minutes of repeating the same stories, Lord Willoughby ended the conversation by handing over a purse full of coins for the family of the fallen Keeper to help with his death ceremony. Mr Poole gave his word to make sure the Keeper had a proper send off. Lord Willoughby didn't actually care but nodded his head as if in agreement.

'So before we leave, gentlemen, where is the control mechanism?' Impatient to be gone, his voice was sharp and demanding. The two brothers looked at each other in astonishment before shaking their heads at the short aristocrat.

'We have no idea, sir. In the heat of the fighting, we didn't stop to look for it. Perhaps you will find it when you move the luggage?' Captain Poole answered in a cold tone of voice. He refrained from glancing towards where the control box was hidden in a locked drawer of his solid oak desk. At the scowl that ran across Lord Willoughby's face, Captain Poole leaned forward and spoke quietly.

'May I have a private word, sir?'

With a slight frown, Willoughby considered for a moment before nodding his head. Both men moved towards the War Room, leaving Mr Poole to answer the questions about Samuel, the slave and the actions of Lord Willoughby and his son. Neither official was impressed at what they heard regarding the aristocrats but felt that this version of the story spoke well for the Keeper and seemed more truthful than the version they had been given when Lord Willoughby had first approached them for justice.

Once inside the small room, with the door firmly shut, the captain asked permission to speak plainly. Intrigued, the Bisranese aristocrat gave a sharp nod.

'Patcher was not as ill as he made out, Willoughby, as was obvious from what I have just told you. In the aftermath of the fighting, I had questions asked of the whole crew and many have come with the same information. Neera is our usual overseer of the ship. Needing almost no sleep, he moves about, keeping a watchful eye on things. Before he was distracted by your son, the Air Elemental often saw Patcher sneaking around, intimately touching the slave girl, stealing food and searching your family cabins. Not, I am sure you will agree the actions of an ill man. Also, he made certain allegations against you and your family.'

'Allegations? What allegations? How dare he!' spluttered Lord Willoughby.

'Well, the first thing he said was that you knew nothing about the slave girl being offered as a bet by your son at the gambling tables. I know, of course, that Lord Markus would never have dared to offer her without your permission. I am very pleased to have won such a prize on more than one occasion. Having her as an attendant meant that I could enjoy special nights with my own lady while your slave prepared food and cleared away, giving us privacy from others and allowing me the precious time to concentrate on Zutana. So I thank you for your generosity.

Although I am afraid your son is under the impression that the slave and I shared a bed, I can assure you that we did not.

Patcher spoke other lies that were much more worrying. One of them was that he had wished to have had the slave more often when you were all back in Harmony but he was unable to drug the Keeper as much as he wanted. He also spoke most disparagingly about Lady Sophia. Patcher seemed almost obsessed with her Ladyship, saying he would have paid anything to have been the first to tup her but he was too late. He also made comments about you and Lord Markus sharing more than just the slave but I know, at least I hope, that most sensible people will dismiss those rumours out of hand.'

Lord Willoughby felt himself growing angrier by the minute as each revelation hit him like a physical blow. The fact that Markus had gone against specific instructions regarding the slave had him questioning the boy's judgement yet again. The rest of the comments made him reconsider some of the times he had noticed certain things that seemed out of place on the journey but he had been so befuddled with drink, he had foolishly dismissed his own intuition. Now he began thinking and seeing certain actions in a different light. The days when they were still in Harmony and the Keeper seemed slower to move than usual and the slave had unexpected bruises, always explained away by Patcher as her being clumsy, yet she was not a clumsy girl. Meeting the butler coming out of Sophia's room on more than one occasion and the look on his daughter's face sometimes when she met Patcher unexpectedly. The way the man kept pushing for a private conversation after he had been in Markus's cabin a few weeks before. Perhaps a good job it had never happened, the damn fellow seemed to have been thinking of blackmail. As for thinking that Polite Society would be generous and believe that Willoughby and his son had not shared Sophia, even though neither of them had touched the damn girl, Lord Willoughby was less sanguine.

The older man's emotions were clearly visible on his face. Captain Poole recognized that they had won the fight. Willoughby believed Patcher was a traitorous dog and that Samuel had been trying to save his Lordship's reputation, as well as his property. The captain gave an internal sigh of relief but kept all thoughts of victory off his own features. Suddenly, Willoughby nodded abruptly before standing up and offering his hand to Levi.

'Thank you, sir, for all the help you have given to both myself and to my family. I fully appreciate your support. Let us say no more about this situation. I am afraid that I have been cruelly deceived by Patcher who, from what I now understand, must have been using the slavey back in Harmony for years. He has been a worm in my bosom, sir, and I rejoice in his death. The Keeper has been maligned badly and I will make sure that all know of his sacrifice at my next meeting with the Preceptor, as is proper. The situation with my daughter infuriates me. I can assure you that if the scavenger was still alive I would horse whip the bastard butler until he begged for mercy. She is, of course, a virgin and will remain so until her marriage. I will speak to her and demand she tells me of his misdeeds. His cunning is amazing in its concept.'

'He had long practice, I think, of deceit and lies. I did not want to speak of these sensitive issues in front of the others, especially the councilman, just in case the gentlemen were not as understanding of the situation. I have no wish to cause you any distress or inconvenience.' The captain's face and voice were bland and soothing, hiding completely the disgust roiling through him at the complete about face in attitude from Willoughby. Steeling himself, he shook the flabby seeming hand, only a little taken aback at the strength it held. The voyage had given Willoughby a much healthier air than he pretended to cultivate. Much of his excess weight had melted away, showing more of the solid muscle it had once disguised.

Leading the way back into the salon, Captain Poole exchanged a quick glance with his brother and nodded slightly. Within a few minutes the visitors were leaving the ship, Captain Daventry pausing only to murmur to his friend, asking for a full explanation another time. The two men with him heard nothing and didn't see Captain Poole give a sly nod before seeing them off. Letting out a huge sigh of relief, he turned to his brother, laying an arm over the brawny shoulders.

'We have done all we can for her, Elias. It is in the hands of the Gods and also in Danielle's abilities. There is nothing else we can do.'

Perched on the edge of the seat in the coach, Lord Willoughby stared back at the ship in distaste.

'I am not sure of what went on back there, gentlemen, but I don't think we have heard the whole truth and I aim to get it. Captain Daventry, I want to know of any women found dead in or near the docks. I also need to know of any good bloodhounds, human or canine, for hire, just in case the bint managed to escape. Patcher is dead and beyond my reach but I must know if this was a plot to help her escape. If it was, I will hunt down everyone who helped her and I will punish them, their wives and their children. No-one touches my property without my permission, no-one!'

Epilogue

A couple of miles away, Danielle was in a small hut, drying herself off behind a wooden screen. Soaked to the skin and bitterly cold, she was grateful for the warm clothing hidden in her pack. The camisole and short legged knickers were the first proper undergarments she had ever known. The long-sleeved shirt covered the knives strapped to her forearms. Her britches covered her to her knees and thick stockings warmed the calves nicely. Putting on her sturdy boots she then strapped on her belt and the large knife in its beautiful scabbard. Shrugging into the coat that fell to her knees, Danielle felt overwhelmed with the generosity shown to her. A sob caught in her throat as she remembered how she had laughed and cried with Samuel over the gifts. Swallowing down her pain she stepped back into the main room and looked at the curious little man dishing up some stew for them both. Both packs had been opened and everything set in neat piles.

'Sit, sit!' the man screeched. No higher than Danielle's waist, the extraordinary creature followed his own instructions and began eating rapidly. He looked even smaller hunched over his bowl, his skin grey and covered in warty growths. He was dressed in a pair of patched britches that flapped around his ankles but were tight across his barrel of a stomach. A loose jerkin covered up the rest of his round body while boots and gloves hid missing digits on either hand. When they left, he would wear a child's hooded cloak to hide him from the sight of Abomination hunters.

Danielle didn't feel like eating but knew she should keep up her energy so began slowly. Before she knew it, she found herself finishing her first bowlful and it was being refilled immediately.

'I am Pandam, lord of all I survey...which ain't much, lady. I know you need to get to the FreeLands and I know you is a slavey cuz of your neck cover. I have been paid generously to get you started and stay with you a week or so, learning you to live off the land and that. Naming what's safe and what ain't, understand?' Pandam's voice was a strange mixture, both hoarse and high pitched, so he spoke in a whispering scream. 'Nice packs with sensible stuff, you won't need some of it and his is no good now. Perhaps just take what you need from his and if you can keep up, put it in your bag. Take food, leave clothes.'

Danielle listened to the gnome as she finished her stew. Nodding at his suggestion, she began repacking her bag with the extra tools, gems and money. Seeing the good clothing left, she added Sam's shirt to the pile to take and looked at the medallion of a spreading tree his mother had given him when he first left home. He was not allowed to wear it as a Keeper but took it everywhere with him. Looking at the silver tree, Danielle almost felt it was alive as she slipped it into her pocket. Taking the extra food package, she put the rest of his clothes to one side after removing the hidden gems. As she attempted to collect Sam's books, she saw the old gnome shake his head.

'Books no good, just weight to drag you down. Leave behind, foolish one. We need to move quick, quick.' Pandam spoke angrily and rapidly.

'I will be carrying the pack so I am the judge of what I can manage. All of what I leave behind you can have. Sell what you can and keep the money. I am grateful for your help but do not presume to tell me what I should do.' Her voice was low and hard as her pain took away her usual musical cadence. Pandam looked at her briefly and shrugged, letting her have her way.

'As you say, you carry,' he agreed before explaining the route they would take and which portal he would sneak them through. Approving of the maps, he took one for his own use. They both lay down to sleep for a few hours and although Danielle did not expect to be able to, she fell asleep immediately, exhausted from shock and emotion.

Pandam didn't sleep. He waited until her breathing grew heavier before taking all that was left from her re-packing and sneaking out with it, taking it to a broker who gave him a tidy price for it all. Getting back to his shack, Pandam made up a pack of food for both of them before waking her and getting her to eat some bread and cheese with a big glass of milk. After cleaning up and banking the fire, the lights were extinguished. Both Danielle and the gnome slipped out of the door. Pandam mumbled a few words before blowing a fistful of magical herbs at the shack. A quick bright rain of sparkling light covered the doorway before fading away, hiding the hut from sight.

'Is magic, keeps home safe,' explained the little man. With a cautious look around, they both slipped out into the night. A few steps away from the hidden cabin and a dark shadow came out from a nearby alleyway. Danielle recognised the huge kat that had pulled at her as Samuel lay dying. As tall as Danielle's waist, the kat was all shades of grey and seemed to appear and disappear as it moved ahead, stopping every so often to wait for them to catch up. A shadow kat, the slave realised, one that really could appear and disappear from view. The gnome walked swiftly but was careful around the kat and Danielle could see that he was nervous of the animal. So, these were to be her companions for the next part of her journey, she thought wryly.

As Danielle looked up at the moonless sky, she gave a quick thought to Samuel and the others who had meant so much to her but were now left behind. Uncaring about what might happen if she was caught, she followed the small gnome and the cat from shadow to shadow as they slipped quickly away into the dark.

Lightning Source UK Ltd.
Milton Keynes UK
UKHW011249110522
402819UK00002B/99